With

compliments

of the

publisher

HARPERVIA
An Imprint of HarperCollins*Publishers*

**UNCORRECTED PROOF
– NOT FOR SALE –**

INTEMPERANCE

This galley does not reflect the actual size or design of the final book. Reviewers are reminded that changes may be made in this proof copy before books are printed. If any material is to be quoted or referred to in a review, the quotations or reference must be checked against the final bound book. Dates, prices, and manufacturing details are subject to change or cancellation without notice.

Also by Sonora Jha

FICTION

Foreign

The Laughter

NONFICTION

How to Raise a Feminist Son

INTEMPERANCE

A Novel

Sonora Jha

HarperVia
An Imprint of HarperCollinsPublishers

This is a work of fiction. Names, characters, places, and incidents are products of the author's imagination or are used fictitiously and are not to be construed as real. Any resemblance to actual events, locales, organizations, or persons, living or dead, is entirely coincidental.

INTEMPERANCE. Copyright © 2025 by Sonora Jha. All rights reserved. Printed in the United States of America. No part of this book may be used or reproduced in any manner whatsoever without written permission except in the case of brief quotations embodied in critical articles and reviews. For information, address HarperCollins Publishers, 195 Broadway, New York, NY 10007.

HarperCollins books may be purchased for educational, business, or sales promotional use. For information, please email the Special Markets Department at SPsales@harpercollins.com.

FIRST EDITION

Designed by Elina Cohen
Chapter art © flowersmile/Shutterstock

Library of Congress Cataloging-in-Publication Data has been applied for.

ISBN 978-0-06-344084-5

$PrintCode

FOR THE INTEMPERATE

Feast on my corpse, oh crow
And pick away at the choicest of my flesh
But do spare my two eyes
I yearn for a glimpse of the beloved.

    —Sufi poem by Baba Sheikh Farid (translation by Sonora Jha)

Contents

The Proposal	1
The License	11
The Invitation	23
The Dance Lesson	36
The Save-the-Date	47
The Astrologer	58
The Wedding Planner	72
The Groomsmen	87
The Skincare	105
The Officiant	113
The Priests	138
The Music	146
The Cake	173
The Videographer	180
The Blessings	206
The Dress	217
The Vidaai	231

CONTENTS

The Bridal Shower	244
The Vows	259
The Cleanse	261
The Garland	268
Oh, and the Swayamvar	273
Acknowledgments	285
A Note on the Cover	287

INTEMPERANCE

The Proposal

I am not the sort of person to throw a lavish party, but this is no ordinary party and the thing that makes it necessary is no ordinary loneliness.

After seven years of a revolutionary solitude (except for a couple of brief dalliances), I find myself a woman in her mid-fifties, caught in the shudder of the planet's mid-2020s, now seeking communion with a man, despite everything we know.

Hum ek swayamvar rakh rahen hain, I say out loud to the dog. I am planning a swayamvar. He cocks an ear.

I am scared out of my mind. Scared of this thing I'm about to do, scared of being a lone voice saying a thing out loud, scared of owning a solitary heart that seeks another. So scared that this enterprise might seem self-serving. But also scared, somewhat, of the kind of loneliness that my physician has warned could be the death of me.

But when I shut my eyes and imagine this event, a giggle erupts from me. Unseemly. That's the word that comes to mind, but then it delights me, this word and its finger-pointing accusation at a late-middle-aged woman as she puts a third teabag into her giant mug, as she stands at her bedroom window in her holey fleece robe. Once the giggle has been gulped down, I imagine Draupadi eyeing the hairs on Arjun's sculpted abdomen. Draupadi, a gorgeous princess born from fire, a female character in the tremendously masculine epic Mahabharata, nevertheless channeling main-character energy at her swayamvar. Sixteen days of princes and kings vying for her hand in marriage. Draupadi feasting on the spectacle of her suitors—at their biceps raising a bow, triceps taut from aiming an arrow at the eye of a fish revolving on a wheel they could only see in its reflection in a pool of water below. A convoluted feat, but who cares, because look at those beads of perspiration forming on Arjun's brow. Focus, my prince. Show me that valor.

Yes, a swayamvar is called for. A swayamvar in this soggy little town of Seattle. I spend this morning imagining Sita picking out Ram from among a slew of contenders. I see Damayanti, who spurns the lined-up gods and instead puts a garland on the neck of her chosen human male. What was his name again? I see kingdoms burst into song, chariots of elephants bedecked in jewels, colored gulal flying in the air, trumpets and matrimonial fires and laddoos on golden platters....

The dog butts up against my shin. I forgot to feed him an hour ago. I shuffle to his bag of kibble. As he eats, I pull on my walking shoes and grab my walking cane and the dog's leash. I step outside onto the side deck of this houseboat I live on. This moment, of stepping out and looking back into my home as it glows from the lamps within, is my favorite part of the day. My own little jewel, this houseboat I bought eight years ago, when Karan was all launched into the world as a responsible young man and I could do something as irresponsible as put my savings into a home whose status, like my own, could not quite lay claim to a patch of land.

INTEMPERANCE

A house on water, tethered by rope to a dock, capable of coming unmoored and floating away in a good thunderstorm.

I wave at my neighbors on the dock we share on Portage Bay, and they wave back as they water their plants placed carefully on the side decks of their houseboats (to mimic foliage on land—this weird desire of Americans to have it all). My own side deck is clear, spare—bare some would say—but I would argue it pretends to be nothing other than what it is: wood on water, mossy if I don't take care, sure, but firm enough under my feet and my cane as I step carefully across it today. The only object I have on my deck is on the other side, the one where the dock juts into Lake Union. It is a kayak, a bright yellow kayak that I take out onto the water on clear days. I've done it just three or four times this summer despite an abundance of clear days. I realize this now with a pang of guilt because it's the dog's favorite activity, sitting on the front of the kayak with his little orange doggy life vest and his short fur catching the little droplets of water that drip from my oar.

I am tired of rowing alone, I whisper to the dog sometimes when we are in the middle of the lake, and I'd like to think my voice doesn't carry over the water. I know the dog understands and forgives me.

I am looking to get married. It's not easy for me to say this. I am lonely. It's even harder to say that. I insisted for so long that I was never lonely, that I was past such petty matters as love, that the company of my books and the dog and my friends was so enriching, so soul satisfying, that I felt no need for a partner. The company of the dog came close to being enough, but it didn't quite seize my soul. It's not as if the company of any man has come anywhere near the soul either. The dog made it farther than any of them.

There is, of course, the matter that I have been married before. Twice. Siddhartha didn't care for the domestic life, so I set him free. Then came Paul, who cared very much for the domestic life, and then he cheated on me and, somewhat to my relief, quickly agreed to my desire to banish him.

More about all that later. I have a party to plan.

To be quite clear, I want no fanfare, but I can't imagine how such a thing as a swayamvar is possible without fanfare. If the idea is to spread the call far and wide, and if men are to assemble somewhere to seek my hand, I will have to make a bit of a thing of it. Oh, it will be nothing like the scale of the emperors and kings of my ancestry, whose kingdoms would drop all other travails and welcome princes with gold, silks, feasts, merriment in the streets to win the hand of their princess by performing duels, archery. Exploits that demonstrated their focus, their might, their potency. Or their wit.

No, my swayamvar is already outlandish in its audacity for reasons obvious to most but increasingly obscure to me. I won't involve a kingdom, for one. Yes, of course, I could always just do this by correspondence. Have the suitors write a letter of application. But how would that be different from a dating app? I have been on dating apps, and the worst part is the writing of the profile, the responding to the questions, the expressing of one's desire for a partner with levity without exposing the ravenous, grasping loneliness beneath it. The getting dressed and meeting just one whole other person has only had me hurrying home alone after, more desolate than ever, to wrap my quaking self in a blanket and rock back and forth. It takes a while for the dog to feel safe enough to come lie at my feet again.

No, this must be different. My goal is to find a prince. Or, well, a king. A king of hearts. My king. Worthy of my hand. What feat would I have for those men? What feat would lead me to a knee-buckling love?

When I was a little girl, my father asked me what kind of man I would want to marry. I said, "A happy man, a laughing man, a man who is rich and handsome and loves me very much."

"And why would such a man want to marry you?"

My father didn't say this unkindly, but my smile disappeared. I remember the disappearance of that smile like muscle memory. My smile has disappeared many other times since. Perhaps one of those muscles I employ in the act of smiling atrophied forever right there and then when I fumbled to find an answer to my father's question.

"Khudi ko kar buland itnaa...," he began, not waiting too long for his daughter to respond.

I'd heard this lesson before from him, this wise poem from Allama Iqbal that my father wanted me to internalize as a guiding wisdom.

> Raise your Self to such stature,
> That even God, before he writes your every fate,
> Asks you, "Tell me, what is your desire?"

Well, here I am then. Statured. Desiring. Godless.

And yet I imagine myself worthy of a swayamvar. Of being sought, hand and heart and soul, by at least a man, if not a king or a god.

Statured enough to make a spectacle of it.

So, a call will go out.

A queen, on her fifty-fifth birthday, seeks a man to wed. Come ye from far and wide. Line up. Perform a feat of her decree. She will garland the man who is victorious.

AND WHAT, THEN, is the feat that a man must perform to win my hand? I will not concern myself with that for now. I will begin, as most of my quests begin, with cake.

My plan is to set up a wedding to immediately follow the victory of the suitor. A lavish affair, just this side of ostentatious, just that side of apologetic for being a third attempt. We will have cake. We will have shehnai, played live, for which I may fly in a musician from India. I will have a wedding dress, to be determined, a virginal white in the tradition of my chosen world in America or a fertile red from the culture from which I hail.

I HAVE TALKED and talked and talked about what I want in men. I have studied and I have schooled. I have been published and I have been promoted. I have built a whole career poking and prodding at men—or, well, at masculinity. I have ended two marriages poking and prodding at men. I have called out their mediocrity, their cruelty, their emotional unavailability. My anger has been righteous, channeled as analysis. *Outrage because we love*, I have clarified.

Lately, though, I have journaled and swiped and vision boarded. To no avail. This will be different, this swayamvar. It isn't calling in The One. This is not a spell or manifestation; this is a straight and clear summons. A call to action.

The swayamvar and wedding will be five weeks from today. It's the day I turn fifty-five years old. It's also just enough time so I don't lose my nerve and back out. It's the tail end of the wedding season. The end of summer in Seattle. Five weeks from now, the

INTEMPERANCE

city has strained itself, exposed its pallor to every bit of warmth from a sun that will soon abdicate responsibility to the Pacific Northwest. In the weeks leading up, all around us are expos and revelations of men cycling down the street with their shirts off, rowing and sculling and kayaking on the waters of lakes, stand-up paddleboarding with their dogs, the richer men on their boats with babes, older householders raking up late-summer leaves dressed in shapeless cargo shorts, grunting to lift the foliage from the sidewalk into the yard waste bin. Men seated on Adirondack chairs outside cafés, their white legs exposed past crisp seersucker and their eyes hidden behind sunglasses as they raise iced lattes to their thin lips.

Look at me, describing mostly white men. Oh, I must not lose heart! I must visualize that men of color—no, kings of color—will be at the swayamvar too. I must examine the heart to see what it truly desires. I must dream of the impossible man being the possible king.

It will be the end of summer; he will be there, in line at the swayamvar, and I will find him among the assembly of would-be kings. People will be ready to sit down to some cake and champagne and shehnai. And a good garlanding.

Dear Mother,

I implore you to reconsider this . . . what should I call it . . . whim? May I call it madness though? I know you don't do things lightly, but this does seem totally flippant and quite out of character for you, don't you agree? A swayamvar? I mean, it works well as, say, a party theme for a big fifty-fifth birthday bash (which, of course, I would fly in to attend, being your adoring son, dear Mama). But an actual swayamvar? An announcement going out in the newspaper? You, sitting in a public place with a marigold garland expecting—what, an assembly of suitors?

As I said, it works as a theme, even better as a joke, a public prank, if you must, although that also would be a bit weird. Please reconsider this. I might even say just please go ahead and nix this idea before your sycophantic friends erupt in squeals and let you go through with it. Will they though? I can't imagine the feminists and progressives will love this spectacle of patriarchal pageantry!

If not for your own sake, for mine? Haven't you hauled me through enough in my life with you? Please don't get me wrong, I have nothing but gratitude and admiration, but you will have to admit it hasn't been easy living through two of your divorces and losing so many people along the way, let alone being a "celebrated child" of a pathbreaking feminist sociologist and all. By the way, I have been reading up on menopause and one of its symptoms—brain fog. Don't get me wrong, dear Mother, this is not meant as any sort of disrespect or dismissal of your beautiful mind. My research is really just for a character in my novel in progress. Anyway, I can't help but wonder if your whimsicality can be explained by this very common, totally physiological, entirely understandable change that so brutally and terribly unfairly (dear God, I am using too many adverbs, aren't I?) body snatches middle-aged women just as they hit their prime. Awful.

Just a thought here—you can fight it. There are medications and other therapies. I have hardly urged you any restraint before, Mother. But this time, I do.

I am always available if you want to talk this through. You know I love you.

Your bastard son,
K.

"WELL, HE HAS a point," I say to my most loving friend on the phone.

"Stop saying 'he has a point,'" her voice interrupts the rush of thoughts that clamor in my beautiful mind.

My most loving friend is named Cat, not because she looks feline, though she does, with her round face and green eyes and slow, knowing smile. No. Cat is short, as it usually is, for Catherine, also known as Aunty Cat to Karan, even though she has always been a bit harsh on him, something he seems to have nevertheless enjoyed. Cat had predicted this sort of response from Karan. She also doesn't like the sign-off to this letter. Karan likes to refer to himself as a "bastard" when he is being contrarian, as a kind of preemptory humor. It has no reference to the marital status of his parents when he was born. I would never have let him use such a term in that case.

"I seem to have disturbed him, panicked him somehow," I say to Cat.

"Where is that son of yours right now?"

"He is away at an artists' retreat somewhere closer to you on the East Coast. He's taken the time to handwrite this letter and mail it by FedEx Priority Overnight. I had indicated in the subject line of my email to him that he didn't need to read or respond until after his return, but..."

"But he wanted no distractions," my most loving friend says.

"He wanted no distractions. He's quite sure this new book he's writing is one to win awards two years from now. I feel terrible to have interrupted his craft."

Cat's laughter mixes in with my own to make one of my favorite sounds. She lets the critique of Karan drop, but I get the sense Aunty Cat will return to it with greater energy sometime.

In the rush of love I feel in the moment, I say, "I miss you. And how is that husband of yours? Is it time for me to come visit yet?"

"Not yet. But likely soon. We are savoring each day now."

"Give him my love, please. And bite those little children for me?"

"I will," she says. "And you go make a list of all the good reasons for this swayamvar thing." She hangs up. The sound of Cat's short laugh and the squeals of her two little daughters in the background—and the susurration of the sports channel underneath it all—clicks out of my ear.

The License

This idea of a swayamvar has been a couple of years in the making. It took the place of the other public event, a much more somber one I'd been craving—a massive communal mourning for the lives lost in the terrible sickness that gripped the Earth. I spent The Great Isolation all alone with my dog. I used the time to steady my heart and save my soul. But when we all emerged, I wanted a rending of the air with cries. I wanted strangers' ears pressed to strangers' chests, listening for the beating of hearts weakened by poor exercise or strengthened from love and longing. I wanted a dirge sung loud by a hundred thousand voices in the streets. I wanted no words but only howls from the humans who somehow stayed behind when so many others were taken.

That desire, unrequited, eventually subsided thanks to the small manner of living I'd chosen. I, along with others, began to mingle, raise toasts, and fly places. I was once again in the presence of humans, which, on occasion, meant the presence of men. For some years, while I'd certainly encountered men—walked past them in the street, shouted them down in meetings, asked them for directions with my car window down (even though, yes, we could look up directions on our phones now, no man needed), and gone on an occasional dating-app date—I hadn't felt a routine flush of wanting, a dwell of the eye on another, iris peering into iris. It wasn't as if the muscle of desire atrophied the way my disabled right leg atrophies with each passing year, a polar iceberg hapless in the inevitability of its doom. No, my desire still flexed and convulsed on occasion, and I resuscitated it with an occasional tryst with a love interest, say once a year . . . or two. But with no customary companion to call on, my own introversion became my beloved until I came to to desire desire itself.

AND THEN IT came right up close when I simply wasn't looking . . . indeed, just a month ago, when I was stuffing my face with bread at a party because I was bored. It came in the shape of a stranger at a get-together on a terrasse. In the small town of Agen in the southwest of France, where I was visiting a friend.

The first thought I had when I saw the man was that I hoped he was Indian. His hair was dark, just a little bit long and a little bit gray, curled from its natural grease and sweat. A close-cropped beard, a moustache on a ruddy face. He was large compared to the smaller builds of the other Frenchmen around him.

I didn't have much time to think anything after that. He looked right at me as he walked in, and it was as if he didn't look at anyone else after. I had to avert my eyes instantly. Nothing had hit me with such force in so long. Besides, an adolescent girl who had arrived at the party by his side was walking right up to me. The girl reached out to place her small hands on my shoulders. She stood on tiptoe to kiss me on one cheek and then the other. I was startled by the girl's tenderness and was unsure if I was to respond the same way. The French are weird, and here was a weird French child.

I took a step back from the girl, and then the man was upon me, holding me by the elbow as he leaned in to kiss me, cheek after cheek. His facial hair grazed open a yearning so fierce I thought everyone in the room could see it burst like a river onto the terrasse.

The girl was his daughter. She was so small, even for a teenager. So achingly pretty. I watched her for a while because I could not bear to look at her father, whose eyes seemed never to lift from me, even though of course they must have to set down the loaf of bread he had brought for the party, to kiss every other stupid cheek there, to greet and grin and give others what I ached he would give me again.

I had wished he was Indian because he came so close to being so. This single thing would have made him so much more a marker of home. He was of a color closer to my own, possibly mixed race. But his intensity was something I had witnessed only in a certain sort of Indian man. A confidence maintained in their silence and at a distance. An openness to their stare, a frankness in their interest. The better Indian men would keep things just this side of lecherous, as this one did. I hadn't realized it until then, but I missed home and didn't know where that was for me anymore. I was assailed by a sense of homesickness while also feeling drawn to the strangeness of this man. Most American men didn't look at you like that. I told myself to be bold, to look back, to hold his gaze. When I did, I had to look away just as a smile started to play at my mouth. He didn't smile back, and he didn't look away. This made it all so much more unbearably pulsating, this attraction, for that was what it was, an instant, unmistakable, unapologetic attraction.

I hadn't heard his name when he introduced himself. I had lost my sense of hearing when he landed those kisses on my cheeks.

The party was in the makeshift, ramshackle apartment of Armand, a man who was helping my white American friend Anabel renovate a château she had purchased during the pandemic, as one does. I had gladly accepted her invitation to visit France. In the two weeks or so leading up to the party at her handyman's home, I had eaten strawberries that were surely meant for gods, not mere humans; cheeses and artichokes and paella from the farmers market; pain au chocolat from the boulangerie. I was fullfaced, glowing from fruit and fat and sleep, my hair shining from leisure. I was dressed in a black-and-white dress of soft cotton that I bought in a boutique in Agen. I wore red lipstick to fit in with French women. I felt beautiful, but it had been so long, years in fact, since I had been so viscerally aware of the presence of an attractive man in the same room.

Armand's apartment was close to the historic center of the town. A staircase of twists and turns went up its side and essentially connected each apartment. The terrasse, though, was beautiful—it looked out over an old cathedral, and I could have sworn the pigeons perched on the stained glass windows were speaking French. Their coos mixed with the noise floating up from the street—young people coming out of museums and boutiques and walking to restaurants and cafés.

It was the strangest party I had ever been to, turned more inscrutable by the fact that I didn't speak or understand much French. My senses, then, were both lulled and heightened by this unexpected assault of desire. The people at the party were a mix of working-class French like Armand, but there were also teachers and graduate students. Armand's girlfriend, Christine, worked for a nonprofit that advocated for women's reproductive rights. She was late to the party because she was at a music festival handing out condoms and flyers to young people.

Soon we were seated at a long table on the terrasse, where the guests had laid out their contributions to the meal. Most people had brought bread, which adorned the table with a rustic brown wholesomeness: baguettes, brioche, fougasse, boule de pain, ficelle, pain de campagne.... Some brought cheeses, and others crudités or dips. The most senior-looking of the guests—a woman who was, in all likelihood, just a little bit older than me—brought a large quiche layered with leeks and ham, covered in a magnificently buttered crust. I had hungrily eaten a hefty slice before the man arrived.

The man's daughter sat close to me, and the man stood at the door that led from the terrasse into the apartment, chatting with a couple of other men. His daughter nibbled on a single potato chip for some fifteen minutes. Many of the guests seemed to be old friends, and they asked her about her plans after high school. She said she was trying to decide if she should apply to go to college in America. The conversation then got too complicated for me to follow in French, which was just as well, since I didn't want to feel compelled to weigh in about American academia, didn't want to think about work or America at all.

A young woman sitting next to me, upon hearing I was a feminist scholar, talked about her expectations from men: "My previous boyfriend was a wonderful feminist man. He encouraged me to dream of a big career and go to graduate school and not have children if I didn't want to. I cheated on him. He wouldn't take me back. Which I understand. Do you think he is a bad feminist for not taking me back?"

At any other time, I would have very much enjoyed this conversation and would have risen to solve the riddle of this woman's situation, but I was more moss than feminist at this party now, my roots weak from lust, everything within me slippery from an unfamiliar confusion of language and longing.

Water, I said, and stood up to go to the kitchen, which meant walking toward the man. My joints ached and creaked as they always did when I'd been seated for a while. But I pushed into the pain, pushed also into the cane that I took everywhere with me, and walked as straight and surefooted as I could. The man's eyes flitted to my limping gait and my cane and then came right back to my face. I savored the perplexed expression he had when it looked like I was walking right up to him.

Anticipation is an aphrodisiac and an end in itself.

"Pardon, je peux passer par ici?" I said, looking past him at the water jug in the kitchen.

He barely shifted an inch from the doorway, and while in the past, I would have seen this as a bit of a cad move, I am a bit ashamed to say it quickened my pulse in this instance. What had changed? Was I just bolder now with greater power to find both mirth and magic in these things, unafraid and unoffended and perhaps no longer misreading men's physical cues? After all, they can't help that they have these bodies.

Snap out of it before you go too far, I told myself. And yet I gave a bit of a thrust so that my hip brushed the outside of his thigh against his jeans. He smelled of soap and sweat and skin-warmed cologne.

I sensed him turn to look at me walking to the kitchen sink. I sensed he loved the sight of my full hips even though they were merely a hint of shapeliness through my loose shirtdress.

I was trying to slake a different sort of thirst from a glass of water I poured myself when the man came up and stood to my right. One arm reached past my waist for a glass. If I had half-circled to my right just a few inches, I would be folded into the man's arms and chest. I didn't move. He reached over to the faucet and held the pitcher I had just emptied, filling it with water at a trickle. For a second, his left side brushed up lightly against my right. His palms encircled the jug at its widest curve. The water chuckled its way into the pitcher, and I could almost feel its coolness seeping into his hands. It was a glass pitcher, so he gripped it hard. Green veins. Knuckles white.

Outside, the voices spun from laughter to murmurs to incoherence. I stood there, not touching, not speaking, not looking, just feeling a rising sadness as the water in the pitcher reached the brim and spilled over. Not impatiently, the man set the pitcher aside and brought his hands to the water, rinsing them. He rubbed the skin on the back of one hand, then the next. He locked his palms together and then rolled and wrung them into one another again and again as our eyes took it all in, the thick fingers and soft nails, the gently wrinkled skin on his wrists, the dark hairs on his forearms, the absence of a watch to remind us that all this was taking too long, just too long, this nothing was also time, and it was a lot of time.

I stood there as a woman, neither salt nor statue, pinned not by the touch of his body but by his presence and by the centimeters of distance. Pinned by a sliver of air and a lifetime of gnawing, caged, fearful desire.

I could be that woman who said something alluring that led

us into an adjoining room, where we would have quick and quiet sex atop other people's jackets and wraps. But I wasn't, so I stood there. When he finally turned off the faucet, I reached my arms up and lifted my thick hair from my waist to let air onto the back of my neck. He shifted just a little and gave my neck his breath, cool and then hot.

And then someone else was in the kitchen and we were just two people filling up a water jug. Two good guests.

As he stepped away from me, for a perhaps imagined second, he placed his cool, damp hand on the back of mine. I could swear that it left a spot that has burned ever since.

The party ended and we looked at one another again. The look was different now, still languorous but also laced with loss.

Later, as I walked with Anabel through the streets of Agen to her car, I asked if she could take a picture of me crossing the street. In the grainy photograph taken in the light of dusk, I am a woman far away, looking to her left, dressed in a black-and-white loose-fitted shirtdress and a chunky chain-link white acrylic necklace. I can see a hint of a smile on the woman's face because she knew then that the photograph could not record how verdant she was within and how something had spored. How a search had begun.

The man had disturbed open some petals of shuttered sentiment. I've carried that feeling ever since in my middle, both light and leaden. I began to look at men in the street everywhere I went, including at home, in Seattle. I listened to them laugh at restaurants or speak loudly into their phones at airports. I watched men as they dug up the road outside my building to lay cables. I watched men walk dogs. I watched my dentist's clean hands; I smelled the soap on them. At the swimming pool, where I swam twice a week, with eyes that stung from chlorine and a vision warped from goggles, I watched almost-naked bodies of men. When I couldn't look into their eyes, I looked at stubbles and chest hair. And on some occasions, even farther down.

"AND WHY AM I only hearing of this Frenchman now?" my most loving friend asks when I call to tell her that I have only one thing to put on the list of reasons she'd asked me to make for the swayamvar. "More importantly, why didn't you say something to him?"

"I couldn't think of the words to express my lust in French," I say.

"The French enjoy even a feeble attempt at their language."

"They don't. They hate it. You've never been to France," I say.

"Whatever. You could have said something in broken French. You could have been a damsel in language distress."

"A *dame*," I correct her.

"A madame," she corrects me.

We laugh together.

"Yes, yes," I say. "But he may have been a married man. The girl's mother wasn't at the party, but who knew? Everything felt unknowable. So foreign."

"If he'd been a married man, he would not have been so open and free around his daughter, don't you think?" she says.

"Aha. You would know a thing or two about that," I say, then add quickly, "Speaking of fathers and daughters . . . How are your people?"

"Meh. Let's just keep talking about you, please? These conversations are a good distraction."

"I should come there, sweetheart," I say.

"Not yet. Back to the Frenchman. What if he had been Indian?"

"I would have said to him, 'What brought you to France?' He and I could have been a little bit foreign together. We would have made some plans to meet, maybe. That is, if he weren't already partnered."

"So, maybe the feat for your men is to be Indian and single?"

"Don't be ridiculous. You know better."

"True, true. If that's what it took ... you'd be hitched by now, in just these few days since you've decided to get a husband again."

Husband. What a loaded word. It could summon up excitement, boredom, comfort, terror.

"Or I would have tried really hard and been crushed," I say. "Or I would have come close and walked away."

We both fall silent.

"Yes, it's sort of your ordinary thing, I guess," Cat says. "Maybe what was attractive about the man in France is that thing they call primal attraction ... desire without knowledge ..."

"Without knowledge of who we were, who we had made ourselves. Yes."

"I'd say men have been attracted to you for what you have made yourself. You know that, right?" she says. "He might have pursued you into the following day if he knew."

"That's a certain kind of man. This man had this sort of quiet fire about him. Like he had to wash his hands to subdue that fire."

"Looks like the feat at the swayamvar will be the opposite: to set you on fire."

"Or turn me into water."

INTEMPERANCE

Dear Karan (very legitimately but often perplexingly my son),

I think every day about that image released recently by NASA, of the cluster of galaxies, our own within it. They say that image represents but one patch of sky as large as a grain of sand held at arm's length, a tiny glimmer of the vast universe. I can barely write this without feeling faint. Some of these galaxies may not exist now, they say!

It's all so beautiful and awesome, isn't it? And yet ever since I saw that picture, I feel somewhat tossed about, as if I am completely inconsequential. I felt disoriented for days. I then drew some consequence from something someone said online, about how, if some of those stars far away were already dead but we are seeing them in this image now, then some life out there might one day see the burning star that we are now, this Earth. Our light will be summoned up somewhere beyond us. I hope we shimmer.

This is why I now return to the idea of love—romantic love and partnership and marriage. I have had this strange sensation that a love that once cried out somewhere in another time or place has now come to sit like an echo in my chest. I don't want to silence that call or get in its way. I don't want it muffled in the structures and quotidian arrangements of my present life. I am putting myself out there, in a ridiculous public spectacle, so a man may find me past my ordinary pursuits. But because I, too, must know if he was the one for me, I will set up a feat that only that man who somehow knows that call from across and around and beyond a universe will be able to perform. Of course, I don't know yet know what that feat will be.

The cries, the stardust, the fathom of a whole universe are bearing down on me so pleasantly, I can hardly move from their gravity, and I can hardly breathe.

It's all making me rather shameless, you know. I do see your point, my child, but I am in awe of and in attendance to the call and response of a sort. When the time comes, of course, you should feel free to embrace your inner Telemachus and come by and vanquish your mother's suitors in battle.

Meanwhile, get out of my way, dear son.

Love,

Mother

The Invitation

I wrote that letter to my son by hand on the letterhead of the chair of the Department of Sociology at my university. *I am the chair of the Department of Sociology at my university.* Still, using the official department letterhead to write a ludicrous letter to my son about love and the cosmos is an inappropriate use of office supplies, even worse because I have smuggled some of these office supplies home for this year that I am on sabbatical. I use this paper now because I do not have any other stationery on which to write letters, whereas once I had a range of monogrammed and embossed letter paper and cards to express every human emotion for every milestone and setback in the human condition—birthdays, apologies, congratulations, celebrations of weddings, celebrations of divorce, regrets for divorce, felicitations for children born, condolences for loved ones lost, wishes and prayers for getting back to good health, thanks and gratitude, religious holidays, nonreligious holidays, graduations, jobs, engagements. But I have years ago forsaken the tedium of delighting people. I once searched in vain for a card that expressed regrets for someone getting married. When I couldn't find one, I deemed all else to be clutter and tossed them, quite responsibly, in the recycle bin.

But here I am, seeking marriage, or something of that sort, and putting it in actual words to an actual adult of a son, twenty-eight years old, at work on his art after a critically acclaimed debut novel. I risk alienating him, but that thought seems to excite me. Indeed, I risk alienating everyone who respects me. I risk professional ridicule. I risk personal shame. The list Cat asked me to make should be of the reasons I should *not* do this thing.

I dive into a bottom drawer on my nightstand to fish out a journal from among the journals I received as gifts over the years. I was never the journaling sort. I remember I held on to a red leather journal someone gifted me from Jaipur. I find it buried in the debris of old letters, crinkled photographs, and scrolls of leftover Arya Samaji wedding vows I'd printed on gold-hued paper and stamped with brocade motifs for my second wedding eleven years ago. We'd distributed those scrolls to our wedding guests so they could follow along in the cross-cultural traditions. It was all so cute.

The red journal is fresh and unused except for a single page, on which I find written in my handwriting these words: *How Do I Want to Live?* I do not remember writing this nor the year in which I wrote this. And yet I feel a curl of regret rise in my chest for a younger woman who must have lived a moment in which she believed she could be intentional. She believed she could begin a journal in which she would chronicle life and ruminate on it, but then she plain forgot. Or she got so busy living life that she never got to document what she desired of it.

I consider ripping off this page so I can repurpose the journal for the new matter at hand, but it feels suddenly like I am muffling a whisper that the woman once concealed on a page. I instead fold the first page into itself, like a secret. The second page, blank, serves now as the first page. I stare it at for a long time. I cannot think of a title that won't come back to haunt me years from now if this journal were once again abandoned. This is what time teaches you. That drops and dabs of moments captured in handwriting or in words said out loud to people will reappear, unbidden, to soak you with regret. I, in the present, think of the woman from the past. I apologize to her. I do better for the woman I will be in the future.

I leave the page blank. On the third page, I write:

Reasons I Should Not Have a Swayamvar.

I am not the first modern-day woman to do this. In August 2010, a fifty-two-year-old woman named Bhanumati Rawal from a village in Anand District near the city of Ahmedabad in the state of Gujarat announced a swayamvar for herself. Bhanumati was a widow and lived in an old-age home after her son, a taxi driver, refused to take her in or care for her. Bhanumati said she had too many good years ahead and wanted to marry again. News reports say Bhanumati sought the help of a nongovernmental organization called Vina Mulya Amulya Sewa—a Marriage Bureau for the Elderly—to spread the word. The bureau was accustomed to introducing older people as prospective marital partners, one-on-one. They weren't accustomed to a swayamvar. Bhanumati insisted, and the bureau acquiesced.

Thirty-six men showed up for the swayamvar. Bhanumati chose fifty-five-year-old Rajendra Rawal, a man who read people's birth charts and predicted their future. Bhanumati said she looked forward to moving in with him, cooking for him, going out with him, and enjoying marital bliss. News reporters asked

Rajendra what drew him to Bhanumati's swayamvar, and he said he was drawn to the stories of her strength in overcoming the odds of widowhood and abandonment by her son. Rajendra was thrilled to make it to the third and final round of the swayamvar and then to be selected winner. He said he wanted to fill the rest of Bhanumati's life with joy.

In a display of shoddy journalism, news reports of the time don't mention why Bhanumati chose Rajendra over the other thirty-five men, which leaves me, almost fourteen years later, bereft. The year Bhanumati took a second husband, I was divorcing my second. If I could meet Bhanumati today, I would ask her to share her selection criteria. If I could have met Rajendra fourteen years ago, and if we assume that his proclaimed astrology skills were not shit, he might have predicted that the heartbreak I felt at my second husband's cheating would rise cold and crystallize into a bitterness, then pool into forgiveness, and that would be the thing that healed me from the horrors of my childhood and the discontent of my youth and gave me the solitary years where I breathed and embraced a deeper intellectual life, a more profound love with my lone self than had ever been possible in the companionship of marriage. Who knows, maybe Bhanumati and Rajendra are now divorced. Maybe Bhanumati poisoned the food she'd wanted to cook for Rajendra. I'm too afraid to look up this fact for fear that it will dissuade me from having my own swayamvar.

So, in the red journal, I write the number "1" and next to it I write: *You are free. Why would you now go and throw it all away?*

I imagine the furor in the Department of Sociology if I do announce a swayamvar. I imagine the outrage of Women, Gender, and Sexuality Studies. At first there would be titters. Shouldn't she be done with patriarchal institutions such as marriage? Didn't she famously write a paper on how women should move past such petty matters as the pursuit of romantic love? Hasn't this scholar of masculinities always hypothesized and surveyed and researched and concluded that marriage serves only the interests and the health of men? Someone might then attempt to articulate this mild outrage on paper, a petition to discredit my work and splash my shame across all platforms. And would they be wrong? Haven't I made a good academic stink over the tales with the awful tropes of the tamed shrew and then coaxed storytellers away also from the tales of the lonely, hardened professional woman whose perfectly manicured life was crying out for a good clumsy fuck followed by a diamond-ring proposal? My upending of all I worked so hard for now could get my reference excised from all forthcoming citations and literature reviews!

My wide circle of friends would be concerned for my mental health. My South Asian married friends would be smug, with their *We told her so; She thought she was so cool with her multiple divorces and her single life traveling and laughing in pictures; She didn't fool us; She was cripplingly lonely all along; Is she out of her mind . . . ? A woman doing a swayamvar at this age; Is she doing this just to find some poor fat fool to take care of her through her years of disability?; Will she marry on the same day as my daughter?*

It has always struck me that the people who lead their lives in response to the prospective shame offered readily by their communities under the pall of *What will people say?* have always known exactly what people would say. The question for our lives should be *What say do people have?* But I digress.

Even if I were to push past what the people at work and in the academic disciplines and the students and the people in our social circles would say, and even if I went through all the way to the afternoon of the swayamvar, what really ought to stop me dead in my tracks right now is the prospect that not one suitor would show up. Or, worse, a few pranksters would show up to make a mockery of it all. Could I steel myself against such an outcome? As my solicitous son had pointed out, would I be dressed as a bride with a marigold garland in hand and wedding preparations all around only to be shamed at an altar of spectacle?

Next, could I really commit to choosing a suitor even if a couple or a handful of them were to show up?

AND SO, IN fewer than thirty minutes, I have scribbled some eighty reasons why I ought not to go ahead with the brazen idea of a swayamvar. That ought to be that then.

I AM RUNNING late for my first day of a dance class and a few other errands. I shove the red leather journal into my red leather backpack and rush out into the rainy day to take a bus to the home of a beautiful kathak dancer. She gave up her acclaimed dance performances in India to follow her husband's tech career in the US. From an airy dance studio in their mansion in the suburb of Bellevue, Washington, the legendary dancer has quietly given dance lessons to little girls and young women for years. On a whim last week, aloft on my speeding train of reckless behavior, I'd walked up to her at an art fundraiser (where her husband had just raised a paddle for a $50,000 donation) and asked her if she'd teach me to dance. A sophisticated dancer trained in facial expression, she'd quickly masked her surprise and heartily welcomed me to a class. I'd told her about the broken bones and atrophying muscles in my legs, told her about my use of a cane, but she'd wrapped my hands in hers and told me I could move as much or as little as I liked.

In anticipation of the pain that would come after the dance class, I take two rapid pulls on the weed I fill into a bong. I found these items in a drawer in Karan's room back when he left for college. When the bus arrives, I hop on swiftly and float into a seat by the window to gaze out at the thick rain, my heart already twirling to the sound of the anklets awaiting me in class.

A PECULIAR WOMAN boards the bus, and with her comes a surge of the rain outside. She's soaking wet and I can tell no one wants her to get on, even less sit by them. Her dampness isn't why. She is trying to bring a goose on board.

"Ma'am, I won't let a goose on board my bus," the driver says.

"It's a fucking duck!" someone shouts.

"It's a fucking swan," the woman says. Her voice is steady but raspy. She is carrying two large bags and a guitar in a filthy guitar case. Everything is soaked and falling and spilling over.

"It's a service animal. I know my rights," the woman says to the driver but also to all of us on the bus.

A commotion starts as a dog on board begins to bark at the duck. Dogs are supposed to be calm on board the bus, someone says, and the woman points out that the dog is a bigger nuisance right now than her swan.

People in the line behind the woman at the bus stop start to complain. Umbrellas smash against each other. The driver mutters something and lets the woman on. She ambles slowly down the aisle, looking for a seat as her guitar slides to the floor, when she clutches on to a bag of books in a tote whose strap has broken in the chaos. A man stands up and helps the woman with her balance and her things. He offers her his seat, but she taps her hand on his head as if he were a child and waves him away. "Not now," she seems to say to him. I crane my neck to see how the man reacts to this, but he's sat down. The back of his neck looks familiar.

I shut my eyes, hoping the woman will think this commuter is asleep and...

"You're in my seat," a voice says, low and very close to my ear.

I open my eyes and am struck by how much space the woman takes up when here up close with her hair in a torrent around her shoulders and her belongings swirling around her with the motion of the bus.

"Seats on public transportation are not assigned....," I say.

People are watching us.

"Just messing with ya," the woman says. "But you okay if I sit here?" She's pointing at the empty seat next to me, where the fabric seems to have been ripped off and patched over with a faux-leather material printed with a messy pastiche of lotuses and frogs.

She has a dazzling smile. I am confused because I had expected her to smell bad. From a distance, she'd looked unwashed, bedraggled, nasty. Homeless. Up close, she looked... sparkling, cleansed, even well-groomed. A spotless white satin dress peeks out from under a two-toned silver-white raincoat that I immediately start to covet. I can't place her scent, but I can swear I smell something familiar but forgotten.... Jasmine, frangipani....

She doesn't wait for me to answer. She shoves her guitar case under the seat in front of her and flops down in the aisle seat next to me. She doesn't seem to care about personal space. Neither does her duck. Its beak is inches from my nose and its eyes stare into mine.

"Swans won't peck at you unless you try to occupy their lake," the woman says.

I shrug and try to seem nonchalant. I look away but nothing in the view from the bus window offers anything as ridiculously intriguing as this woman and her ... things.

She doesn't seem to mind my return to staring at her. She seems accustomed to it, even expecting it.

"Do you have any questions for me?" she asks flatly.

I shake my head, unsure of what she means.

"Here, hold this," she says. She hands me a clear acrylic water bottle as large as a pitcher that she seemed to have also been balancing in one of her hands. It is filled to the brim. Heavy.

"Here's a question," I say. "How on earth are you carrying all these things around in two hands?" I regret my question as soon as it's out of my mouth.

"I'm not," she says.

I wait for her to elaborate but she doesn't.

"You're not carrying all these ... ?"

"Not in two hands," she says.

I blink at her, and when she doesn't explain any more, I let it go. I have already interrogated an unhoused woman about her need to carry all her belongings. I'm not about to prod her about her mental health.

"Do you have any questions for me," she says again, taking the pitcher from my hands. This time, it sounds like a statement.

I am getting used to staring at her. "I mean ... lots? But ..."

"Ask me one."

"Let's start with your name."

"Really?"

"I ... what? Isn't that what one ..."

"It's Sara. She/they pronouns."

"Oh. And my name is . . ."

"Next question," she says.

She doesn't seem rude. She's fixed me with a frank stare. I am stunned that I hadn't noticed it before, but her lips are red, a familiar red lip color.

"Is that Red Carpet Red from Charlotte Tilbury?" I hear myself say.

Her eyes jump into a frown. The duck quacks at me and I could swear it sounds like the duck said "fuck."

"These are the wrong questions," the woman says.

"That's a line from a Woody Allen movie," I say, grinning at her. "*Stardust Memories*. My son loves that movie, and he forced me to watch it because . . . you know . . . I wouldn't watch a Woody Allen movie unless forced by someone I love. In the movie, there's a scene in which these aliens come down to Earth and this guy, the protagonist, asks them . . ."

"'Why is there so much human suffering? Is there a God?'" she drawls, moving her head from side to side, her voice mocking but still not rude, somehow.

I stare at her. "Yes. Those were the questions. . . . You've seen the movie. . . . How do you . . . ?"

"Look, could we not talk about a rapist, please?" she says. "I was raped by my father, sweetie. Remember?"

"Jesus," I say.

"No. Brahma."

I scramble for words, but now the goose clambers from her lap onto mine, which allows me to tear my agape eyes from her face. I don't dare protest about the goose. Besides, it's surprisingly light in weight, and clean. Its webbed feet are spotless. If it poops on me, I could use the woman's water...

"Silence is not our friend, pet," the woman says, and I can't tell if she's talking to me or to the goose, because she's caressing the bird's wings as she speaks. A ripple of sensation carries from the swan to my thighs.

"Unless you are in a forest by a river. Then silence is silver. But you already know this," she says.

Her voice is down to a whisper now and she is leaning in close. Her face is no more than a couple of inches from mine. The bus is moving fast, but I feel like if I were to lift an arm, it would float slowly away and carry me with it, like I was in a spaceship.

"Don't you mean golden?" I say, stupidly.

"I like hues of white and silver. But you already know this," she says.

Her mouth is dancing with laughter now, red, teeth white within.

Her hand brushes against my thigh. This feels entirely different from all the times in my girlhood and youth when a leering man's hand would brush against my body on the bus. This feels lotus soft down in my bones, all light and silken in my brain.

But her hand is merely on its way to her tote bag placed atop the guitar case, carefully, not on the floor of the bus. On the outside of the tote is printed: WHAT IF IT ALL WORKS OUT? The tote is filled with books, so many books it couldn't be possible for her to have been carrying all that weight.

"You can have this," she says, handing me a book with a cover that's white and red. Before I can read the title, she says, "The answers to some of your questions are in the book."

"But I didn't ask..." I can't speak anymore. Her hand is pressing the book into my hands, and the book is damp. I feel her warm skin, feather soft against mine.

I lean into the last two inches of space and her lips are on mine. I smell Rajnigandha, or is it the scent of some forgotten fruit from some orchard I'd once roamed?

Then she breaks away, slowly, as if setting a child down in its cradle.

I say, "This is the first time I have..."

"...kissed someone on a bus?" she says, laughing. "No one cares."

I shake my head, and she places her hand on it to still it. "Voyage," she says in that raspy voice. "Don't believe everything you read. Wonder. Say 'yes' more. Meet new people. Eat more cake. Meet old stories. Hydrate. Ask for what you want. And for goodness' sake, ask better questions," she says.

Or maybe she says, "Ask him better questions."

She stands up, gathers the swan from my lap, picks up each of her five belongings, balances them as she teeters to the front of the bus, taps the head of the man who had offered her a seat, thanks the driver, and disembarks. The man's head resembles the head of a man who swims in the lane next to me at the swimming pool.

When I turn my head to watch the woman from my window as the bus pulls away, she is standing there on the corner of Third and Pike, smiling at me with those lips still moist from mine, her water bottle missing its cap and dripping its contents onto the street, her swan screaming, "Fuck!"

I am alone again. Land spreads out all around me and it is as if I am trying to hold on to the sound of a waterfall long after it has faded into the distance. I have the sensation of water in my ear.

I look around for the man whose head she had tapped so we

INTEMPERANCE

can commiserate over the strangeness of the woman, confirm that she was even real, but the man seems to have disappeared, or perhaps alighted with her at the stop. When I descend from the bus, I walk steadily to a mailbox and post the letter to my wise son. Then, standing there with the stem of my large red umbrella balanced against my neck to shield me from the pouring rain, and the handle of my cane resting against my right thigh, I fish out my phone from my bag, place it on the damp book the woman gave me, log into my social media, choose a picture of a dahlia that I took on my walk a few days ago, upload it because pictures work better for the algorithms, and type out:

> In completely sound mind and with a dancing heart, I announce that I will host a swayamvar on the morning of September 25th somewhere by the water in Seattle. Men are invited from far and wide to seek my hand in marriage upon successfully performing a feat. This feat will be announced to suitors at the event. I will garland the victor and we will wed that afternoon with pomp and splendor. For full disclosure—I am fifty-five years of age, own my home but am otherwise modest of income, am twenty pounds overweight and face increasing disability in my legs as my age advances. My wit and charm, however, will only dim on my deathbed.

I post the damned announcement.

The Dance Lesson

As I begin to walk in the rain toward the address of the woman who will teach me to dance, I am aware of being in a heightened state of romantic arousal. I can no longer tell if the encounter on the bus was with a woman or a vision, a mendicant or a goddess, but I know my hunger for another human form in close proximity to my own is generally and achingly called for. A conversation that disorients me orients me. I want more of that thing. I want to be teased and I want to be touched. I want a swan or to be someone's swan. I want to know and be known by a someone who sits beside me on a bus. *But you already know this.*

I get lost in my thoughts and get lost in the rain. When I arrive at the address in the enclave of the gated community where Shakti lives, the guard at the entryway must phone the dancer's home to verify my credentials. I can hear Shakti's voice over the phone sound indignant, and I become aware that she is not accustomed to having guests who might look dubious to her doorman. The doorman is apologetic to her but remains brusque with me when he hangs up. I don't blame him. Few guests must come here on foot, even fewer soaked to the skin and looking like they'd lost their way midlife.

INTEMPERANCE

Shakti is waiting by her door, looking radiant and dry. She is stricken by my state but recovers quickly and ushers me to a guest room. She has an attendant bring me a fluffy white towel and a change of clothes—a lovely yellow chooridaar kurta. When I emerge, dry and eager, Shakti leads me by the hand to her living room that has a sweeping view of Lake Washington. Even on this dreary day, the expanse of sky and water annexed for the uninterrupted view of a single dwelling is stunning. I sense others in the room but must first take in the resplendent interior with its sleek fireplace; brocade-upholstered furnishings; jewel-toned original art; furniture that's wide in girth, deep in story, heavy, rooted, sure to have traveled over willing oceans, not needful of any assembly upon its arrival. Everything about this room looks settled in, like these people would never have to move anywhere in a hurry. They belong here, and here belongs to them.

As much as the home is awe inducing, the hostess is homespun, or at least achieves such an air. Shakti has the sophisticated warmth of old wealth, old Indian wealth, and the word tehzeeb comes to mind from a smattering of Urdu with which I was acquainted long ago. Her own garb is no more ornate than the one she has lent me.

"Come," she says. She leads me by the hand to an adjoining room, which is her dance studio. The room is large, well lit, minimally but tastefully decorated with mirrors. Two large swings hang from the ceiling and are furnished with silk bolsters for dancers who want to take a break or observe other dancers. Around the room, fresh pink rose petals float in squat bronze urns filled with water. In the air, the scent of agarbatti.

She introduces me to her assembled pupils and then asks them to practice their mudras while she readies me. The pupils vary in age, race, and gender—two Indian females around my age, three younger Indian females, one Indian male, one young white female, another female who could be Korean or Japanese and possibly the youngest of us all. They display a camaraderie and a reverence with one another.

Shakti asks me to sit down on the gleaming hardwood floor. She walks over to a basket and picks up a pair of ghungroos, anklets. She ties the string, the dori, around my toe and then swiftly, firmly, adorns my ankles, round and round, with rows of the ghungroos. The sound of the little bells tinkling against one another and gently quivering against my ankles reaches deep past the broken bones and seems to whisper against the steel and titanium within, bells meeting cells. Some ineffable emotion gushes hard from my feet into my face. My eyes well up.

Arre, Shakti says. Her face is beaming, surprised. She puts a cupped palm against my cheek.

The first lesson is a salutation, a structured namaskar. I set my cane aside and stand up. Chin up, hands to heart, hands to head, left knee to floor, right knee to floor, shift weight to left foot, push up, wrists swirl around each other, arms above the head.

Over and over, I stumble and fall. Over and over, Shakti smiles at me with kindness, holds my arms, pulls me up. The other dancers avert their gaze and practice their moves. Out of the corner of my eyes, I watch them twirl, their footwork like fireflies in flight, their arms the necks of peacocks, their eyes . . .

Shakti clicks her fingers in front of my face, draws me to focus. "Do you want to move like them?"

I am accustomed to being a teacher, not so much the taught. But I nod.

She teaches me to clasp my palms, right laid onto left, below my chest. She teaches me the basic footwork. Right foot flat, left foot flat, right foot flat, left heel thrust. I do this together with her, standing side by side, four, ten, sixteen times. An hour goes by, maybe two, and no one seems to be in a hurry. This is what it feels like to tend to an art.

Ta thaee thaee tatt

Aa thaee thaee tatt

"Ta is the male energy. Thaee is the female. Tatt is their union," she says.

I don't tell her that I think the union of the male and female energy, the goddamn tatt, just broke the titanium ankle replacement that took two surgeries to assemble into my shattered joint some years ago. I point, instead, at the single bell that comes undone during the slam of my foot and rolls across the studio to hide under a chair. I offer to scramble to the floor and fetch it, but Shakti isn't having it. It happens more often than you'd imagine, she says. Let the ghungroo be suspended in time and space. She smiles.

I flinch against the pain in my leg and ask if I may simply observe for the remainder of today's class. She kindly agrees. I recover my cane and limp over to sag into the vermillion silks of one of the swings. I am sure I hear the internal bleeding from my ankles throbbing in my ears. I hold my facial expression in what I hope reads as enchantment as I watch the other dancers converge at the center of the studio now to dance in beautiful synchronicity with their teacher. Whatever supposed error they make, and their teacher corrects, is lost on me, for all I see is beauty, once and still now unreachable to me, the grace of bodies unbroken, unshrinking, uncrippled, untaunted in the streets of their childhood.

When the class ends, Shakti offers us freshly made chai, pistachios, and dates brought in from her kitchen by the attendant. I cannot bear the kindness ladled out onto my inharmonious presence here, and so I excuse myself and say I must get home to get dinner started (a lie, of course, because I plan to eat crackers and leftover dal for dinner). My hostess is solicitous. So many reasons why I should stay, she says, not just for the snacks but for an early dinner together with her family, for a warm soak of my feet, for . . . I can smell the aroma of dinner being prepared in her kitchen—onions sizzling in ghee, cumin and red chilies being ground to a paste, cardamom and saffron suffusing creamy warm milk.

I hesitate for too long and the moment is lost. Shakti is saying something apologetically about inviting me properly with ample notice next time.

One of the pupils, one of the Indian women somewhat younger than me, offers to give me a ride home. She says she lives in Seattle not too far from my place. The last thing I want right then is to make small talk with a lissome and light-footed dancer, so I try my best to get out of it, but in the end, my protests sound suspicious, so I acquiesce. My hostess folds me in a warm, sweet-scented embrace, hands me a canvas tote with my own clothes all washed and dried (so swiftly by the omnipresent attendant), and insists I keep the borrowed chooridaar kurta so I won't need to bother with changing in a hurry now, and the anklets so I can practice tying and untying them at home before the next class. I have neither the heart nor the nerve to tell my generous hostess that I have no intention of stepping into this paradise again, so I decide to let that wait until we are at email distance.

INTEMPERANCE

THE WOMAN WHO offers me a ride introduces herself as Janaki. As we head out the door, she notices my hobble and offers me an arm to descend the steps. Her grip is firm and her arm strong as a mallet. The throbbing in my ankle has subsided, and nothing seems broken internally (as I'd imagined earlier, in a state of drama-queenhood). I wouldn't have to ask poor Janaki to drive me to the ER.

Janaki tells me she lives alone. "Don't you love the single life at our age?" she asks.

She seems to be trying to pin my gaze down with hers, but I am distracted by the stunning simplicity of her Tesla's interior. The inner screen of the car's expansive sunroof silently slides open, even though Janaki doesn't seem to be pressing any button. I am encased in a warm glass egg.

"Umm, yes, sort of," I say. "Totally," I add quickly, so this line of conversation can end.

She purses her lips and touches some buttons on the screen and the car starts to drive itself. Now I want to get out of this contraption right away.

"Why would you go and throw it all away?" she says.

"What did you just say?" I am definitely meeting her eyes now. They are lined with thick kohl, which is the only makeup on her still-young-looking face. She appears to be in her forties. She is slim and is dressed impeccably in a pale-yellow pantsuit I had been admiring earlier, when the dancers changed back into their non-kathak clothes.

"I had a brutal divorce," she says. "It killed me. I lost custody of my twin boys. You'd think after I spent years raising them all by myself while separated from my husband, they'd choose to stay with me in their teens. But no, they went with their dad. He's a powerful man. Everybody loves him."

"I'm so sorry," I say. I can visualize it, her loveless marriage to some tech CEO. I want to warm up to her, show compassion, but I am unsettled by her previous comment.

"Would you like to listen to some Lata Mangeshkar?" she says. She isn't smiling. She taps a finger, and the car fills up with "*Aaj Phir Jeene Ki Tamanna Hai.*"

"Oh my God, I love this song!" I say, despite not wanting to get too chatty with Janaki. On the other hand, talking about Lata Mangeshkar's songs would definitely see us through the rest of the ride. "*Aaj phir marne ka iraada hai!*" I sing at the top of my lungs. I move my head from side to side, urging Janaki to sing along. Come to think of it, how sweet that would be, this new friend and I singing along to this classic song.

"It's sort of my anthem," Janaki says. "It should be yours too. Break all ties and let your heart soar. You could decide to live today or die today." She's translating the song.

The car picks up speed. I don't even know where I am now. I never really know where I am when in suburbia, but this seems even more disorienting. We're definitely going uphill somewhere.

"Oh, is your car driving you on autopilot to some hike or something?" I say, chuckling nervously. "I don't think we're heading to Seattle."

"I am a tornado or am I a storm...."

"Hey, Janaki? I know the song. Could we turn the music down? The car is..."

"...Someone tell me where I am...," she continues to translate.

"Yeah, I'm trying to do that!" I am shouting now. The car is going at seventy mph around curves. Janaki has closed her eyes.

I know nothing about this ludicrous car. I have no idea how to turn this thing around. My driver is my only hope.

"Men suck!" I say. "My second ex-husband cheated on me!"

Janaki opens her eyes. They fill with tears. "Right? There you are, one day, young and lovely, perfectly strong in yourself, and then your family says you must marry someone as strong as you so he can do some of the heavy lifting..."

"Hey, would you like to go get coffee?" I say, trying to look at my abductor as if there's nothing I'd love more than to hear more about her ex and her exile.

"I'd like that," she says, and the car magically slows down. With it slows down my racing heart. But I still hold my breath.

The next song on the album is "Bindiya Chamkegi." Janaki jabs at the steering wheel and the music stops before Lata can sing about teasing her lover's self-control with her bindi and her bangles. It just happens to be one of my favorite songs, but do I dare tell Janaki that? Hell, no.

She drives us smoothly to Irwin's Bakery and Café, not too far from my home. I jump out of the car as soon as it comes to a halt.

"Are you fucking crazy?" I shout at Janaki when I'm safely on the sidewalk and she's safely out of her murder machine. "You almost got us killed back there!"

"I was in control," she says, looking hurt.

"Yeah. In control of our death plunge!" I scream. "Were you taking us to drive off a cliff somewhere? It sure looked like that. Look, I don't care what happened in your marriage or divorce; you have no business taking me with you. I should report you to the cops!"

Her face darkens. "You wouldn't do that to me. This has happened too many times." She says this thing almost to herself.

"What do you mean?" I say, lowering my voice. "You've been reported to the cops? Jesus. Who are you and what did you do?"

"No, not the cops. People gossiped about me and reported false accusations to my husband. He constantly thought I was cheating."

I sigh. "Okay—look, lady, I am really sorry all these terrible things happened to you. Truly. I've been through a lot myself. But I got help. A good therapist and a few good friends can set everything right. Promise me you'll do that?" I am backing away from her and walking away from the café. "And I really don't feel up to getting coffee right now. Maybe another time," I say, waving at her.

I walk away from her as quickly as I can with a cane and a painful ankle. The next thing I know, what feel like two hands thwack me on my back and I tumble hard into a ditch. "I'm sorry!" Janaki sings as I fall.

Commotion. Dirt in my mouth. Mud on my face and hair. I scream for help. I feel my body for pain, feel my ankle for the metal inside to have thrust out alongside any broken bones, for my head to be severed from my torso, for my guts to be spilling from being impaled on a pole or something. My body has kept the score from my car crash two decades ago, and my brain has crossed over with every slasher film and Scandinavian noir television show I've watched in the past year.

Construction workers. Large, burly men with strong arms lift me out of the ditch they have dug up to lay cables or start a new condominium project, who knows? They ask if they should call paramedics. I can sense their relief when I refuse. It's probably been a long day of work for them. They readily agree to hold me in their arms until my Lyft arrives. I lay a cheek against one man's chest and lock arms with another. This way I can be sure I don't fall. This way I realize how much I love men.

INTEMPERANCE

"You don't suck," I say to one of them. He asks if I have a concussion.

I seem to be largely unhurt. The ditch is muddied from all the rain, and it softened the impact. My physical therapist has trained me to break my fall to save my head and my limbs. That training kicked in stupendously. Even the single dance lesson may have readied me. I am not dead. Not today, Sita.

"WHAT DO YOU mean your goddesses are coming after you?" Cat says with understandable incredulity. She's relieved I called her back. I'm relieved she doesn't have bad news from her end. I saw four missed calls from her, but only after I'd showered and scoured off all that mud and then attended to a couple of scrapes on my knees and palms, massaged Biofreeze into my ankle, and then fed the dog after giving him the shortest walk known to dog-kind.

I never want to miss calls from Cat, this sister I found so late in life. We live on different coasts now, and we'll never really agree on whose fault that is.

"Look, I know I sound crazy," I say. "But I just had to be lifted out of a ditch into which I was pushed by ... I don't know ... a woman whose story ... you've got to know these Hindu mythologies to get it ..."

"Okay, slow down. I'll read up on whatever these stories are. Send me links. But you're telling me a woman from your dance class tried to drive you off a cliff? Like, tried to pull a *Thelma & Louise* on you and then pushed you into a ditch, and you're not calling the cops because you think she might be a *goddess?*"

"Yes."

"Setting aside the goddess thing, which—sorry, but it doesn't

45

make sense. I'm calling the cops. But just in case they want to know why she'd do this, am I going with mental health issues, or can you give me something else? Not the goddess thing. Not telling the cops that."

"You're not calling the cops, honey. I don't think I'll ever see her again. I'm not going back to the dance class anyway. Too hard. Too beautiful. But yes, I'll watch my back in case she looms up."

"Why would she try to kill you?"

"I don't think she was trying to kill me, exactly. I think she was trying to get the earth to swallow me for my own good."

Cat is silent.

"She had a bad marriage that started with a swayamvar," I offer by way of explanation.

"This woman did?"

"Well, this goddess."

"I see. Speaking of the swayamvar . . . that's why I called you so many times. Have you looked at your socials?"

The Save-the-Date

It hasn't been a deluge but a steady trickle. Nevertheless—the ground is giving away beneath my feet.

When I open my social media, I realize that a kathak dance class, a death plunge, and a bath to wash and clean tiny, fresh wounds yields enough time for a middle-aged woman's reputation to go from stellar to shit to straight up celebrated. I had expected a few encouraging shares from friends and followers on my modest Instagram and Facebook presence, a few forwards to any single men in their circles, some gentle joshing, a bracing feminist debate or two in the outer circle of academic associates.

Indeed, a few thousand followers had afforded a few gentle likes, a couple of loves and shares and forwards, and then someone on X took a screenshot and wrote—

What a circus.

I don't know the person who posted those words, but I have to admit they are an efficient lure. If I'd seen them pop up in real time, I would have engaged, hurriedly conceding that yes, a swayamvar could be seen as a circus, but you see, if you'd examine the history with the lens of feminist... As it turned out, any defensive chatter from my end had been unnecessary due to the flood of comments from acquaintances and strangers either supporting or ripping apart the intent of the person who had reposted my announcement. People loved or hated the circus comment.

> Ummm... I am all for a mid-fifties woman claiming her space and all, but doesn't she have girlfriends to tell her to save herself the embarrassment? Who the hell is going to show up?? Not any guy *I* know!

> She knows she'll be expected to commit to the guy who wins this "feat," or whatever, right? No matter the rest of what he's like? Please tell me she's thought this through?

> What, Netflix turned down her pitch for a reality show, so she took it to the real world?

> She could of kissed some frogs.

> Is this some sort of academic experimental study? Did she get approval from the IRB?

> *Institutional Review Board.

> *IRB protects the welfare, rights, and privacy of human subjects.

> Wait, men need their welfare protected?

> #notallmen

INTEMPERANCE

Men are discriminated against, specifically with child custody and alimony, reproduction rights and access, domestic violence against men, circumcision, conscription, education, suicide, and health policies.

Is this a religious thing? Is she promoting Hinduism?

Jai Shri Ram. She is not promoting Hinduism. Our religion has beautiful stories of young princesses and goddesses selecting a suitable husband from among their suitors. It's not for a dented-painted, damaged old woman who has lost her way. She is making a mockery of Hindu culture.

Just when American women are starting to walk out of their marriages, this woman is embracing a capitalist institution. Why marriage, ffs?

She is also an American woman. (This one from Cat.)

Could we give her a break? Y'all know what dating apps are like for women these days? Especially women in their fifties??

The comment that tipped everything in a whole other direction was from a particularly badass feminist who has millions of followers and drew everyone's attention to the backdrop against which my post had been "offered."

The feminist pointed out that the photograph in my post was the cover of a book by none other than bell hooks, and the juxtaposition of my bare and wrinkled ring finger against the words "female search" was no accident. The feminist had performed a textual and visual analysis of my post. Amazing—but. I realize that when I'd stood in the rain by the mailbox on the way to the dance lesson, I had posted not the picture of the flower as I'd intended but an accidental and awkward picture of the book in my hand.

A red-and-white cover with the words *Communion: The Female Search for Love* by bell hooks.

Where the heck had that picture come from? I did not own that book. I certainly was deeply acquainted with hooks's work, beholden to it in all the literature reviews I'd ever assembled, grateful for her concepts I'd seized and cited on panels with brilliant intellectuals and arguments with undeserving civilians, modeling my own aspirations as a social scientist on the phenomenal example offered by this luminous philosopher . . . but this particular book had never made it to my desk.

The feminist commenter had referenced the large drops of moisture on the book—tears, she concluded, "although this queen had absolutely no reason to cry."

Oh. Raindrops.

This was the book the woman on the bus had thrust into my hands. She had saved me from ridicule. As bell hooks had saved so many of us.

"Fuck the patriarchy" was the most common comment on the post after the feminist commenter mentioned tears. Even now, when I refresh the feed, more of those have popped up.

This is no circus, they said. This was a clarion call. A middle-aged woman claiming agency over her desire for communion. This is at once an academic power move and a coquettish come hither. This swayamvar (misspelled and autocorrected variously as samovar, sambar, Sammamish, savory, swagger, sadomasochism, Samuel, and so on) was both a liberatory kick in the pants and full-on foreplay....

TWO DAYS HAVE gone by, and if I was shaken, although somewhat flattered by the fanfare, I am now charred by the skewering. It appears there are men on the internet that do not admire this sort of thing. This old woman is taunting men, they have decided. Men are not monkeys, they say. Some of these gentlemen seem to hate academics in particular. While it warms my heart that they took the trouble to peruse some of my publications, it chills my soul that they don't go beyond the titles. So much fun to be had, they decide, with the term "hegemonic masculinity." So much more with "marginalized masculinity." These tweets of theirs get more than a hundred thousand likes, and I am sorely tempted to go in there and point out the ironies.

So-called intellectual women who live alone are dangerous to the minds of the children of America, they say. The paper with "White Male America" in its title, while having received a gentle buzz in my peers' literature reviews in 2015, gets a major surge online (once again, only in its title; not even a link provided to JSTOR, and totally bereft of my carefully nuanced and compassionately posited arguments). "Take immigrant professors out of our classrooms" is trending. The discipline of masculinity studies is being dragged now. My peers in academia, while they love to spar at conferences about the state of men, are quiet as mice at this rampage.

Someone unearths that, while I understandably haven't been able to keep a husband, I indeed have a son. Men, and now also apparently some women, weigh in on how terrible it must have been to be raised by this man-hating mother. I now live in terror that they will discover my child's name and bring his critically acclaimed book into...

I call Karan, but it goes to voicemail.

So, instead, I apologize to the dog because the internet has now decided I own an army of cats. I also apologize because our walks are now quick and functional. *Do your business*, I mutter at him through gritted teeth a few feet of land away from the houseboat. I can swear neighbors are looking at me with wonder—of which kind, I can't tell. I don't know if my recent notoriety will be a good or bad thing in the fraught politics of the houseboat owners' association. Will Denise's husband from two houseboats down look at me funny when I ask him to help me restart my generator?

I know this is a time to get a good night's sleep; eat fresh, whole foods that list only one ingredient; keep my heart rate up with outdoor activities in abundant sunshine; sit out on my deck and warm my feet; moisturize; stay offline; and most of all, hydrate, but I have been scrolling my feeds at the devil's hour and feeding my rolls with angel food cake. I've been ordering delivery of rich malai kofta and aloo paratha, and I can swear the Uber Eats delivery guy's smirk is because he recognizes me from the awful memes.

I would never have agreed to get my voice on *The View* if it hadn't been for Cat.

"You can take back the narrative," Cat says when I finally answer her call. "What do you have to lose?"

"My mind? I don't even watch this television show, and..."

"Stop right there. You don't watch *The View*? How am I only now learning of this?"

"I don't know. I know Whoopi Goldberg is one of the hosts,

right? But that's all. I mean, what time does it even come on? There's so much good television these days. They say it's the golden age of..."

"All they're asking is for you to do a fifteen-second video message to your potential suitor. It's so romantic! Look, they're going to discuss this whole viral nonsense anyway. They're actually making room for you to say your bit."

"Seriously, this has already been so much of a spectacle. I'm a professor. I'm not some fame seeker." Even as I said the words, I realized how they didn't square with the situation I had created.

"You know I don't like academics saying things like 'but I'm a professor.' Enough with the self-aggrandizement."

Cat's husband is a professor. This is not an argument I will win against her. She's had too much practice.

"Cat, they're going to refer to me as 'One Woman.'"

"What?"

"One Seattle Woman has gone viral for announcing that she will... blah blah blah."

"But you *are* one Seattle woman. And just to clarify, they're probably going to call you 'one Seattle woman who lives on a houseboat.'" Cat laughs.

I sigh. I imagine how Seattle may now be mad at me for drawing attention to Seattle being so Seattle.

"Okay, look," Cat says. "You're doing something unusual and also something important. You can talk about it on your own terms. Get ahead of this kerfuffle on social media. Claim your story and tell it in your own words. Take back control."

"And what *are* my terms? What's my goddamn narrative? I'm losing sight of what I was seeking in the first place!"

"Well, maybe I can remind you? You are having an event

through which you may summon a partner who is also seeking you. How does it hurt to spread this word far and wide?"

"I'll tell you how. It could make the whole thing sound trashy. It could bring in a whole lot of psychos to the swayamvar. Fame seekers. Woman haters. Serial killers."

"True."

"*True?*"

"True."

"So, I shouldn't do it, right?"

"Or you could trust yourself to say the right thing. To speak to the right one somewhere. To be heard for what you want to say. And to make the right choice on the day of. Ask for what you want."

"I could," I say, a little disoriented. *Ask for what you want.*

"You could. You could. You could trust yourself the way I trust you."

"Damn you, Cat."

"*Thank you*, Cat."

"And you're sure *The View* is . . . highbrow enough?"

"It's not that at all. But I will get a kick out of seeing you on it. Do it for me. I need something fun right now. My husband is dying."

Damn you, Cat.

When the segment airs, the women on *The View* are kind, especially Whoopi Goldberg. Together, they egg men on to take the bait. "Tear yourself away from going after women online and go perform a feat or two," they say. Laughs and cheers all around. And then, my video. God, I look harried, but I did get my hair done and rocked a red lip tint. And I did tap into something deep within and say, "I have stopped searching. But I have started expecting that you will show up. I don't know what feat I will ask you to perform on the day of my swayamvar, but I know you will breeze through it. I am doing this thing that is so scarily public so I can improve the odds of reaching you somehow. I promise you that when we find each other, we can both disappear into our world."

NOW I WANT two days of unplugged silence. Now the dog is walked by a dog walker. A text from Cat declares that she and her husband thought my television debut was a roaring success. Someone has delivered flowers, and I'm certain the pollen in the lilies is coated with anthrax. The phone is ringing off the hook, if that's even a phrase anymore, and I've been foolish enough to take some of these calls. When it's been from someone I know, they've simply wanted to gather information of the kind I just don't have right now—logistical or legal or the more solicitous mental health queries. And, of course, the main question seems to be: *What have you decided for the feat?*

Meanwhile, the mail is piling up on my dining table. Cards. Handwritten letters. A few from India. Definitely not opening those. One letter from an inmate at the state penitentiary. I have a writer friend who teaches yoga to men in prison, and she would want me to treat this letter the same way I treat the ones from people who are not incarcerated, so I do. I let them all sit there in a heap, awaiting trial.

Feminists of all stripes from my homeland and from my current land of citizenship are sending messages, mostly of support and some also of caution. As is their wont, several are seeking to complicate the question, problematize it some, intersectionalize it, queer it up a bit. They send me readings so extensive they would see me all the years to my grave (so to speak; we Hindus cremate our dead). All the years to my pyre.

Given that I am on a sabbatical, I have developed an aversion to reading. I just can't be bothered anymore. Oh, I know it will come back, my academic, inquiring mind, but for now, I am enjoying the intersectionality of menopause and time off. I sift through the throng of messages with an eye only for the delightful or the frighteningly disdainful.

My dean does write with a message asking if there is any particular way he ought to answer any media inquiries coming his way, for there have been a few, and they are hard to ignore. *They want to know if the university supports this action on the part of their celebrated feminist faculty, and I plan to say this is a purely personal decision and the event is not a university-sponsored event. Is that fine?*

Yes, I respond. *It's fine.* I want to add that Women, Gender, and Sexuality Studies ought to be contributing some funds to the swayamvar.

I haven't heard anymore from the son yet, and I imagine it might be because he is in thrall to a Muse at his writing retreat or perhaps a Fury if the virality has reached him. Either way, I'm relieved to not have to explain, although it would be soothing, wouldn't it, to just hear my child's voice.

I am conscious that the worst thing for a tiny houseboat is clutter. I scan the pile of mail. I see flashes of bright yellow. DHL courier. Two such packages, one indicating a thin document within, the other a hard little object.

Now, what could be so urgent as to warrant a pricey international courier service? I reach for the one with the object. The name and address are unfamiliar. Ananya Kumar from Patna. I sometimes get emails from names like these, or LinkedIn requests, but never a . . . despite my best judgment and perhaps as part of the self-destructive streak I seem to be on, I find myself slowly cutting open a corner of the package. When nothing explodes or sprays or fumes out, I cut further, inch by inch. Inside is an exquisite little silver filigreed box. I pry it open, bit by bit. Inside, a black goop smelling of camphor and ghee. To be eaten? No way.

The aroma does that thing that happens to me with scents from what once was home. I am unsteadied. I root my feet to the floor, although fully aware that beyond the few inches of wood below is not land but water. I have to look around my living room space and glance at my books, my lampshade, the hydrangeas on my dining table, the two red velvet footstools that spark joy and all, because I am here, and outside my window is a sun-dappled Portage Bay. But if I close my eyes, I am on summer holiday in the home of a sweet aunt in Patna in 1979, when she scorched almonds and cotton and ghee and camphor and turned it into soot to make kohl for her girls and for me.

Why has someone from Patna sent me homemade kohl?

I set the silver box aside. The aunt is a distant memory and the cousins grown and gone to several parts of the world. My own parents and brother are kept at a distance, and this other DHL courier had better not be from one of them, although I can't imagine them reaching out to me after all these years of estrangement. On the courier, a different name and address, again unknown. Inside is a handwritten letter.

The Astrologer

Dear Madam,

I hope this letter finds you in the pink of health. I am couriering it to you from New Delhi with the highest urgency. You don't know me, but I am your distant cousin-brother, Dr. Brajesh Chandra Thakur, residing in New Delhi. We met many years ago in childhood when our families joined together for Dussehra celebrations in our mutual ancestral property in the village of Bhagalpur in Bihar. You will not remember. You were a small little girl running around in your kachchi. I am elder to you by around ten years. Even though our families have lost touch, I am pleased to have been kept updated as to your accomplishments over the years. We are all very proud of you overcoming the misfortune of your physical handicap and going on to be bestowed with a PhD, that too from a US university. Very well done.

It is with this esteem and regard for your intellectual achievements that your elder brother is writing to you today. I have been informed about your proposed project of holding a little swayamvar ceremony in your locality in the city of Seattle. As a learned lady, you must have researched the history of the swayamvar, but upon

INTEMPERANCE

inquiring into the research available on this matter in US research databases, I am certain you must have fallen short.

Before I inform you on the practice of swayamvar itself, I will tell you a story that might give you some caution and dissuade you from this path you are on. You may not be aware, but there is a curse upon our family, especially your branch of our family. It mainly befalls the ladies. The most heartbreaking part of the story is that the curse was pronounced not by a daayan (do you know about the witches that still to this day run amok in Bihar?) but by a Brahmin woman who had lost her mind. She was none other than your own great-great-grandmother. Yes, madam, you have been cursed by your very own great-great-grandmother.

She was the mother of your great-grand-uncle, Alokendra Thakur. This boy brought shame upon our family, a shame from which we are still trying to recover. He cut off our noses in the intoxication of something he is said to have called love. Not only him but our entire clan was undone by it. There is a saying in our parts—Baadhe poot pitaa ke dharm, kheti upjay apne karm. If I may attempt a translation: A father's good deeds will reap fortunes for his son, but one's own deeds may reap our misfortune.

We cannot blame his father, the great landowning zamindar Ishwar Nath Thakur. They say he had some hopes even for this son of his, who was already showing signs of being a weakling. They say that if Alokendra hadn't been sent by his father at dawn one day in the summer of 1892 to amble through their acres of litchi orchards, the terrible fate would not have befallen our clan. Alokendra was supposed to go and walk around as a warning to any errant laborers who might try to steal a nap under the trees. The branches were bursting with ripe fruit that needed to be picked before their peels threatened to crack. This litchi empire was one day going to be his, after he returned from a prestigious education for which he was soon going to leave for Calcutta. But because of his wrongheaded ways, his life—and therefore now yours—took a different turn.

Alokendra is later known to have said that "matters of love and longing are fated," but you will see how this was just the beginning of the many blasphemous things he had said. Meanwhile, his elder brother was doing the responsible work of the family, sent by his father to their mango orchards. As you well know, mango is the king of fruits, and keeping an eye on those laborers is paramount to the work of a zamindar's son.

In the coolness of a late-June morning, in the season of Ashadha, Alokendra is said to have stopped in his tracks upon arriving in the litchi orchards. He was struck by the sight of two dark-brown arms. They say he described those arms as "moving with the grace of a dancer" through the boughs of the litchi trees. Yes, these trees and their yield were meant to be Alokendra's someday, but he wanted to lay claim only to those feet that jumped from bough to bough.

The sun crept up slowly on the orchard, but the face of the litchi plucker stayed hidden from Alokendra's view. It is said that people saw the picker become aware of being watched. Beneath the trees, sat rows upon rows of ladies, their own nimble legs discreetly crossed under their saris. They kept their eyes on Alokendra at a slant.

Madam, you have never seen this kind of sight, I am sure, but it is your loss. I am told you have not been to our village since that time when you were a toddler. The season of litchi picking is a beautiful one indeed, and I am fortunate to take my wife and grown-up children to see it during summer months. I can easily picture how those ladies all those years ago quickly covered their heads with the pallu of their saris when they saw the young thakur approach. Their voices must have fallen to whispers. Their fingers

INTEMPERANCE

must have turned more attentive and moved more deftly, reaching for the litchi among the leaves and branches laid out at their feet. Their slender hands must have plucked each fruit with the gentleness demanded from the task. They must have softly plopped the pink-skinned litchi and crimson-skinned litchi into separate baskets and thrown the brown-skinned ones into a waste heap as they do even today.

To continue with the story of your great-grand-uncle, Alokendra is said to have widened his shoulders, crossed his arms at his chest, and leaned against one of the trees that were to one day be his. He is said to have watched the ladies with a fixed, sharp gaze but let his peripheral vision wander desperately to keep a single spectacular being in view as it moved, sure-footed and taunting, in its prance above.

They say that beads of sweat started to form on young Alokendra's face. He watched as the litchi picker's arms expertly plucked off the twigs and not the thicker branches. On the picker's arms was a jute bag. When the picker saw Alokendra gazing up into the trees, the bag slipped, and they say that the tender perfume of the litchi fruit, as it dropped from the air, assailed Alokendra's senses so deeply that he did not realise that the picker, who jumped down to land an inch from him, was a male and not a female.

The villagers like to make up dramatic parts of this story, but they say that a whole bag of the fruit fell to the rich red earth of our famed Mithila land and the plump fruit broke through the skin with its pearly white arils lying bare between the two young men. The women are said to have gasped because the litchi picker was an Untouchable, and he is supposed to have known not to let even his shadow fall on the young Brahmin landowner's body. He was already trained not to let his fingers touch the litchi itself, only the branches. Untouchables were not allowed to touch our food. Anyway, they say that after their gasps, the women giggled that their najuk (delicate; in case you have forgotten your mother tongue) thakur turned into a Shahi litchi himself (this being the name of the variety of litchi grown in those orchards) and that, like the litchi, his seed was small.

Please forgive me if this story is offensive to your senses. I wanted you to be transported into that time and place to understand how the shame and curse befell our poor ancestors and follows us to this day. The "love story" of Alokendra and Heera (the name of the litchi picker) was not just doomed because of the difference in their castes. It was doomed because of their same gender. If it had been merely about caste, and if Heera had been a Dom-caste girl instead of a boy, people would have looked the other way. After all, a lower-caste girl who slept with a Brahmin man was said to be elevated in her own social ranking and was also said to have earned a place in heaven.

The Manusmriti, which you may or may not know is the ancient Hindu text that prescribes the moral and legal screed for men and women in family life and public life, says a Brahmin boy can marry a girl in any caste—Bania, Rajput, Kayasth—and the child will be allowed into the father's upper caste. The child will be honored as a Brahmin. In Maithil Brahmins, if you must marry outside the caste, you can marry a Kumhar girl or a Teli girl. The castes of potters and oil makers are clean castes.

As you must be well aware, no casteism exists in India now. These days, even people from the Chamar caste, whose ancestors until recently did the disgusting work of tanning leather and disposing of animal carcasses and hides, are now magistrates and collectors! They have even gone so far and banded together to form

INTEMPERANCE

a national political party whose members are chief ministers and MPs, and their leader is a lady. Madam, perhaps you know a lot of this already, but my point is this: India is not the same India you left behind. So much progress had been made in our proud nation. And yet a lot of it is getting out of hand because people have forgotten their place in the divine and delicate order of things.

Even today, you will agree that the kind of impure desire that Alokendra showed for that boy, Heera, will make your stomach churn. And a bestial desire for a Dom-caste boy! In the nineteenth century! It is no surprise that terrible things befell poor Alokendra. It is said he was under the spell of Heera's sister, a young daayan whose witchcraft made it impossible to retrieve his senses as he became entangled in this "love" for Heera.

I will stop here with their story for now. It may be too much for you take in the matter of why Alokendra's own mother put a curse on her husband's family, a curse which dogs you today, marriage after marriage, man after man, decision after wayward decision.

Please do not mistake me. I am not judging you. I am a progressive man. As early as the 1980s, I allowed my wife to take up employment as a Hindi schoolteacher after our children were grown up. I celebrated the arrival of Goddess Lakshmi in my house with the birth of my two daughters. They never once saw me raise my hand to their mother or even raise my voice at her. I taught their brother, my third child, to respect his elder sisters like avatars of Goddess Durga. I educated my daughters all the way to postgraduation and gave them the same privileges as I gave my son. Like you, my daughters are settled in the United States after receiving good marriage offers by the grace of God. My eldest daughter is a dentist in New Jersey and my second daughter is a pharmacist in Houston. Both of them are happily married. I have very good sons-in-law who provide well for their families. My daughters have been blessed with two children each. My youngest child, a son, was too precious to his mother and she has kept him close to us here, in Delhi. He is a civil servant.

As you can see, my side of the family escaped the curse. I am saddened to see that yours did not. Such is the way of curses. I would not have written to you if I did not feel the obligation, given what you are about to do with this mockery of a swayamvar. It pains me to hear that my dear (even though distant) younger sister has lived such a life of turbulence and poor decisions. There are some who say that if you have had two divorces, the problem must be with you, not the men. But I am not one of those people. Still, when I heard that you have not only been possessed by the curse that marked the ladies and the ladylike men of our ancestors but that you have also been cursed with twisted ankles like the daayans of our villages, I put a stone on my heart and put pen to paper.

You are afflicted, but you have the inner power to break the curse. You have the blessings of Goddess Durga Mata, whose temple is just outside our ancestral village home in Bhagalpur and draws people from far and wide for worship.

I am not happy to write this letter. I cannot proceed any further in my explanations of our family history. The matter of Alokendra and his illegitimate lover is too shameful to write in full here, especially to you, my sister. Some of the men in the family were given a horrific letter that Alokendra wrote to that disgusting litchi picker. This letter has been passed down to men in our family as a caution. The language is too appalling for the delicate ears and eyes of most ladies, but I am willing to share it with you, owing to the high level of your education and your senior age. I know you will want further information about this, so I will await your phone

call on 91–9512047111XX. I also invite you to join our Thakur family WhatsApp group, where everyone is very respectful and if they are not, I will take issue with them on your behalf.
  My salutations to you—Jai Shri Ram.
  Yours sincerely,
  Dr. Brajesh Chandra Thakur

IF THE LETTER had indeed found me in the pink of health, it has left me in a state of fuck-this-guy. Why is it that no matter how far away a woman might run from the voice of her father and brothers, the structures of flight and postal services and virtual clicks could still deliver their boom into her chambers? I had little doubt this man was indeed some distant cousin of mine. His words were too familiar in their caution and their cadence. A thrust in their intent. A watchfulness and a monitoring of the sisters' lives. Men like him have slapped me in the name of protecting me. My father. My brother. Somewhere, those men are still slapping the women of the family I left behind in what they call a modern city.

I toss his letter under the other mail. I stand up, scratch the dog behind his ear, and ask him to find his ball for a game of fetch. I make myself a pot of Assam loose-leaf tea and take it outside to the deck. There, I the toss the ball into the water and the dog jumps off the deck and swims to it, back and forth and back and forth in a rhythm the two of us have turned into our very own meditation. Here we are, woman and dog afloat, content, safe.

If this dog hasn't met the Brahmin men from the shores of the Ganges who ate and married and raped and plundered and loved and fed and toiled and murdered all along that river, those people who nurtured and slaughtered and cursed daughters before me, then do I need to turn my attention to them at all? This quiet life of books and bookstores, a break-even academic salary that feels like wealth nonetheless, a smattering of good friends of regions and races I would not have known so dearly had I stayed a Brahmin girl of relative privilege in Bombay, this teapot and this lick of Lake Union, these sights and sounds seem beyond the reach of some old, meandering curse.

When the stars start to appear in the sky and the dog has shaken off the lake from his fur and enjoyed a towel rub, I return to the warmth inside. I am struck once again by the beauty of my odd little home. Standing here, on the threshold between outside and inside, I am nevertheless displaced from my hard-won ease. I am reminded that the upper-caste Brahmin girl from Bombay was aided mostly by her privilege into the jewel tones of this life. No space she inhabited could be casteless.

I stare at the silver box on the dining table as it glints in the blue bath of twilight. Surely nothing can happen if I simply pry the lid fully open with the corner of my thumbnail and sniff at the kohl carefully pasted inside?

The scent goes straight to my head and kicks open a door of memory in which the aunt in Patna puts a little mirror in my hand and, with the soft tip of her ring finger, gently traces kohl into the rims of my young eyes. "Never leave home without some of this in your eyes, she says. You will see the world as it really is, not as what the men tell us it is. And with this lining your eyes, you will always have beauty. The kohl will draw people's sight up to your pretty face. No matter how badly you limp, you will always be the most beautiful woman walking down the road."

INTEMPERANCE

I look at the glistening charcoal paste in the little silver box in my hand now. Would I be blinded from lead? Should I research the shit out of this before rubbing a tiny bit on . . .

My lower lash line—the waterline—stings a little from the camphor, but the sting is not unpleasant. The water that rushes to my eyes is only to be expected. I blink, blink, and am overcome by the urge to curl up on my bed and lay my head on my pillow. A cacophony of . . . wedding sounds . . . starts up around me. Everything turns dark for a moment and then light.

I am barely holding on by a thread. I am spun and rocked and swirled in a dizzy revolution around what seems like a vast and terrifying planet. A metal planet. I scream, but the sound comes out as a tinkling . . . bell. I clutch at a thread of deep red velvet to which I am tethered. All around me, tiny brass bells. All of them more secure than me in their belonging. More embedded. Help, I say, but they are all singing in a rhythm. My scream is also their song. I succumb to my form as a bell and sing along. Chham-chham. Jhunnak-jhunnak.

Outward in my vision, a throng of people. Feasting. Women dancing in silks, their heads covered. A bride, a groom, a priest. People I have never seen before, people from another time. Humans, servants, scampering with copper plates laden with . . . laddoo. When I glance at round things, I feel comforted for a moment. A brotherhood of roundedness.

Brothers, so many of the men here look like brothers. Whose?

Angry faces. One man looks right at me. No, not at me, why would he look with such rage upon a poor bell falling away from her sisterhood of bells? No, he looks a little above me. I am tethered, barely, to red velvet, a dancer's ghungroo wrapped around a human ankle. I am small, too small, trying to keep up with the beating of the dancer's human bones within and a human . . . heart. Who is wearing the ghungroo? He is in love. I feel it in his bones.

His father glares at him and the way he is dancing. He swirls and now, in place of his father, there is his mother, her face half covered with her orange sari, seated, trying to look away from her son, trying to push a smile up against muscles tensed with terror and . . . shame at her dancing son. The shame is round. Complete.

Ta thaee thaee tatt . . .

Alokendra, someone whispers.

And the swirl slows down. Another young man, this one in the shadows. Carrying food-soiled plates made of leaves. His eyes locked on the dancer. His muscles taut. He is trying to push shame upon his smile, but the shame won't stick. The plates in his hand quiver.

Tatt.

I am ripped from velvet and roll across the floor. I roll with the speed of a universe asunder. I roll with no control toward the soiled plates on the ground. A foot stamps down on me, holds me there for a moment, muffling my screams in a passion so forceful I am sure my own ridges will rip through the flesh of his sole and draw blood. But then the foot shifts and I am in thrall of the face in thrall of me. Heera's fingers pluck me like a fruit from the sole of his foot and tuck me into the damp and dirty waistband of his dhoti, cushioning me and carrying me away from the riptide of wrath in this feasting home.

When he takes me out again and holds me in his palm, Heera is singing by a river. I don't know the words; I am but a bell, but I have danced enough to know this is a song of love. A ripple on the water and then a shadow springs out against the moon. It splashes back into the water, then surges again, a giant fish.

The young man calls out to the creature. I have given my heart to *someone, he sings. He jingles me, rolling me round and round on his flattened palm in a revolution that feels safe. I am no longer small. I am a whole galaxy. He makes a rhythm from my chime for his song and for the dive and the breach on the water, the clicks and the whistles that come in response from the sweet blind beast that lives in the Ganga.*

The Wedding Planner

The dog is barking into my face. A sensation on my skin, as if I have just returned from elsewhere. Not much time has passed, and yet I feel older and also younger, I am here and also there, then and also now. Muffled. Aroused. Disoriented. Unearthed.

Where did I go these past several minutes? I can't quite summon up a recall.

The dog pees on the rug in front of me as I watch. He only does this when he is frightened. Did I frighten him? When my motor skills return from the fugue state, I rush to the mirror. The kohl is a mere smudge around my eyes. Has it absorbed into my skin and retina?

I find towels to soak up the pee on the rug.

I MUST DISTRACT myself from the residue of muddied sights in my brain. And yet there's something I'd like to allow to linger—a wisp of a feeling of longing. It's as if someone else's heart skipped a beat somewhere, and it landed like an echo in mine. A soundless song is lodged in my ear, neither music nor lyric nor clear memory.

I think of calling Cat, but I am afraid to tell her about rubbing non-FDA-approved kohl in my eyes. I want to see some of my present-day, human, available-in-person friends in Seattle, but I don't want to have to fill them in on my plans for the swayamvar.

As I skim my email past the literature reviews on offer and the cautions in the clutter, it's a message from one Demi Yante that catches my eye, with its unabashed directness at wanting to capitalize, quite literally, on my swayamvar.

LET ME PLAN YOUR SWAYAMVAR FOR FREEEEE!!!

I hadn't thought or even desired to hire a wedding planner for either of my first two weddings, and I certainly don't need one for a tiny, scaled swayamvar, but Demi is offering her labor for free. Something in my ancestry compels me to approve of this, but that is why I must resist.

She'd emailed and called and slid hard into my DMs after two whole days of no response from me. She says she knows I'm not trying to be rude. She is aware that I have probably been deluged with messages.

I correspond with Demi. I talk on Zoom to ensure she isn't a bot or whatnot. Demi is exactly what you'd expect a wedding planner to be. She is in her mid-thirties, dazzlingly pretty, and preemptory of my every if and but.

She admits to me right out what's in it for her. "A little bird tells me that your swayamvar is the next enchanting thing in the world of weddings." The wedding industry is always looking for firsts, she says, and after interracial weddings and queer weddings and interracial queer weddings, this swayamvar is something she was "born to do." She says she wants to be the first one to get in on it.

"You know, you may even start a trend," she says, clapping her hands.

When I frown, she assures me she gets the gravitas of the whole thing and will not mess with my vision for the event and will only provide support. When I say I'm not sure I need support, and all I plan to do is show up somewhere by the water in bridal attire with a garland and a three-tiered cake, she lifts her pen from her furious note-taking, points it at the web camera on her end, and jabs the air with—

So, you have a city permit for a waterfront venue? You'll need that for even the smallest event.

And you have a dress?

And you have a florist who makes garlands—you will want marigold and jasmine, right?

And you squared away your cake order six months ago, I presume?

She says we should meet in person. I am suspicious of this. She sends me her testimonials and her privacy notice to reassure me. She mentions she is culturally sensitive, being biracial herself. Her mother is Latina, and the Yante last name is from her Filipino father, she says. She offers to set up a call with a satisfied client if I'd like a reference.

I brush away that offer and tell her that, while I'd love to meet in person, I probably need to be hiding out. I don't want to be out and about, drawing attention. She giggles and says that out and about is the only place we're safe from attention. "Being online has a way of making you feel that you're in the center of the gaze," she says.

"Right."

"When you're out and about, unless you're a real celebrity, no one's aware. No one cares. Everyone's on their phones. It's a loopy paradox. You get off your phone and go out, you're safe from everyone because they're on their phones. You hide in plain sight."

INTEMPERANCE

"You're a philosopher," I say to her. "And I believe my swayamvar demands a philosopher wedding planner. Let's get ice cream."

DEMI IS WAITING at Frankie & Jo's ice cream shop when I get there. I order my favorite, California Cabin, whose name isn't half as delicious as its description, which I like to read every time I patronize this establishment—"A whimsical smoked vanilla & pine ice cream with bold, delicious black pepper cardamom shortbread cookie throughout." This time I must have read this out loud, because Demi laughs and reads out loud the description of her own choice of scoop—Salty Caramel Ash, "A luxurious, imaginative salted caramel ice cream blended with activated coconut charcoal and sea salt."

Somehow, despite her mirroring, Demi's demeanor doesn't feel like practiced charm. She doesn't seem to be attempting an agreeable disposition. She seems to genuinely love her job and has an enviable manner of surrender to the present moment.

Outside, it's the kind of day for which Seattle aches nine months. The sun is mild but warm, maybe around seventy-four degrees with a light breeze that makes skirts billow and bones heal. Demi drives us to the nearby beach at Golden Gardens Park in her cream-colored MINI Cooper convertible. It could be a great venue for the swayamvar, she says. My hair is a mess when we arrive, and my heart is beating fast because Demi has been driving poorly: she'd like to eat her ice cream before it melts. I smooth my hair down, clutch my cane, and we start to stroll on the beach.

"You still don't recognize me, hunh?" Demi says.

Startled, I peer at her. I frown and shake my head.

"Professor! I'm Demi Yante! Class of 2011?"

"Oh! Demi!" I say. I still have no recollection, I want to say, especially since that was the year I was getting divorced from Paul, but I have a rehearsed response for students with this kind of thing. "Of course, I remember! You always paid such good attention in class. Such an irony that your professor's own memory is fading!"

"Oh, it's really all right," she says. "I didn't want to say anything earlier because I didn't want you backing out for some reason. You know? Like, the familiarity and all. And it could seem a bit stalkery."

It absolutely does, but I laugh heartily. I feel a bit guilty for not being able to recall her. After all, it's not as if Seattle has sent me that many students of color over the years. She continues to reassure me. Yes, she'd recognized my name in the social media shares, she'd hesitated but then taken the chance. She'd wanted, for years, to write to me and say how much my classes had meant to her.

"I do what I do today because of your teaching," she says.

I laugh and then realize she isn't joking. I don't want her to think I look down at her line of work, so I say I can see how but would love to know more.

A child in swim trunks runs up to us and asks to lick our ice creams. We both giggle and say no. The child, no more than three or four, starts to cry. We look around for an adult to claim the child, but no one seems to be in charge.

"*Excuse me?*" Demi calls out in all directions. The child is now pulling at the skirt of my dress and wailing. His face is red and snotty. He starts to cry for his daddy. I am a little surprised at this but don't have time to think about it because the child is now kicking sand onto my feet. He doesn't have much power in his plump little feet, so I'm not disturbed by this, but both Demi and I are now concerned about the child's rising levels of distress.

Just as I start to lower my ice cream toward the child's mouth in confusion and perhaps from some long-ago instinct of appeasing Karan in this way when he was a toddler, a man comes bounding up to us.

"Hey! Hey! Lady! Stop that!" he shouts.

I'm disoriented and look around. He's waving his hand at me. His sweaty face comes close to mine. "You can't just give someone's child your half-eaten ice cream!" he says. "What do you think you're doing?"

I'm trying to find the words to explain, but the man won't stop talking loudly into my face. He starts to escalate everything, speaking as he tries to put the picture together in real time, but all wrong. He is now accusing me of luring the child away from him. He starts to shout and call out to people. Strangers start to look over, but no one moves. They are assessing the credibility of the people involved. This is Seattle. A white man is screaming into the face of brown and Asian women. Not cool. But wait, could the brown woman have been trying to kidnap the child? Not cool. Let's wait and see.

Perhaps sensing my urge to punch the man square on his nose, Demi steps between the man and me and says in an even tone, "Sir, you need to back off. This woman is a faculty member at the university. Your child ran up to us. She wasn't feeding him. She was trying to trick him into quieting down. I'm going to call CPS because you let your child get lost on a public beach."

The man disappears with his crying child.

Demi shakes her head. "Single dads," she says as she dives one hand into her purse to pull out a wet wipe for her other hand, on which some of her ice cream has melted.

Despite my political objections to her comment, I start to laugh. Demi laughs along. I remember her now.

"Sorry," she says. "I know that's wrong to say. But, like, dude!"

"Demi. You used to be a dead-serious young woman back in college. Quiet, almost stern. I recognized it just now when you spoke to that man. I remember you shutting down a male student so eloquently once. I can't recall what he said, I think he kept interrupting a female student, and you suddenly spoke up and said..."

"Listen twice, speak once," we both say together.

"I was paraphrasing Tupac Shakur, and he was paraphrasing a Greek philosopher, I think," Demi says, smiling.

"Well, I remember the class laughed and the young man laughed along sort of grudgingly," I say, returning to my rapidly melting ice cream. "That's a rare gift, you know, to win both sides and offend neither. And you were so quiet yourself. So serious. You're sort of different now. I mean..."

"So chirpy?"

"So lighthearted."

We sit down on the sand and watch people frolic in the water. Only a few are swimming. I feel a breeze bathe my face and play with my hair. I slowly lick the last bit of my ice cream, savoring the cardamom cookie bits. I nibble on the nub of the cone.

I thank Demi for her presence of mind with the strange incident with the child and the man. I ask her what she had started to say, about how my teaching led her to be a wedding planner.

"Oh, yeah," she says. "You know all those books and papers we read about masculinity and marriage? Well, it stayed with me. I became an assistant to a wedding planner, and I noticed how, in cis-het weddings, it was always the bride-to-be approaching us and leading the whole wedding preparation. This didn't sit right with me. Of course, you'd think that the bride is the one invested in having the wedding a certain way, but well, so much of that is socialization, right? And then, she gets more and more stressed out because, one, there's too much pressure on her from all sides for the actual logistical pieces, and she's feeling let down in one way or the other emotionally because this is maybe her first experience with how her fiancée is socialized to not be involved. Then she gets labeled as a bridezilla. Ugh. My boss at the wedding planning agency would routinely make bridezilla jokes. I'd keep bringing in the studies we read about heterosexual partnerships, but my employer wasn't interested. I mean, she straight up told me to shut the eff up."

So, Demi had found an investor and started her own wedding planning agency. She now has two employees who work for her.

I ask Demi what she'd like brides to know. I don't look at her as I ask, so she doesn't feel like I am invested in her response for my own sake, but I am surprised that I sort of am.

Wonder.

Demi is happy to be asked. "So many brides talk about how their groom is kind and smart and funny. And I don't see these guys bring these things into the wedding planning process. I have to listen over and over to how he proposed. How he buys her gifts. How he whisked her away to a vacation in Paris. How he makes her laugh. How he cooks and cleans and does his own laundry. How he reads antiracist books because he wants to understand her experience in America. At some point it starts to sound like a justification for marrying that guy, you know? Like he's some sort of God."

"I know," I say. "Go on." I fill my fists with warm sand and pour it down my shins, something I did as a girl on Juhu Beach in Bombay. I watch as it sandclocks its way through the ridges of surgical scars on my ankles.

"What I often don't hear is how *she* is loving *him*," Demi is saying. "How she showers him with affection. How she dotes on him. What is she doing for him? It's like we've all been socialized into silence around this. We're so afraid of not being loved or not being seen as loved, we've forgotten that we, too, have the agency to love unabashedly and wholeheartedly. And to talk about it. Not in some hashtag tradwife way, not performative, but in a . . ."

I blink at Demi. This is not where I thought she was going.

Neither of us has the word she was looking for, so we let it be.

She looks back at me earnestly. "But a little bird tells me you know all this. It's what bell hooks said in that book, right? That when women embrace the art of loving, it's, like, the biggest threat to the patriarchy. When I saw your post about the swayamvar and saw that it had been inspired by one of my favorite books, I was like, whoa!"

I don't have the heart to tell Demi that I haven't read the book yet. Why haven't I read the book yet?

"In my first meeting with the bride-to-be and whoever accompanies her, I tell them my philosophy—everyone will participate in the planning because a wedding is the first or one of the most significant celebratory partnership exercises for the bride and groom. Right? And doing it together will foundation a memory into how to be there for each other hereafter," she says, looking

INTEMPERANCE

pleased with her choice of words that are probably verbatim from her website mission statement. Her clientele has grown by word of mouth, and her agency is much sought after, she says, smiling shyly at me.

This time, even though I have the stock sentence to speak at such moments when former students tell me of their accomplishments, I am caught a little off guard by how sincerely I mean it. "I am so proud of you," I say. "Truly, Demi."

She beams, then says, "Well, a little bird tells me I don't have to have that pep talk with *you*."

"Right," I say. "Because there is no groom yet." I can't help smiling at how often and sometimes bafflingly she uses the "little bird tells me" phrase.

"Well, sure. But I meant because you practically write papers on all this. And the bell hooks book and all."

I smile and shrug. Sheepishly.

"What's troubling you, Professor? Please talk to me," she says. She puts an elbow on her knee, her chin in her hands. An image flashes into my head of a Raja Ravi Varma painting of a woman leaning dreamily on a banister in her palace balcony, speaking to . . . a swan, I think?

I shake my head and grin at her now. When she doesn't look away, I turn my face from her searching eyes to the water. The light is dancing on it. It's easier for me to talk into this view. I tell Demi how clear my intention had felt a few days ago, and now, with so many people weighing in, and the whole vitriol online, and even the cheering, things are getting cloudy. I may be losing sight of where this all began and where I'd want to see it go.

This is common, Demi tells me, even for those not planning a swayamvar but just a little wedding. And she says she is sorry she assumed I should "have it more together" just because I "rock this thing academically." You're entitled to be like just any other bride for whom this whole approaching-date thing can feel like a runaway train, she says.

Demi says there's something she wants me to keep in mind. She wants to tell me the story of her own marriage that is no more. She tells me she had listened her whole life to women in her family telling her she was pretty and could have whatever she wanted in a man. But then they had also talked so much about what she should want in a man. "They told me to dream and then they rushed to fill in ideas. I didn't have the chance to wander in my own dreams. They gave me a checklist—wealthy, handsome, caring, smart, funny, blah blah."

And then she'd found just such a man and married him. Her family loved him. He "treated her right," so she thought he was right. "We were mismatched," she says. It wasn't his fault. He was raised with a checklist, too, for what he ought to be as a man and what he ought to find in a woman.

"We grew bored of each other so quickly. We were relieved when we both arrived at the decision to divorce. Everyone was so mad at us and making them mad was the most fun we ever had."

She laughs hard. I join in. My goodness, I am glad to have met her.

"We have to stop looking for Gods in men," she says.

That sounds to me like an odd thing for her to say. She reminds me of a myth I once knew of a woman who was tricked into marrying a God but yearned for . . .

"Next time, it will be just an average guy, and he will be The One," Demi says.

I laugh out loud and slap my knee.

"What?" she says, looking hurt for just a second, then covering it up with a professional smile. "A little bird tells me he's on his way!"

I realize she's dead serious. She tells me she knew her marriage was over when she saw how in sync one of her clients was with her wife-to-be and yet they kept asking one another questions. They leaned in to listen with curiosity. "And it wasn't just because they were a lesbian couple. They were both pansexual, actually. Those people have, like, PhDs and Nobel Prizes in partnership dynamics. They've experienced the whole spectrum." She laughs. "But of course, I won't romanticize them. There's always room for human error. People can be assholes to each other no matter their socialization or orientation. But it just so happened that I saw them so in love with one another, so attentive and clear-eyed about their love, I just wanted what they had."

Demi had married at twenty-five, ended her marriage at thirty. After a couple of years of dating and letting go, she'd decided to spend a few years solo. She was now thirty-seven. "But a little bird tells me to still *believe*," she says. "And every wedding I plan teaches me so much about color palettes and about relationships, not just between partners but between extended family." Demi wants to have children one day, she says, but she must find the best father for her children. And the best father will be a flawed and fully complex human. So, she's frozen her eggs and will wait years if she must. She has no checklist for the kind of partner she wants, she says. "But, like, be a good human . . . and also sweep me off my feet."

"So, you believe in such love," I say.

"Yes," she says with that same shy smile. "You do too, right? I mean, look at what you're doing. You're putting yourself out there to say you're aching for the right partner. And sure, you're gonna tweak it and help the whole thing along with like a feat or whatever. You're my hero."

I squirm a little. "Aching? All right, aching. I am aching but I am not going out in search. I am asking him to find me. But these past couple of days, with all the chatter, I don't know if I truly believe."

Demi is nodding hard. "Got it. You may be wondering if you're all in. Sure. Understandable. You also may be afraid to show that you *want*. You may be vigilant that you don't show it too, like, *visibly*."

I smile. "You know you should be charging therapist-level fees, right?"

Demi chuckles. "Who says I don't?' she winks.

We come to the matter of the feats. She says I should keep her informed as I decide on them, so she can get any city permits required. Archery? Sword fighting? Wrestling lions? She knows people who know people.

We laugh again.

"If I may . . . ," she says. "I'll give you a piece of advice I give to other brides. Decide on one thing you plan to do for your wedding on your own." She tells me that some of her brides decide they will make their own headpiece or go buy their own flowers on their wedding morning, or bake their own wedding cake or, best of all, do something for their partner for their wedding day. Sew their initials on a handkerchief or cook a single cupcake or mithai for them.

"This will keep you focused on the love that is building up in you," Demi says. "Can you think of something? You don't have to tell me if you don't want to; just think of something."

I say I will, but I can't imagine what such a thing will be without knowing the man I would choose. No sooner have I said this, it comes to me. My cheeks are flushed, and I gasp.

Demi laughs. I tell her what it is.

"Perfect!" she squeals.

"In the meantime, how do you show that you are not afraid to want?" she says.

I take it she is going to tell me.

"You show it in the cake," she says. "Go meet my cake person. Get the best cake you can afford."

I narrow my eyes. Demi sighs and says: "I know what you're thinking. Aaaargh... *Professor*! I'm not trying to get you to spend money for some sort of commission! You will not pay me. And you will have hearty discounts with the vendors. But you will have to do one thing. You will have to trust me. At least trust me. And trust the process. You came up with the idea of the swayamvar for a reason. A professor of mine used to say, 'Trust your instincts.' M'kay?"

I smile. I say I will do that if she lets me pay her. I've skimped and saved all these years, and even though I walked away from the two marriages with no wealth, I've built a nest egg. I'll put some of that nest money toward this antic of bringing home a bauble of a man, I tell her. How's that for trusting the process?

"You have a beautiful laugh," I tell Demi.

"Strange you should say that. My husband thought it was too cackly."

She smiles at the frown on my face and continues: "I stopped laughing around him."

"Dear God, this breaks my heart." I try and imagine Demi swallowing her laughter. It's a hard thing to imagine. I want to put an arm around Demi sitting there next to me. Do the rules of not touching students casually still apply even when they're former students? I decide to damn the rules and hug. She squeezes into my hug.

"Did he make you laugh?" I say.

"My ex-husband?" she says. "No."

"Thank goodness, then."

We both giggle.

The afternoon sun is lower in the sky, inching toward the water. I have spent longer than I'd expected on this little strip of beach. I sense I should look at my watch, gasp at the hour, stand up. But I find myself saying, "Have you heard the story of the princess who wouldn't laugh?"

Demi shakes her head.

I tell her the Russian tale about the czarevna who wouldn't even crack a smile, so her father, the czar, sends out a call far and wide for a man who can make his daughter laugh and win her hand in marriage.

"A Russian swayamvar," Demi says.

I nod. "Serious men and successful men and silly men came vying for her hand. Clowns and jokers and jesters."

"But to no avail," Demi says, cackling.

"But to no avail. And then there's something in the story about this working-class guy who impresses his boss so much the boss tells him to take as many gold coins as he can. But the man only takes one. Or maybe one a year. He wants to travel. But instead, he gives the coin to ... let me think ... a beetle, a fish, and a mouse."

"Why?"

"I don't know. It's a Russian folktale. I just never know what's going on with those."

She cackles. The sun catches the glint of a small pendant around her neck. It's a bird of some sort. Golden wings.

"And then one day, the man is walking by the czar's castle, and he slips and falls in the mud. But the beetle and fish and mouse come to help him up. Don't ask me how their help makes a difference, but it does, because this is a fairy tale. The czarevna sees this and smiles."

"Just smiles? She doesn't laugh?"

"I don't know. I mean ... what if she laughed and the man thinks she had laughed upon seeing him fall?"

"That would be rude. And it would depend on how much time went by before the creatures came to help him up. Their help would be more smile level than laugh level."

"Unless it's all slapstick and there's a lot of mud flying around. Anyway, you get the gist. Man-who-makes-you-laugh-is-man-you-must-love-and-marry. Or the other way around. The man you must marry is the man who makes you laugh. Although I have come to a point where I really don't care whether ..."

I trail off. I don't want to appear cynical to young Demi.

She is looking closely at my face. I keep my eyes on the people splashing about in the water.

"Professor?" she says.

"Yes?"

"Have you ever wondered why the czarina ..."

"The czarevna ..."

"Have you ever wondered why the czarevna didn't smile?" Demi is plucking at her pendant. A golden-winged bird flies away and back to the hollow of her neck.

"But she did smile!" I say, wondering if she hadn't understood the ending. "When the common man and the beetle..."

"No, I mean, before. Why didn't she smile all those years before? Does the story tell us that?"

The Groomsmen

Demi asked me something, what was it, something about the feats and whether I had a type. She'd asked if I knew what I was looking for in the body of the man who would win the swayamvar. Perhaps that would be a good place to begin to lead me to a list of possible feats.

I decide to turn my mind to the matter of men's bodies. After all, it would be the one clearly apparent feature at the point of purchase. I could rely on primal attraction and go right for an in-person thirst trap, but my menopausal body serves me mixed messages these days. If ever I had a type, I don't anymore.

To aid my senses, I cook myself a meal. My fridge is gorgeously stocked now thanks to deliveries I've ordered as a self-soothing strategy to see me through the viral meltdown. I get to work as I listen to my grand playlist of most loved Hindi movie love songs. This music rises like gold dust around me, seeps onto the lake outside, flirts with the ripples of blue-gray water.

I cook nothing too elaborate, just a prawn curry simmered in a paste I grind in my stone mortar and pestle with fresh ginger, dried red peppers, and whole coriander seeds mixed in with a tamarind emulsion, sautéed onions, and coconut milk. When the curry is cooked, I fold in a ladle of hot tadka—mustard seeds and tiny green curry leaves sizzling in ghee. I top off the prawn curry with a garnish of coarsely crushed black peppercorns. This will go so well with a vegetable, so I make a jeera aloo. Soft potatoes cooked in sweet sautéed onions and chopped green chilies with cumin, turmeric, cilantro, lemon. My houseboat fills up with the aphrodisiacal aroma of spice and basmati rice as a woman prepares to think closely of men.

The first time I looked at a man with any curiosity was when I was eight years old. Muscles on his back, sinews of his arms, veins on his temples, sweat on his neck.

My father took the family—his wife and two children—to a temple in the Himalayas. The temple was in the town of Joshimath, where he was posted as a major in the Indian Army. The family was staying with him for the summer holidays. He planned outings for us—to temples, scenic destinations high in these skies, hot springs. Sometimes these outings were with other families that were either stationed with the officers, or families like ours that lived away while the officer-father served out his postings.

I was happy to be in this place, this cold mountain town instead of the heat of Bombay, with my father at last, and with the family while it was still intact, before it splintered into memory.

But my father wasn't the man I watched. The man who caught my eye was a villager, or he may have been one of the priests of the temple. Thousands of people had thronged to the temple that April morning. They came from far and wide for this event that happened once a year at the Narsingh Temple. All the army families piled into the Jeeps and Jongas driven by army-employed drivers. Orderlies had been sent ahead to reserve seats for the army families.

INTEMPERANCE

We were ushered into an arena and seated in rows of steps ascending around a courtyard. A man told us the history of the temple. I didn't listen to much of it except a part that frightened me. The deity in the temple was in the form of a half lion and half man. For a part of that afternoon, my eight-year-old-girl brain thought we were gathered to see this strange creature. I wondered if the part that was man would have control over the part that was lion.

Drums started to beat around us, and temple priests and villagers started to chant. I kept my eyes on my father and mother, seated close and among other adults, while I was among the children. They were talking languorously with the adults. I could hear my mother's tinkling laughter, which was often punctuated by a familiar shriek that delighted me. My brother, just a year older than me, feigned an air of calm.

A priest, fat and bald with stripes of sandalwood and vermillion on his forehead, stepped into the arena and told us in Hindi that this annual festival was about to begin. A goat was brought to the middle of the courtyard. I watched as a man stepped up to the goat while another held it down with pressure at its neck. The crowd roared and something happened that I could not see because some people stood up in front of me. When they sat down, I saw blood on the floor of the courtyard and the goat's limp body being dragged away, leaving streaks of blood on the ground.

My parents were not looking our way. Why.

A thin man appeared in the center of the courtyard. I would not have known that this man was special in any way. He was the kind of man I had already been trained, at my young age, to see as the servant class. Lower than an orderly, lower than a Jeep driver, a bit higher than the young man who cleaned our home.

The man was given a basket. The priest from before stood by him and told me that the man would now eat the whole flesh of the goat that had just been slaughtered.

I watched as the man's body started to shake. He was dressed in nothing but a loincloth. He looked clean. But now his arms were quivering and his face was turning red. He picked up the basket and drew it to his face. He swung it upward so the chunks of raw meat jumped into the air. He caught some chunks in his open mouth. The flesh and the bones. He chomped on it.

He swallowed.

He growled.

I was scared. I looked at my mother. She was watching me. She smiled and shook her head.

I knew this signal. *Don't be afraid. This is nothing. We are here.*

For the next hour, the drumbeats and chants rent the air. The sun rose in the sky above me and I grew thirsty. The man ate and ate and ate. Such a frenzy rose around us. There was nothing I could do but watch the man.

I wondered about his throat. I watched it distend as the meat and bones went down. I wondered about his stomach. I watched his stomach—flat, with no fat of the kind that made my father's stomach so funny to me. The man's stomach did not grow fat with the meat. I watched closely. I saw hairs that grew under his navel. They seemed to be thicker as they grew in a line down into the tuck of his loincloth. I wondered what would happen if the loincloth came undone from all his shaking. I started to want that to happen because it would be funny and then this crowd would laugh instead of shouting and chanting.

When I looked back up at the man's face, his mouth and

INTEMPERANCE

cheeks were bloodied. He would wipe that blood off with the back of his hands every now and then. Was he hurt? He didn't seem to be in pain.

The blood was from the flesh of the freshly slaughtered goat.

I grew thirstier. I looked at my mother but now she was looking away. Her head was resting on my father's shoulder and her eyes were shut. She didn't have a bottle of water near her.

The man's legs were strong. They paced all over the courtyard, faster and faster around it as the meat in the basket dwindled. Strong legs. Not like my legs, uneven from polio. I saw symmetry. I was transfixed by the balance—thigh to thigh, calf to calf, foot to foot. I had never looked at another human's legs like this before.

This was what normal legs looked like. Not like mine. I pulled the skirt of my frock to stretch it past my shins.

Then the drumbeats stopped, and the chanting stopped, and the man stopped eating. Only a few bits of flesh remained in the basket. Was the man going to die?

His face stopped twitching, his body stood still as a statue, and then he fell to the ground. He opened his eyes and looked much smaller now. The priest asked him if he felt sick. No, he said. He felt hungry. He said he wanted to go home for lunch. His wife had prepared khichdi.

The crowd roared.

We were told the man had been taken over by the deity. The lion wanted to feast on a goat, and the man was the deity's channel for the feast. The man had done a divine thing, my father said as we filed out of the temple.

I could think of nothing but the man's very human legs.

As I walked out slowly in the line of crowds, the temple around me started to swirl. The sky grew dark, and my face turned cold. I gripped our mother's arms and fell to the ground.

When my eyes opened, I was lying on a cold floor and a crowd was screaming around me. Someone was pouring something in spoonfuls on my mouth, and it was trickling toward my ears. I parted my lips open. I felt sweet water on my tongue. I closed my eyes and slurped at the offering.

I had fainted, my parents told me. The crowd had gathered around us, joining the priest in his declaration that this little girl had been possessed by a deity and needed to be carried on their shoulders to be worshipped as a goddess. My parents had held the crowds back and shouted that this was nonsense, their daughter was clearly dehydrated, and if anyone laid a finger on her, they would be shot dead by the Indian Army. Some of the officers and their families had helped push away the frenzied crowds. Others had stood by and watched, afraid to upset any deity if indeed what the priest said was true.

Someone had brought me sugar water to raise my glucose level.

Could it have been true? I asked my parents on the way home in the Jeep. Could I have been possessed by some goddess?

They laughed. Don't be silly, they said. These backward people were full of unscientific beliefs. You are never to think such thoughts again.

But what about the man, I said. I spoke to my parents about the sinews bulging on the man's arms, his reddened face, the sweat that I had seen crawl from his jumping throat to his navel to the tie of his dhoti at his waist. I didn't get to the part about my wonder at his physical form devouring the raw goat. Their faces darkened at the details I recounted.

I was not to look at men that way, they said.

THE NEXT TIME I looked at a man was when I married one. In the years until then, I was a thing being looked at. Watched, taken in, ogled, but never long enough to be regarded, never deep enough to be seen. The year after that summer in the Himalayas, I started to be touched by men. A man on the bus. An uncle who came to stay a while. An army officer in an elevator. A physician examining my ten-year-old legs to tell me how much to exercise the one that was atrophying. A trusted family friend who had a daughter of his own and had so much access to me because my parents loved his company and enjoyed his parties. These men touched me between my legs or squeezed my chest that was yet to grow breasts or took my hands and wrapped them around the mouse-thing that bulged in their pants. It was understood that I was not to talk about these men, nor tell lies about them, because I would draw attention once again to myself as a girl who probably did something that drew these men to me. A girl who gave off a signal or a shameful perfume.

Is that what you want?

I thought this was happening only to me. That if I just averted my eyes, looked away from them and even from my own body when it was in their hands, I could make it stop. I didn't know that at that very moment, a million girls around the world thought this was happening only to them.

I have in my collection of old photographs given to me by my mother (as if she couldn't bear to hold on to the very few pictures taken of me in girlhood and emerging youth) a picture of me as this girl in the time when she was being touched by men. The girl is ten or eleven. She is wearing a dress that stops just above her knees. I remember it as blue, the color of the Indian Army swimming pool where she loved to dive and rise like a dolphin.

The picture, though, is black and white. She is with another girl. I remember the other girl as Nancy, my classmate, the Catholic girl from the thirteenth floor of the building in Bombay in which we lived on the eleventh floor. Nancy is wearing her school uniform. I wonder now why Nancy was in uniform and the other girl, the girl who was me, the girl who was being touched by men, was wearing "civilian" clothes. Ah, probably because it was her birthday. She looks happy, this girl who is standing with Nancy. She looks gleeful. Her hand is on her waist, like a little supermodel. Her other arm is draped around Nancy's shoulder. Nancy is not smiling. She looks at the camera as if arrested by it. Nancy is not what would be considered a good-looking girl. She is probably accustomed to being the girl who is not looked at, not photographed even as infrequently as the other girl, the Hindu girl from the eleventh floor.

Look at these girlhoods. Girls being looked at or not looked at. Who took this picture? My father? Yes, because his girl is standing next to a bicycle he bought for her tenth birthday. Did he look at Nancy the way other girls' fathers looked at his daughter? Was Nancy looking trapped by the camera because her body had at some time been cornered by my father?

What hell these two girls could have let loose if they turned to one another then and said—I see you; do you see me? I don't want to have this picture taken. Do you want to have this picture taken? I don't want to look at myself the way they look at us, one of us understood to be a pretty girl and another not, each one pinned down by her relationship to their gaze now and for years to come. Let us go play somewhere where our eyes and our eyes alone are on our own hands, in cool water, picking soft and sharp things from around rocks, our skin turning browner in the sweet, unmerciful gaze of the Indian sun. If a man reaches for us, we scream and find the other girls and turn the world almost deaf until they are forced to make him stop.

When I sometimes gaze at this photograph, which is unframed and lies scattered in a shoebox with other stray photographs, I want to gather these girls up in my arms. I don't know where Nancy is today, not even when I tear through social media in search of her. But I breathe love at her, this girl commanded to freeze in this moment for the documenting of the gleeful state of her classmate. Nancy D'Souza, a girl who simply was in the company of her friend on her birthday, living a girlhood like others' where you sometimes just end up in the wrong place at the wrong time.

I breathe love toward myself in that photograph. That girl will grow accustomed to being looked at. She will keep her head down and her mouth shut. She will be in other photographs. When she is seventeen, she will be approached by a modeling agency and her parents will be pleased by this. So, she will have her picture taken for modeling shoots and will be in advertisements for things like detergent, potato chips, tea, and even a barbecue grill. At these shoots, she will be surrounded by handsome men, men who are being photographed alongside her, men who will talk to her and tell her she is beautiful, but she won't look at them. She won't look at men when they speak to her or she to them.

At home, though, in all those years, I would rush home from school or college and insert VHS tapes of Hindi movies into the player and gaze upon the leading men. The heroes. I would study the breadth between the shoulders of Dev Anand in a red cardigan as Waheeda Rehman wraps her arms around him. What an unusual camera angle this was, focused on his neck and back arched over the actress. So, this is how a man softens his body when he is in love! I would watch Dharmendra as a handsome young doctor fall in love with Nutan, an inmate in the prison where he works. He offers to marry her, this murderess! She spurns this God for a coughing, hacking, dying man who abandoned her years ago. Cut to Dharmendra's stricken face when he learns she is gone. So, this is what heartbreak looks like on a man's face! I watch Amitabh Bachchan playing a hick—a boy from the shores of the Ganga, he says in his song—his mouth red from chewing on paan, dancing with Zeenat Aman. He falls in love with this woman more westernized, educated, and sophisticated than him. Look at this man taller than most Indian men dance in the manner of the lower-class men on Bombay's streets, channeling both romance and anger. Look at those long arms. Look at those long hairs on those long arms. Look.

In my twenties, I watched men closer to my age. Aamir Khan with his twinkling eyes, fair skin, innocent smile. Sanjay Dutt with his narcotic-heavy eyes, clumsy stance, large hands. And then, Shah Rukh Khan, short, zany, reaching out a confident arm to pull Kajol onto a running train she is about to miss. Shah Rukh Khan, showing up to find his beloved woman no matter where in the world she goes. Shah Rukh Khan, with an outrageously boyish charm and a sumptuous mouth I wanted to kiss until I bruised it beyond any makeup man's repair.

I was ready for the real stuff.

I'd allowed a boy to kiss me when I was fourteen. I wouldn't recall this until I met him forty years later to rekindle an innocent love. I wouldn't recall because my body had been taken since then, and any ripples of sweet sensations had been washed away in the tidal wave of dissociation. I allowed myself a boyfriend in my early twenties. I mostly spent my time staring into his eyes. Nothing would be legitimate or pure until we were married. I had willingly entered into this pact with whoever was in charge. When I married Siddhartha, I stared at my husband's sinewy arms, lost myself in his honey-brown eyes, marveled at his muscular legs ("meant for climbing coconut trees!" I teased this man from Kerala), rested my fingers on his Aamir Khan lips, halted my breath at the sight of his dark cock against the beige of my thighs.

I looked only at him. I stopped looking even at the leading men. I was filled from looking at only this one man.

When he started to stray away, it wasn't to another woman but into himself. His eyes looked through me. I didn't know how to be when I was not being looked at by men. I tried to hold his head in place, but it fell away. I thought I might hold it under water the way I did with children when I played as a girl in swimming pools, release it for just long enough for him to come up for air. So, I gave into the wolves of depression that had yipped at my limping leg for years and drew Siddhartha into my drowning, as the frail and beautiful object of his compassion. This worked for a bit, but he looked so far away I finally placed my feet on his broad coconut climber's chest and kicked with all my Ganga-shore womanly might and swam away. I didn't turn around to see which of us swam faster away from each other.

I swallowed up a considerably younger man. He looked drunk on me when he entered me. He wouldn't stop looking. When his intoxication terrified me, I found Paul. Quiet Paul, white Paul, American Paul, professorial Paul. We looked at each other just enough. Such fondness. Such regard.

And then I turned my eyes to other things. Raising Karan. And when he was raised, motherhood had left me tired. Education and my professorial pursuits left me exhausted. My gaze turned inward, and I fell into a long, deep sleep from which no prince or kingdom was to wake me.

I opened my eyes just long enough to watch Paul leave. My eyes brightened from the rest that came after, I have emerged a decade later and I can't stop looking.

I watch the way men jump to hold the elevator doors open. The way they check me out quickly as I walk into the elevator as they hold the door open. They let me in. Threshold. Claim.

Men who dance bhangra and men who dance kathak. Men who look like Osama bin Laden and don't strike terror or revulsion in me the way they do in certain Americans.

Men in charge of the gurdwara line at the Golden Temple in Amritsar. On a visit, I requested one of them to please let me into the line for the disabled. His eyes ran over my body and returned to my eyes—was he looking to uncover a lie or undress a liar? He let me and didn't step aside as I squeezed past him. Like the man in France. Men the world over.

Men who swim. Men inside water. Men I want inside me.

Men who run and won't step out of my way as I walk my dog because they are men who must keep their heart rate up. Heartless men. Men who are worse than dogs.

Men with stubbles. Men who know what to do with a stubble.

Men who sing. Average-looking men. Kishore Kumar. He married three times—beautiful women, movie stars in their prime. Men who aren't handsome or suave but whom a Madhubala will marry.

I watch the way men listen to me on a first date. The way they can't stop talking about themselves on a first date, men who are full of themselves and then the men who are just terribly nervous. The way they crave a meal of dal bhat tarkari or a grilled cheese. Men seeking comfort. The way they will wear brown shorts because their job requires them to deliver packages in brown shorts. Men who turn women into sad princesses or queens consort and men who leave kingdoms to honor their woman. The way a man can kiss you with the tenderness of a woman. Men who can't.

I watch the way a man stands out in a scarf, the way he shines in a sherwani. The way his muscles strain against silk, the way they relax into flannel, the way they turn subtle under a white cotton shirt. The way he looks in a suit. The way he looks in a loosened tie. I have never liked men in a leather jacket. The way he looks dangerous in a simple thread looped across his torso, this janau on an anointed Brahmin man.

The way he looks with a towel tied around his waist.

The way he looks asexual when he runs. Undistractable, driven, panting for the wrong reasons. I don't like to look at running men.

The way a man lets another man lather his face with shaving cream and take a blade to his throat. The way he looks smooth, baby faced after this ritualized encounter with death. Men leaning their faces inches away from the faces of other men, lathering them with promise, men arching their necks to receive, tender with trust.

I sometimes follow men riding bicycles. I don't go out looking for them; I happen to see them because this is Seattle and we have bicyclists and bike lanes, and we are all idling at a traffic light. I am in my car, and they are cycling in front of me. I must slow my car down in solidarity with this man doing his bit for the planet. For the air I am breathing so rapidly now. At my respectable distance, I marvel at the taut glutes that only cycling seems to offer. I follow as they rise and pedal in a standing stance. I don't admire the men in cycling shorts; I like the ones who cycle in business casual. Cement poured into khakis. I turn to khaak. I rise from the dust.

I watch men look past me in the street. I watch the men at a construction site nod and call out to a young woman sauntering by in a shift dress. I attempt to catch their eye as I walk by in my wide-leg linen pants that the internet promised me was the rage this summer. The men nod a wordless hello, and I understand, because these are working class men whose boss just told them to focus.

When on a work trip in Mumbai, the auto-rickshaw driver still watches me in the rearview mirror, but of late, it is just to ask us if my children have grown up in the US or some such respectful question. A masseuse in Goa presses his groin against my limp hand on his massage table and asks if I would like a deeper massage, and when I gasp in outrage, he tells me women of my age usually do.

I watch men love. I watch a man kiss his woman in the crashing wave of the Arabian Sea on the Marine Drive I loved in my childhood. On a vacation in Paris, I watch an older man at a café in Montmartre emerge from a toilet and walk past a younger man seated on a barstool. I watch him land a peck on the top of the young man's head. The young man doesn't look up, doesn't look at him, and I sense they are together, are at the end of their time at the restaurant, have already said their goodbyes. (For the day? Forever?) I watch the older man's face, and it is restful, self-assured as he walks out of the café. I build story upon story about the two men, but each of these is a love story, I find.

Later that afternoon on that trip to Paris, at the Musée d'Orsay, I watch a man some ten years younger than me stare long and deep into my favorite painting in the world—*The Laundress* by Honoré Daumier. When I have come to this painting in years before, once with Paul, who asked me why I loved this painting and then listened closely and said nothing, but kissed me on the cheek and moved on, I have felt unmoored by the image. I have imagined Daumier seated at his studio on the quai d'Anjou, watching this washerwoman ascend the stairs near the laundry boats moored on the Seine. I imagine Daumier moved to document this moment in the life of a tired working-class woman. A man watching a woman who doesn't know she is being watched and will be looked at for centuries after, not unkindly, but still, in her moment of exhaustion.

In the gaze of the man looking at my favorite painting now, I see a frown, a peer at the use of light, perhaps. I see him look past the stocky woman in the painting. I want to follow this man around the museum, to watch him as he looks at the nude women in the garden painted with suited men by Édouard Manet or the sculptures in various states of sensual surrender. I decide against it. When the man moves on from my painting, I let him go. He didn't see me seeing.

Where once I was in hyperfocus and wanted to disappear, I now watch myself fall away in the depth of field and yearn to be arrested in a single gaze.

If men should gather and vie for my hand, I will feast my eyes on their form.

I CALL CAT the next morning, dying to tell her about Demi. She texts back to say she cannot talk; her husband is asleep. He isn't doing well. I ask again if I should go be with her. No, she says. She wants this time alone with him. She says she would love some distraction, though, so I should text her an update on the swayamvar.

"Do you think I have a type?" I ask her.

"Well...," she texts back.

"Do I?"

"Well, you seem to like some muscle on them. Like, wiry but muscular."

"Okay, but should I have them perform a physical feat at the swayamvar?"

"It's your swayamvar. You can do whatever you want. Just, like, stay within some bounds. You don't want to be fired or arrested or something."

"What? Jesus. What kind of physical test were you thinking...?"

"I don't know! You have a wild side. It's getting wilder. Wouldn't you say?"

"Maybe. Okay, should I ask them, 'How far can you swim in this body of water at whose shore we have gathered? And how fast?'"

"What would that achieve? Apart from making you sound like a pastor giving a sermon. I mean, how is his swimming ability going to be relevant to the years you have together?"

"Maybe it is, maybe it isn't. But I will get to see him with his shirt off."

"Don't make me come there."

"Okay, how about this one, 'Can your body devour the raw flesh of a whole, freshly slaughtered goat?'"

"What the fuck?"

"Never mind. Okay, bestie, how about you help me come up with something better?"

"Anything would be better than the goat thing. You'll have to explain that to me some day. But how about, 'How may you hold me and never let go?'"

"That is weird. He's going to hold me then? Like, a row of men getting to hold me one after the other? Or do I get to choose which one holds me?"

She is silent. "..."

My heart sinks. She was talking about herself and her husband.

"Dear God, Cat. I'm sorry. I didn't realize you were ... I'm so sorry for the pain you are in and the pain to come."

"Thank you, hon. Okay, back to the questions. How about, 'How do my eyes drink you in?' Then you could just stand there and stare at each one openly."

"Show us what your body can do."

"Show us how you can lift me up. Show us how you set me down."

"Show us the hair on your chest. Show us your calves. Climb a tree, quick."

Cat is laughing now. Lolololol. I didn't have to try too hard.

I go on. "Show us your thrust. Show us the rhythm of your tongue."

She says, "Show us how you stroke my dog behind his ear."

"Nice one. Show us how you start a fight. Show us how you stop a fight. Do you throw your body into it?"

"Show me how you hold my gaze. And when you look away."

"Show us how you dance. Do you have a swing to your hips? Do you smile?"

"Show us how you chop wood."

"What? I don't care how he ..."

"You have a thing for forearms. This way they have to roll up their sleeves and you get to see their forearms. You're welcome."

"Okay, that shows potential. But it's sort of too macho. How about, Show us how you embrace a man. How long can you hold that embrace?"

I AM ALL quivering, translucent fruit flesh, peeking out from behind a stiff curtain of peel cracked open from today's rising heat in the orchard. I cling to the stem of my family of fruit, which clings to its great clan on a branch on the big, rooted world of a tree. Below, two lovers writhe and grunt, then softly moan.

I am spoiled, they will say tomorrow and throw me in the pile of rotten fruit. But for now, I am ripe, and it is my will that I push my perfume out into our summer night.

Yes, this is what I want.

The Skincare

I wake up with a start. It's daytime outside.

I look down at my phone. The text with Cat is still open, but there's a "You still there? Okay, sweetie, we'll catch up again later. Bye?" from Cat. That was three minutes ago.

I don't even know when I put the kohl in my eyes again, maybe absent-mindedly while chatting with Cat? I see it in the smudge around my eyes in the mirror now.

Something about being on sabbatical makes my imagination porous. Impressionable. The kohl just seems to aid some temporary leap of imagination.

Either that or I'm having some sort of extended stroke. I would google it, but if I go online, I will be treated to another blast of public opinion on my life choices. I would have asked my therapist what's going on, if I hadn't let go of her in the wildly confident notion a few months ago that I no longer needed therapy. Everyone always needs therapy. Which is why my therapist no longer has any openings to take me back.

I summon up a sense of the vision. Two people in love, making love. Even the residue of the vision is enough to take my breath away.

THE LAST TIME I had sexual intercourse, I screamed, and it wasn't in pleasure.

This was almost two years ago. Just a little tryst mid-pandemic. And at the time, it had been over a year since I'd last had sex, which had been with a man I met on an app, a brief relationship. In that time between the two sexual encounters, menopause had crept up like a demon in my vagina.

The sex that made me scream was with a man as handsome as the last time I'd seen him, which was when he was sixteen and I was fourteen and we were the cutest little kids holding hands and sitting quietly by the Arabian Sea. The boy I'd allowed to kiss me. I was nowhere close to being ready for anything more than that, and I know now that his own body must have hurt from longing. But of course we couldn't do anything but watch the sun set on our sweet little romance. His family moved away. Forty years later, we reconnected over moony video conversations for hours a day during the pandemic. When the love grew too much to bear and I found myself about to do irresponsible things like undressing over a video call, I flew down to Malaysia to meet him. He was doing well in life in his corporate job there. He flew us to a spectacular vacation on an island with turquoise waters.

This time, I was aching and flushed and ready.

When the resort staff had finished showing us around our suite with its private infinity swimming pool and an outdoor rainforest shower, I pushed him onto the mile-long bed.

Wait, he said, pulling me down beside him. Maybe we should take it slow?

Forty years not slow enough for you? I said, straddling him.

He laughed and reached his hands into my hair. This sexy laugh, no longer carried on a Zoom audio, but right here, coming from his throat against my hand, coming from his eyes locked on mine.

What do you want to do? he asked, choking on his words but not looking away.

I swooped down to his mouth and kissed it. I knew he'd enjoy feeling my hair curtain our faces and turn everything even more humid.

I kissed him like a lynx drinking water from a stream. When I pulled away for a breath, he drew my head back to him instantly, thirst transferred. We kissed again and I fell off him, fell back beside him. His hands touched my neck, and we took turns at being shy and hungry. I sat up so he could pull off my dress. I leaned in to inhale at the collar of his white linen shirt, where I'd smelled his cologne all morning. Now my bra was off, and his hands were on my breasts, and I was thankful that he had only dated within our age demographic since his divorce some years ago, so he'd know what to love about these breasts softened from the arcs and loops of sex and lactation and gravity. I fucking love my breasts.

He wanted to touch my belly the same way he'd kneaded my breasts. I tried to gently guide his hand away, but he put it back on my belly and said, "I like this. Tell me if you really want me to stop."

I discovered that I didn't. I lay back and let this man massage my belly, let him trail his fingers on the stretchmarks and nibble softly on my fat. I drew my knees up and my right leg flopped out to the side. I pushed it back up, aware of my muscles quaking from the effort to keep this leg symmetrical and sexy with my left. He put one hand on my right knee and, holding my leg in place, took little chunks of my fleshy inner thigh into his mouth and grazed his teeth in bites that I wished would cut through, but they didn't.

When he broke away to look back up at me, his facial muscles had turned slack from that look men get when they can't bear to wait anymore. I made sounds new to me. I begged him to keep doing what he was doing to my belly and my thigh. So, he did and he did and he did. And then his hand was between my legs, and I thought it would all end much too soon, and his jeans weren't even off yet, so we worked on that, and I feasted my eyes and my mouth on his form.

"Now. Please," I said, lying back naked and opening myself up with my fingers. He pressed in.

And that was when I screamed.

He yanked away and sat back. I shook my head in confusion and touched myself to see if I wasn't wet enough. I was wet and ready. I had him try again and I recoiled again, this time with just a gasp. He touched me and we grew crazy again and I asked for another attempt, but it was all so painful and my desire was retreating inside me, clamping shut doors upon doors behind it. There was no recovering from this terror in this moment, not even for our mouths or hands to finish what we'd started.

We spent that day holding each other and singing our favorite vintage Hindi film songs. That night we swam naked in the pool surrounded by bougainvillea. He lifted me to seat me on the pool's edge, spread my legs apart, and went at me with a hot tongue. I leaned back on my palms and looked up at the night. I didn't scream. I sighed and shuddered and squealed against his quickening rhythm. As I came, he nuzzled his whole face against my flesh. I savored the feel of his damp hair and warm scalp under my fingers. The thing about sex as you age is that it teaches you to quietly gather up sensations to later stroke in memory.

BACK IN SEATTLE, Dr. Liang first congratulated me on the new relationship. Dr. Liang is my physician, and she makes notes every time I tell her about the absence or renewal and expiry of a sexual relationship. She asked me what I thought of Malaysia. I asked her to please tell me if I was dying.

She said I wasn't dying. "Your vaginal walls could be thinning," she said.

"*Thinking?*" I said with awe.

"Thinning," she said slowly, and inquired if I was also experiencing brain fog.

"Yes," I said, "that too, but brain fog doesn't feel like someone taking sandpaper to my thinning walls, so could we please focus?"

"Actually, it's always a good idea to first rule out imminent death," Dr. Liang said and sent me for an ultrasound and a biopsy of my walls and the rooms beyond. Drink plenty of water before the ultrasound, she said.

The ultrasound technician was annoyed that I had drunk too much water and she had barely enough time between the two back-to-back ultrasounds to grab an image.

The ob-gyn who entered me with hard metals and cold gels took a piece of my soul. My biopsy came out clear. It was only then that Dr. Liang suggested hormone replacement therapy.

I was reminded of a news report on a study that showed that human wastewater is delivering chemicals from the medications we excrete to fish, and that hormones from Estradiol in particular are leading to male fish developing eggs in their testes.

"Surely that's an urban myth," I laughed.

"It isn't," Dr. Liang said, her face expressionless. "Even female fish are being affected. Their reproductive cycles are thrown off. They're often developing eggs later and missing the spawning window."

"Jesus. Sorry, Mrs. Salmon."

"Yeah."

"Well, I'm not going to add to this terrible assault on our fish population," I said. I felt virtuous and wanted to let nature take its course on my body. Of course, it helped that I wasn't moving to Malaysia to build a life with my childhood crush. That relationship was short and sweet because we were old and wise and had jobs and lives and routines on different continents. As for my skin and hair and vagina, I'd keep it healthy with a diet of cantaloupe, seeds, and, well, fatty fish.

But now I'm readying for the possibility of a suitor. I no longer want the occasional tryst. I want to know a body as it ages and I want my aging body to be known by a chosen one. With a chosen one would come an unknown penis.

I imagine there are those who believe I ought to have had my fill of love and penises, that I don't deserve another indulgence of intimacy and passionate lovemaking. Perhaps I am gluttonous. My reach for a third husband, especially in a manner that implies a slew, an array, or an assembly of suitors, is deserving of the accusation of gluttony rather than lust. Lust implies the presence of a libido. A woman of fifty-five is not expected to have the welling up of moisture anywhere in her body to flood her with such lust.

Her vulvar and vaginal mucosae is expected to appear pale, shiny, and dry. Her vaginal canal is atrophied to be shorter and thinner (in this my vagina has companionship from my right leg). Her tissue is less elastic. Her genitourinary syndrome wakes her up multiple times a night to pee.

But fuck you and fuck me. My desire wells up from a place far deeper than a vagina, from a centripetal force operating outside the circle of my canals and my reason, but the way to that place will be through my yoni, and I'm damned if I'm going to let her be lashed with broken glass again.

"WHAT ABOUT TESTOSTERONE?" I ask Dr. Liang at today's appointment.

"You want testosterone?" she asks with a frown and consults her notes, probably wondering if she'd missed something significant in our last few visits.

"No. I just want to know if any of those hormones from men's erectile dysfunction medications are finding their way to fish? Testosterone?" I say, as if two years hadn't passed since my last conversation with Dr. Liang about hormones and the aquatic population.

She puts her notes down. "Those studies haven't been done as much. Research has been mostly following the panic over male fish getting feminized."

We look at each other.

"Do you want it?" Dr. Liang asks, straightening up and glancing at her watch.

"Are the male fish at least turning kinder?" I ask her as she writes the prescription.

THE ESTROGEN PATCH comes in a wrapper that can be mistaken for a condom wrapper. From inside, I remove one side of a sticker film, then put this little round, sticky patch on the fatty-fleshy part of my ass. Then I remove the other side of the sticker. Then I press in the sticker on my skin and count to ten. Then I spend five minutes trying to remove the staticky film from my fingers. When it's time to change out the patch, I stick the old patch sticker on the bathroom tile. I recall what an older friend had said about how, over time, her shower cubicle has become dotted with old estrogen patch stickers like a planetary constellation on her CHANI app, telling her to bring gentle attention to her inner radiance.

Dr. Liang has also prescribed a cream that I must deliver into my vagina with the help of an applicator. I learn the technique on YouTube, send the cream along its way, and then attempt to wash the applicator. This takes almost twenty minutes, and the residual cream is still stuck on the plastic. I wipe it down with a facial tissue.

I look at my face in the mirror. I am weeping. I feel bad about the weeping. Hadn't I promised myself I wouldn't lament the loss of youth? That I'd be grateful that I'd survived polio that tried to take me as a child, and survived a car crash that came for me when my child was a child? What is this moisture doing running down my cheeks then?

It's just that I hadn't *noticed*, I tell the wicked queen in the mirror. I hadn't savored. I'd gobbled up time and now it was inside me, gobbling me up right back.

The Estradiol is to be taken in conjunction with progesterone. Those come as pills that look like little pearly eggshells. They will help me sleep through the night without being woken up by the urge to urinate, Dr. Liang has said, and from the way I climb into my bed, kiss the dog good night, and start drifting off, I can tell.

For a moment, I want to reach out for the kohl again. I think of the two young lovers under the tree, and I decide to let them be.

The Officiant

The swayamvar is four weeks away. Demi has acquired permits for all sorts of activities on the beach at Golden Gardens Park to account for any leaps of imagination I may throw at her for the feats.

She also wants me to be prepared to change the venue at the last minute "in case there's trouble."

"Trouble?"

"Well... it's a good thing you've been staying away from socials and apparently not answering emails and calls for comments? It's on traditional media too now. Drew Barrymore did a nice bit. A few good hot takes on all the smart media platforms and feminist podcasts and such. And some local news reports. Like, *Seattle Times* says the mayor is in full support of your event. So, we can have a couple of cops standing by."

"I don't want cops at my swayamvar. Defund the..."

"Okay, okay, you just let me handle all that. They also need to make sure you're not endangering the lives of these men, right? You focus on getting me the feat. I need to get any equipment, props, and all. And we will need to make some announcements a couple of weeks in advance, so I have to set up a website."

"Dear God."

"Don't worry. All privacy is in place and under control. I'm going to send you some contacts and links to find your dress and order cake and other good things. You focus on deciding the feat."

"It might be feats. Plural. That's what happens if I'm not allowed to endanger their lives."

"Oh. Okay. The feats. Wow. Trust the process, I guess?"

I STOP TO browse books in my office and in the university library in search of clues to a good set of feats. Searches on the university library databases like "masculinity" and "relevance" have yielded some new literature I could do well to take a look at.

There's a daunting pile of mail in my department mailbox. I sigh and gather it all up in a large envelope. I decide to sit down at my desk for a bit and open an envelope or two, even though I really shouldn't be here on campus in my office, interrupting the bliss of my sabbatical.

A man bursts into my office. Ah, well, perhaps I am exaggerating when I say he bursts in, because he does knock. But he doesn't have an appointment, and he isn't announced to me by the administrative assistant in the lobby, which may have been, granted, because they're running some errand.

But still. A stranger walks in. White. Male.

The man walks in and says hello. I raise my eyebrows, express surprise at his entry at first. Then, recalling some of the threats from men online, I feel the room darken. I wonder why the university has not equipped each office with a panic button to buzz for security, given the things that happen in schools and campuses in America.

He seems to sense my panic. He takes a couple of steps back.

He quickly tells me he's sorry for barging in, he's not a threat, look, here are his hands, up in the air, and he'll keep a distance. I realize I have stood up and have been gripping the edge of my desk. He doesn't reach out a hand to shake mine, but I sense that he would, if I reached out for his. I don't.

He says his name is Sylvan Wilson. "Yes, a bit of a tongue twister," he says with a shrug and a smile, and I wonder if he says this every time he introduces himself, a built-in icebreaker in his opening line.

"Mr. Sylwan Vilson," I say, mixing up the "v" and "w," an Indian slip I still carry in my speech, something that embarrasses me. I am flustered but I cover it up quickly with an icy, "Do we have an appointment?"

"No, I'm afraid," he says. "I apologize. I should have made one. I can explain."

His manner and speech are oddly formal. They are also self-effacing, which is incongruent with the sense of entitlement one would expect from someone who has, well, burst in.

I stay standing, so he does too. As he speaks, telling me about what he does for a living and such, I take in his appearance. I don't know if that is an indicator of the level of threat, and surely that would be profiling, but it helps me focus. Maybe it will be helpful later, if I need to identify him in a police lineup. He is dressed in a well-tailored linen suit in light blue. A navy cotton shirt within, no tie. He seems to be in his late fifties or early sixties. What might have once been piercing blue eyes have faded a bit. A medium build and medium height are slumped into that suit, which is perhaps why I didn't think of him as an attractive man the moment he entered.

"I don't come from the manosphere," he says.

I am taken aback. He is referring to the wide and thriving online sphere of men who revile women. Men who have recently been reviling me. He says it in a manner that almost makes me smile. He pronounces it slowly—man-o-sphere. And it's like he's saying, "I come from the future." Although, quite frankly, I hope the manosphere soon becomes a thing of the past.

"I said I *don't*," he says, his hand reaching out in front of him in protest when he sees me reach for my phone. I cross my arms over my chest.

"In fact, I distinctly keep away from those revolting communities," he says.

"Why are you here?" I say coldly, making a note of his grand choice of words.

He tells me he wants to talk about my plans for the swayamvar. He adds quickly that he is not here to be confrontational or critical, and he is aware of how it must be alarming to have someone walk off the street and walk up to me and demand to talk about a post I had made online.

"Yes, it is. So why do it?" I look him squarely in his faded blue eyes.

"I can come back another time," he says, taking another step backward to reassure me that he means it. "And I can explain why I didn't just email or call. I assure you I mean no affront or harm. And I know that is difficult to believe."

I am about to leave my office, I tell him. I'd prefer he email me.

He nods, tells me he harbors no expectation of a response to the email if I don't desire it, and turns around to walk out of the department offices.

"Hold on a second," I hear myself say. "What's the gist of your ... objection?"

INTEMPERANCE

"Oh, it's not exactly an objection," he says. He has turned around, but he still expects to walk away, so he doesn't reenter my office. He stands outside the threshold and says, "I am simply intrigued by your choice to pit men against each other to perform a feat of some sort. I am curious about what those feats might be. I'd like a conversation, but I am fully aware of my audacity, because you certainly don't owe me one."

I regard him for a moment, this strange and mild-mannered man who stirs nothing in me, neither desire nor distrust.

"Would you like to join me for a drink?" I say. So, this is how my organs will end up being harvested and sold on the internet to paltry bidders. But I have some questions for him. He may have answers I can't find in the books I've gathered.

His eyes jump in surprise. He looks flustered, but he says yes.

To be safe, though, I tell him I must take a picture of him and send it to a friend "or two," so they will be witnesses.

He hesitates for a second. I take the picture anyway. I have earned the right because he is trespassing in my space.

He sighs. He says okay, I may send it to a friend. . . .

"Or two," I say, sending it quickly to Cat with a shrug emoji, which is our code for "I'll explain later."

"Or two," Sylvan Wilson says. "But I assure you I intend no malice, and when we are finished talking, when you see that everything was safe and fine, please refrain from posting something random."

"Random? Are you suggesting my posts are . . ."

"Oh no, no. That's not . . ."

"Let's go," I say. I suggest a place I sometimes head to with friends from work—A Low Bar. It's walking distance (so I won't have to enter anyone's vehicle), it also offers coffee (so I don't give the impression of intending to make a night of it), and it usually has people across gender, not an overwhelming number of men who sit sideways on stools with one hand on their drinks on the bar and their crotches and eyes aimed at this woman or that.

"How did you know I would be in my office today?" I ask him as the two of us wait at the crosswalk on the busy street.

"I didn't," he says. He hesitates and then adds, "At the risk of alarming you and having you walk away right now, I will tell you the truth. I have stood outside your office every single day since you posted the announcement of your . . . selection feats." He points at a spot across the street to indicate where he's been standing in wait.

The light has changed. This man is a stalker. I could stay where I am and refuse to take one more step with this man or . . .

"Please do not walk away," the man is saying. "I have principles. I had your home address because people have posted it online, but no matter how long I had to wait across the street from your office, I would not do the same at your home." He really just wanted to talk to me, he says. Email would have gone unanswered. A phone call would feel awkward and intrusive.

With barely six seconds left on the traffic signal countdown, I step into the crosswalk and snap my fingers at him to follow. On the next block over, I am not watching my step, and I trip when my weaker leg forgets, as it sometimes does, to keep pace with the strong one. My cane slips. Sylvan Wilson's arm shoots out instantly to clasp my hand. He steadies me with one eye on my tread and the other on the traffic. I thank him quickly and we fall into step again.

I watch his face in profile. He shows no signs of being aware of any gallantry on his part. He has barely paused in his speech. His reflexes have been trained to hold, to steady, to protect. A woman always has a sense when a man's body has been trained in masculinity. It sort of clicks into gear, one way or another, protector or predator. I know it would have been different if he were a woman and I had tripped—a gasp, more talk, more questions, more solicitude, not merely a reflex.

The bar offers an early happy hour, and Sylvan Wilson and I settle in on barstools. I hate barstools because my right leg struggles to offer me balance on them. But I decide to be seated on them now, to build in a somatic discomfort so I won't be tempted to stay too long. I order a strawberry margarita and Sylvan Wilson orders whiskey.

"I am familiar with your work on masculinity," he begins.

This is usually an opening line for men who are going to tell me about their problems with my work, so I sip my margarita and hide my smirk in it. But he, in turn, sips his whiskey and is silent for a while.

"I agree with all of it and learned a lot," he says when he realizes I am not going to say anything and am waiting for him to talk. "I especially appreciate your focus on the ill effects of the expectations of resilience on masculinity."

I perform a mini eye roll. I hope the whiskey gets him to loosen up a bit. I look around the bar. On the other end of the counter are two women who seem to be watching us. When I peer at them, though, I realize they're simply looking around at all the people in the bar. One of them is a white woman with graying blond hair. She has a strange contraption laid on the bar counter in front of her, a small loom of some sort. She is idly weaving something on it. I look over at the bartender and it doesn't seem to bother him. We're all so tolerant now of people's pets and objects brought into public for emotional support or anxiety alleviation. The woman next to her is talking animatedly. She's wearing a red dress with a plunging back. She is faced away from me and I can't help but notice her curves. The woman with her leans over and whispers something in her ear and the red-dress woman throws her head back and laughs. Her thick black hair swoops down to her hips at this move.

She turns around and looks right at me. I look away quickly but not before registering that she looks familiar, a bit. Like a Bollywood movie star. Lips in a luscious red tint and large almond eyes. The two women avert their gazes, and yet I move from feeling watched to feeling watched over. Odd.

"It's been a lifelong struggle of mine," Sylvan Wilson is saying.

"I'm sorry, what has?" I ask.

"I struggle with the paradox of acknowledging men's institutional privileges while resisting the burden of masculinity on men."

I nod, encouraging him to say more. I feel a bit guilty for being distracted. But I'd like to know more of these burdens he's talking about.

"In the 1970s, you'd characterize men like me as belonging to the men's rights movement. You know? We wanted to be free to be more human than traditionally masculine. But that movement became anti-feminist, and I rue that even today. I am pro-feminist, pro-choice but am very concerned about gender and power."

"Okay," I say. "So, what do you want to know about the swayamvar I am planning?"

"I'm getting to that. Look, I used to be a child-custody lawyer for fathers."

"Oh, dear."

I glance at his ring finger. It's bare. He sees my glance.

"Yes, yes, I know," he says. "Quite predictably, I started practicing that aspect of law after I lost my own son in a custody battle with my ex-wife. I mean, you have to agree that several cases genuinely needed that sort of representation until the courts became sensitized to gender equity in whether the mother or the father raises the kids."

I shrug and nod.

"And yes, I got disheartened when my law firm insisted I get more aggressive in destroying mothers' reputations in the process. I quit that job and am now a forensic psychologist for the courts. I make recommendations on custody based on mental health. I'd like to think I do that without a gender bias."

"But you . . . your training?"

"Yes, I gave up the lucrative lawyering career and got an education in psychology," he says.

I smile at him. I take kindly to men seeing the error of their ways, even more kindly to those who seek out new education. I ask him about his son.

His eyes get misty, and he looks away. His son earns good grades and is an athlete, he says. He rows for his college crew team. Two years ago, his son was accused of date rape.

"His mother and stepfather asked me to help find him some good legal representation. My son barely knew me, but when I asked him if he did it, he said yes. He said he raped his classmate. And then he said it wasn't his fault because the girl was a tease and was drunk."

Sylvan Wilson had refused to help his son in any way.

I wait for him to say that his ex-wife had failed in raising their son better. I wait for the vitriol against the stepfather. I wait for him to say women are manipulative.

If Sylvan Wilson believes any or all these things, he doesn't say so. The man sitting before me is crumpled into his seat. He downs the last sip of whiskey and orders another.

I don't ask him what became of the case.

I clear my throat and ask him, "So, about the swayamvar..."

"Ah, yes," he says.

He is bothered by my plan to pit men against men. He asks me if I have thought about how this oppresses men and pushes them into old competitive roles in patriarchy. "I would wager it probably feeds right into the delusions of those men online who believe men should be providers and women should be, you know, tradwives."

That is not my intent, I manage to offer.

"How will you ask them to compete? Isn't the very nature of competition gendered? Men competing for your hand? Early men's rights movement activists protested men's beauty pageants. Help me understand how your swayamvar is different."

I have been impressed, so far, at how accurately non-Indian Americans have been pronouncing this word. Sanskrit scholars, all of them.

"I haven't decided yet on what the feat will be," I say. "It certainly won't be a feat of strength, at least not physical."

"So, you are not looking for a gymcel," he says.

I frown.

"Aha! The scholar of masculinity studies does not know that term," he says with a chuckle. I discern friendliness, not mockery. I'm also just relieved he has finally cracked a smile, although that is perhaps owed more to the second shot of whiskey, neat, than any wit I may have exhibited.

A gymcel is a contemporary term for an incel who spends a lot of time at the gym, he informs me.

"Well, a man in good shape is not off the list," I say, grinning. "All else being equal, why shouldn't I pick someone who is easy on the eye?"

I tell him about my body, the rapidly atrophying muscles in my leg, the looming possibility of spending my later years in a wheelchair. "Which is to say, I am not one for being ableist, but would it be so wrong to want a man who might be able to carry me around?"

"Yes, it would," Sylvan Wilson says, without missing a beat. "What you need is good healthcare."

"I'd like to have both," I say. I have been gripping my right leg at the knee, and he has noticed. He asks if we should move to a table.

I refuse.

I watch him closely. He wears his age around his eyes. They would be what are often referred to as "kind eyes," except that he doesn't hold a gaze long enough for the kindness to be turned on someone. Granted, I am a stranger to him, someone with whom he is sparring, even. And yet I get the sense that he eschews the intimacy of locking eyes.

He glances around the bar, and I follow his gaze. He casts a quick look at the woman in red, who is now attracting a lot of attention because she is throwing darts at a dartboard in the bar. I watch her for a bit. I had tried this activity here once and, after a miserable loss, stopped. She, however, is hitting a bull's-eye each time. Cheers are going up in the bar. Men have joined her. Some are competing with her, laughing a bit too loudly when their darts miss the mark.

I glance back at the bar at her friend. She is sitting there, and I am startled that her hair seems to have turned grayer. She looks older, tired. She's still picking at that loom, oblivious to the raucous spectacle her friend—or lover, perhaps, or colleague—is causing.

"Look at them," Sylvan Wilson says, nudging me and drawing my attention back to the men around the woman with the impeccable aim. "They know they are competing with the other men in the guise of competing with her. Tribal-minded gentlemen. Also look at who is *not* competing."

I look around the bar.

He doesn't wait for me to discover it for myself. "The Asian men," he says. "Let me qualify that," he adds. "You have the South Asian-looking man throwing his hat in the ring," he says, pointing with his chin at the group that's thronging around the woman in the red dress who is laughing throatily and working it. "But not the others. I don't have to tell you, of course, about how Asian men are emasculated and infantilized by white women, yes, and even women of their own cultures."

"Well," I say loudly, forcing his gaze back at me. "I am not looking for any particular race of man. And I'll go for dreamy eyes before I go for a square jaw or square swagger. Most of all, I'd go for wit."

"Ah, now we're talking," he says, turning his face and body fully back at me. "Do you have questions or puzzles for the men? A riddle, perhaps?"

"Here's a riddle for you. In mythology or in fairy tales, why is it always the father who sends out a call for men to win his daughter's hand in marriage?"

Sylvan Wilson grins and shrugs. "Good one. I don't have an answer. But I think it speaks to the point I was making..."

"Maybe it was because men wrote those stories. Men made those templates for tales where men grant their daughters a tiny bit of agency, some sort of choice to push the story along, but the kings and princes were the ones orchestrating the transaction. Keep male protagonists on the page, keep male supremacy in the world."

"So, will you use this riddle in your swayamvar? Why did you tell me the answer?"

I lean back and look at him. I shake my head. What a peculiar man.

"I don't know that this is the answer," I say, laughing. "It could be one answer. But I do appreciate that you didn't try to argue it down. It gives me hope."

"Now, *that's* a low bar," laughs Sylvan Wilson.

The bar is so noisy by then; I am almost shouting. Sylvan Wilson excuses himself to go to the restroom. I take this opportunity to shut my eyes for a bit, shut out the stimulation of so many people, the sound of glass as the bartenders do their thing, the music I can almost never recognize, the laughter rising in a language I never learned.

A strong perfume wafts close to my inhale and in the next second even closer. Rose? Sandalwood? I inhale deeply.

"Naag Champa," a woman's voice says. I'm startled to hear Hindi. It's the woman in the red dress. She's leaning over the bar, smiling right into my face. She clicks her fingers at the bartender. The gesture feels rude, entitled, but she turns her smile upon the man, and he puts down the drink he's mixing and comes right over. I cannot hear her drink order because she almost whispers it into his ear, the universal coquettish move of leaning over and lowering your voice to draw a man's ear close, his nose close enough to smell your perfume—Naag Champa. Frangipani.

She looks back at me as the bartender heads off to fix her drink. She reaches over to pick up my glass, pins the cocktail napkin with her index finger, and slowly trails it toward her, her eyes locked with mine all through this. She looks around for a pen. I find myself shuffling in my purse for one, but when I look up again, the bartender has already brought her one. She scribbles something on the cocktail napkin, trails it back to me, picks up her mai tai with what looks like a ... lychee skewered through it ... and glides away.

On the cocktail napkin, in Devanagari script:

I picked the wrong men. Should have married the other guy. Prejudice, like karma, is a bitch. Love, D

I shove the napkin into my purse as Sylvan Wilson returns from the restroom.

"And this final riddle you will come up with ...," he says, totally unaware that a whole little drama has played out in the moments he was gone. "It won't need a certain level of arcane knowledge or a higher education?"

I am silent. Naag Champa. Red manicured finger. Good-looking bartender almost oblivious to me and infuriatingly attentive to the other woman. Inexplicable meaning in the message from ... D?

"I don't like this dynamic of offering corrections to your plan," Sylvan Wilson says.

"Oh yes, you do," I smile.

But he is looking genuinely uneasy at whatever he is seeing on my face, misreading my thoughts. "But you are well aware of how class works," he says. "Not to mention our elitist education."

INTEMPERANCE

"Yes, I am," I say, snapping back to attention toward the man of the moment. "I'm not prejudiced. But you see, I wouldn't want to attract a Jordan Peterson."

"Or a Žižek," he says, grinning.

"Or a Houellebecq."

We clink our glasses, pleased with our learned selves and our references.

I look over to the crowd in the bar. I see flashes of a red dress somewhere in there, but I can't catch D's face.

"I will admit that most feminism, even the best of the intersectional sort, stumbles when it comes to class," I am saying to Sylvan Wilson. "It's intensified in recent years with the rise of the neoliberal girlboss ideology. Good call, Sylwan Vilson."

I have pronounced his name incorrectly on purpose this time. If he has noticed that I sound a trifle cold, perhaps even bitter, he doesn't let on.

I ask him if he will serve as an advisor for my little enterprise.

He smiles. Then, realizing I am serious, he says, "I am flattered, but no."

Why not? I ask. "Do you think no one will show up for the feat?" I lean into his space, lower my voice, smile. Am I flirting, or am I listening keenly for a dismissive tone or a sardonic twist to whatever he has to say next?

"Oh, they will show up all right," he says.

He seems to be all in on the idea that this swayamvar will happen, although I cannot tell whether it is because he hasn't stopped to wonder at my eligibility or given me any thought at all, or whether he is just too bothered at the implications, the ethics and politics of the whole thing, that he doesn't wonder about its subject (me) and its object (me).

"As will I," he adds.

I'm not sure if I blush or whether the margarita is kicking in, but he seems to have noticed some color in my cheeks, because he suddenly looks flustered.

"Oh, no, no. I'm sorry. I didn't mean to suggest that . . . that I would be one of the contenders . . . or whatever. Dear God, no."

I purse my lips.

"Oh hell, I'm making a mess of this. But see, that's another thing. There's an unrelenting demand upon me and on most men to have some sexual response or the other to women at the ready. Why is it that I feel like I must reassure you of your desirability?"

I want to retort in some way, say something cutting, but he isn't wrong. I am mortified and also have had enough of Sylvan Wilson.

As if sensing my impatience, he signals to the bartender for the check.

"I know you aren't asking for an explanation," he says, imploring me to engage one more time. "But under our globalized neoliberal austerity technocapitalism," he says, "I lean toward being asexual."

I squeeze his hand, smile, and insist on picking up the check.

OUTSIDE THE BAR, Sylvan Wilson shakes my hand. Just be really careful, he says. "Traditional masculinity is predicated on performance of activities. Of manners and attributes associated with maleness. Men will show up to perform your feats. If you pick the feat with care, you may, hopefully, find the partner you are looking for beneath the performance. To be honest, I'm quite excited about your swayamvar. I think it could point us all to something."

When I have wave him goodbye and am waiting at the light to cross the street, I see the two women from the bar. They hug each other goodbye. My gaze follows D as she meets up with a group of ... five men. I don't recognize any of them from the bar. She seems much smaller suddenly, not in height but in stature, in her manner or something. She seems plainer, her dress more maroon than a blood red. The men with her don't seem threatening or overbearing, just mediocre. One of them stands out a bit among them because he looks like a bodybuilder. A gymcel. Yet D seems to disappear as she walks with them, her previous swagger uncherished and up for a gamble.

As I cross the street, I see the other woman go by in an Uber. She has the rickety loom on her knees, with a beautiful cream-colored silk fabric flowing from the contraption. A shroud. She rolls down her window, looks me right in the eye, and pulls on a thread, smiling as the whole weave comes unraveled.

MY RIGHT LEG quivers at night and I struggle to fall asleep. I wonder again if the brain fog I'd been warned about as a consequence of menopause has had me imagine recent encounters with the two strange women and even, perhaps, with Sylvan Wilson. But I have his business card on my nightstand to tell me at least that part was real. And I have the strange cocktail-napkin note from D.

I massage my inner thigh and my quad with rose oil. I bring my knee to my chest and stretch my aching leg as far into my heart as I can. The muscles continue to shudder and twitch in a familiar ache. I move my fingers between my legs. Maybe sexual release will help with the pain. But then I start to think of my sabbatical writing project and all lust is lost. I am meant to be finishing up a book on loneliness among men. I had pitched this book to my publisher after the pandemic—"It may be said one day that this nation's creatures died alone together of an invisible disease driven not by a virus but by their inability to find each other." I have received a major grant to do this research. But here I am, planning a sort of wedding. Perhaps the book could be about what antidote is germinated when I pit my own loneliness against the loneliness of a man somewhere out there.

I mull over the conversation with Sylvan Wilson. I have studied what happens to men under the pressures of masculinity. But perhaps I have been fooling myself into thinking that my study was tinged with compassion for men. My examination of the vulnerabilities of men and their increasing loneliness, alcoholism, suicide was driven by a need to expose the toxicity of stoic masculinity. Was my lifetime of study spurred on by the energy of a mere gotcha?

When you have built a brilliant career out of anger, where do you go when the anger is gone? And when you have spent decades studying masculinity, you can't help but fall in love with men a little.

MY MIND GOES now to a speaking engagement I was invited to in India, in a private college in Bhopal. At the end of my talk on toxic masculinity, a young man had asked me, "Wouldn't you say that feminism these days is just well-disguised misandry?"

My brain had to swim swiftly down to the riverbed of my knowledge to retrieve the kelp in which was buried the word "misandry," so long had it been that one had heard this word said out loud. I fished it out and swam to the surface just in time to look like I'd given the boy's question some thought. "Feminism was always accused of misandry," I began, with a sardonic drawl. "But may I quote to you from a superbly eloquent meme I came across on Insta the other day?"

INTEMPERANCE

Laughter in the young audience, as I'd expected.

"It said, 'Don't let men who hate women define feminism as an ideology in which women hate men.' Feminism, as I have been saying in this past hour of my lecture here, is a loving call to men and boys."

The young man sat down as his peers applauded my pithy response. And yet I was left with a troubling sense of being a charlatan. Back in my hotel room, I couldn't stop seeing more of the setting of the young man's environs than I'd noticed while at the event. In the picture being etched and filled in in my head, I saw the boy, dark-skinned, with a couple of seats between him and the others in his class with no body language of camaraderie or cohort-ship from the boys around him, let alone the girls.

If I hadn't been so glib back then, perhaps I could have picked up on more. Perhaps the boy could have done with a nuanced discussion—forth and back—about intersections and hierarchies of power. White women, Black men. Black men, Black women. Lighter-skinned Indian girls, darker-skinned Indian boys. Caste and color.

I couldn't shake off the feeling that this wasn't just my guilt—a generational guilt for sure—for being a light-skinned Brahmin-born girl who had looked right through dark-skinned boys in school and college, taught to conflate skin color and caste. In any case, in all the realm of possibilities for why the boy had asked that question, my response had been incomplete. It served as a singular and somewhat skinny idea—feminism is love.

How did the response serve that boy except to shut him down? Did it calm him into examining his own misogyny? Did he feel dismissed? Would he have received a slap on the back from the other boys, seated two seats away, for asking the controversial question? Would he attract the "cool chick" of the class, the one who didn't call herself a feminist? Had he wanted to say to me that feminism was nothing if a woman like me could talk down to a boy like him? That feminism should be his, not mine?

I would remember him forever. I hoped he'd forget me at once.

I toss and turn for hours. I make a mental list of feats. Cooking? No. Both Siddhartha and Paul were excellent cooks. Some friends had even pointed to that as reasons not to leave the men. Such good men. I'd remembered the good man that was my father, beating my mother's head against a wall; my mother hiding her face away from her children so they wouldn't be frightened by her blood. I remember my father washing his hands, then cooking the most delicious mutton rogan josh for his children. I remember licking my fingers.

But my husbands were nonviolent men who cooked. Such good men. Ailed, nevertheless, by some or the other thing that made me too much of a woman for them, in one way or the other. There is a man out there who wants this too-muchness, and I will know him from the feat.

Ask him to describe his strengths and weaknesses? Set up a scenario where he must step aside so a woman at work can take the lead? ... What does he do next? Talk for a half hour about my philosophy of life and then ask him to recount what I'd said to see if he is a man who listens? I chuckle. Ask him when was the last time he'd called his mother ... and what they talked about? This last one makes me think of Karan and how he'd laugh and cry as a child, how he'd stayed tenderhearted in his early twenties and then developed a stoicism and sarcasm in the past few years, grown a bit distant and hard to access, as if a shroud of masculinity had

INTEMPERANCE

been thrown over his head and a malevolent force had dragged him away from me, his mother, a scholar of masculinity.

When I can't sleep and even the dog doesn't want me in bed, I decide to get up and add a layer of serum on my moisturized face. I hold my serum-soaked palms over my face the way the commercial has shown, so the warmth helps it all seep into my pores. When I flick the bathroom switch off, I see the glint of a silver box and, despite myself, I reach for it. With the soft pad of the tip of my ring finger, I lovingly trace the kohl all along the riverbank of my eyes.

I AM SLITHERING, *dark, indigo. I appear on white and yet am nothing until I am pressed into place. I am ink taking shape with such urgency sometimes I swell and spill. I am all curl and point and straight lines. Slanted lines upon straight lines, meanings and miscommunications and corrections, rolling into . . . what . . . a script. I am words, I am language, and I appear, and I appear, and I appear. I am growing stronger and stronger and making meaning and sense. Of love. As I grow longer in my unfurling, I see a tender face above me, eyebrows furrowed. The writer. He is giving birth to me, and I am making sense of him. I am making sense for his sake.*

Praanpriye . . . (He writes me in Mithilakshar, yet I am all the languages of the universe in this word now, until I am all the languages of the universe in the next. Soul beloved, he writes.) I turn a deeper hue, for here I am, a love letter—

PRAANPRIYE, I HAVE *found you like a diamond in the earth. You are my Heera. And I am Alokendra, Lord of Radiance, but dull without you.*

I will snatch you from the earth, the sky, and every realm in between. I roamed like a misfit until the day you looked down at me from a tree, dazzling me.

Your body is like the sandalwood I wear on my forehead.

You inhale and exhale the scent of my sandalwood paste as if smudging the sins of my people upon yours.

Should I tell you of the exquisite terror I feel when you wait for me in the branches of the litchi tree and leap down on me in the dark? You unwrap the one cloth around my waist with a tug as thrilling as the undertow of the Ganga in full flow, the river-mother that almost drowned me once when I was a boy who floated too far. But now you swim with me in the river that forgives us all. You splash me and you make me swim farther and farther out, and I follow you in the fluid silence that ripples with our story. Our friend the glorious blind fish seems so happy to leap and dive and swim with us. Will you both drown me in our river-mother one day?

Your dark skin is made for the stealth of the night. And what do I do with the way my skin glows and attracts unfriendly eyes? They say you are an Untouchable. Touch me so hard that you hide me in you. Hold me everywhere, wrap me, enter me, cover me from within to without so we can stand full and proud, and everyone mistakes us for a single shadow, your shadow on me and mine on yours. And if they must catch us and turn their wrath upon us, I hope we melt into one, your skin and soul into mine. I hope we shimmer.

I run to my orchards at dawn, and I discover that they are your orchards. You know them better than I ever will. Each tree here has grown with you, from sapling when you were a boy to sturdy young tree, taut and proud like your spectacular manly form. How the branches and trunks lift you and bend for you, doing your bidding. How they gift your hands their fruit.

INTEMPERANCE

My brother and his friends say you are an Untouchable, that you should not touch our food. Should I tell them how sweet your fingers taste when you place a litchi in my mouth?

I arrive with my heart thumping in my chest from running and from anticipation. I slow my step when I get close so that the women sorting the litchi don't giggle and nudge one another and raise their pallu to hide their smirks. I make a pretense of chiding them for being too slow, but I never chide your mother.

Or does my mother know I was bringing the food to you, to feed you with my hands and be fed by yours? Next time I will bring you your favorite brinjal and halwa.

Can I run to Ma now to tell her of my ecstasy the way I did when I was a child and first discovered that the Naag Champa flower in the courtyard gave off a scent that felt even to my childhood sense forbidden?

You say such talk fills you with dread. You say I am too innocent and that I don't understand. I will be nineteen years old soon. My father has invited the British officers to a celebration. You say you have seen these men do terrible things. I have seen some things and not others. You have seen more than me. I don't know what you have seen, and you won't tell me of it all, especially what my Brahman family has done to your caste. I know your ancestors have suffered blows from the fists of my ancestors. I know your women have been raped by men like my grandfathers. But how you chilled my heart when you said my father had tried to plunder your sister. How can that be? Would my mother not know and say something? You say my elder brother spat on your father and kicked him. I believe you because he looks at me, too, with seething rage. We played gulli danda all day and pachisi late into the night as children and he fed me the mangoes that were sweeter than his own share, but now he looks at me as if he is ashamed of my singing. I fear him.

If my sorrow could heal your generations, I would spend the rest of my days shedding tears. And if my love for you could burn down my own men who are in rage, I would fan the flames.

My Heera, how will I leave to go study at the university in Calcutta? I will go and then I will return for you.

Yesterday I stared at you too long as you teased me by letting your fingers linger on one litchi after the next. You stroked them like a musician on his sitar and then you did the same to my little fruit at night.

You are an idol and I want to worship you, but you bend and twist and turn me into a bride on the loamy soil of our meeting place near Ganga. Our river goddess gives us the same silence and solace that she does to any of the other lovers who must have sighed and moaned near her waters.

In the daytime, the koyal sings with greater urgency these days in the orchards. I fear she is telling everyone about what she saw you do to me by the river.

Ay Heera, you know everything. Tell me, are there humans who understand the language of the koyal? If they do, will she tell them how much you want me?

AND THEN THE writer stops, and his face is no longer my moon. I am words on this letter folded into myself, word of me meeting word of me, embracing even though we don't make sense pressed up like this against each other. Our writer is running. Our home, a parchment page rolled and folded to fit into a silk pocket. And then we are in the air again, and our writer's face is above us and he is reading us, and as he reads, he is kissed over and over by his lover.

I am now wholly new, a new story, formed word by word as I am pressed into shape not on parchment but on the earth by two hands.

INTEMPERANCE

This is what must be lovemaking, our writer's hand pressing upon his lover's hand upon a stick that gives birth to us in mud. We unfurl a word in ecstasy—Heera.

We are not as firm as when we are written by our writer's hand. The hand beneath his is fearful. This is forbidden, the shake of his hand says. This touching, this writing, this learning of writing even one's own name as an Untouchable, is forbidden. This Knowledge, this literacy, is for Brahman to own. And this love? Forbidden.

The Priests

I wake up from a deep and long sleep. This time, no terror. Something has soothed me, yes, but also dislodged some of the timber of a dam I have built against the people and stories that came down from my family. I want to know more.

I rummage about in my accumulated mail like a desperate little witch in her recipes of spells. Surely, the obliging Brahmin cousin-brother, my very own twisted cultural informant, has written more? These kinds of men don't wait for you to respond. But I find nothing in envelope after envelope I tear open.

Aha! He's migrated from international courier into my university email now.

Dear Madam,

I hope this letter finds you in the pink of health. I have awaited your phone call but to no avail. I had thought I will not bother to write to you again, but upon seeing the vile WhatsApp cartoon of you that has gone viral here in India, my sweet wife counseled me to reach out to you again. We were both having to hang our heads in shame. My wife has never been exposed to such visuals and was unable to keep her eyes open alongside me.

INTEMPERANCE

Perhaps you now see the way the curse of our family is intensifying upon your insistence to go ahead with the swayamvar ceremony and bring shame upon yourself. Since you seem to have not paid heed to my gentle retelling of the story of the family curse, I will tell you about the more tragic happenings now. I had wanted to save you the distress, but perhaps it is necessary.

Alokendra and Heera are said to have been caught in a compromising situation on the bank of the river late one night. It was none other than Alokendra's elder brother, Maheshwar, who came upon the filthy sight.

I want you to imagine his horror when he came upon those unnatural acts being performed by his younger brother with a boy of the Dom-caste. This was in the sacred litchi fields. Are you aware of our family's heritage? As you know, our Maithil Brahmin family is of the priestly clan and we were also landowners, zamindars, who owned litchi farms starting in the seventeenth century. We built a litchi empire. We had the luscious rose-scented litchi and the Shahi varieties. Even today, we have some of these orchards remaining.

The trunks of litchi trees are tall and the branches bear leaves on high. The human form is visible within the trunks of the trees on these acres of land.

I am saying all this to give you a picture of the bodies of two boys performing their act among the beautiful hanging fruit in the trees. You can picture the pride with which the elder Maheshwar must have walked through these trees only to suffer the shock of seeing his brother engaged in unmentionable behaviour.

It is said he let his younger brother off with a warning at first, but he asked his assistants to keep an eye on the young Alokendra Thakur. When whispers in the village became too loud to ignore,

Maheshwar could not abdicate his responsibilities to his father and their family nor to the family of Asavari, the girl to whom Alokendra was promised in marriage.

 Madam, you probably do not know of the rich and complex tradition of matrimony in our clan. You have chosen to marry outside our caste in your first marriage and then marry a foreigner in your second attempt. You have strayed too far away from our family, so far that even your parents cannot tell about the glory of our clan. You have probably never heard of a place called Sabhagachchi, where thousands of Maithil Brahmins would congregate to make matrimonial matches for their offspring. Matchmakers would keep busy introducing families of Maithil Brahmin boys and girls. Here, you would find esteemed genealogists called the panjikars. These men meticulously catalogued and maintained records of marriages of us Brahmins to maintain the purity of our lineage. This tradition was established in the thirteenth century. The panjikars wrote down the genealogy on beautiful parchments of palm leaves. In those days, it wasn't the girl's family that paid the dowry. It was the boy's! This was not a patriarchal place. People forget how much stature was given to ladies even before marriage in those days. These Brahmin ancestors of ours would offer to marry brides of a lower stature, though also of Brahmin caste. Of course, the practice is said to have been misused sometimes by some Maithil Brahmin zamindars who were so rich that they could afford up to twenty brides, each one younger and more vivacious than the next. When the Britishers came, some people complained about this practice, and the Britishers made some half-hearted attempts to stop all this. These days, we have the horrific instances of the pakadwa vivah, in which a groom who might have cleared his examinations in the Indian Administrative

INTEMPERANCE

Service or medical or engineering is kidnapped by organized gangs and forced to marry a girl whose family cannot pay dowry. These marriages are next to impossible to annul.

Anyway, I bring all this up to note that during that prestigious and respectable time, young Alokendra's marriage had already been fixed in front of the community by his father in Sabhagachchi. Backing out would be ruinous for generations to come.

So, as was his duty, Maheshwar reported his brother's sick acts to his father.

I TURN MY eyes, my head, away from this vile letter from the cousin. My heart is slamming open and shut like a window abandoned in a monsoon.

Those boys in love. This man's hate. I wanted some clues to my visions, but this is not the story I want. What does this Brahmin want from me?

I minimize the window of his email and start a search for the effects of prolonged use of non-FDA approved kohl made from camphor and ghee...

Convulsions. Blindness. Death.

Wild exaggerations, surely. Look how beautiful it looks when I trace it more thickly around...

Smoke all around me. In wisps and in clouds. Sticks and cones of incense cloud my vision. Closest to me, yellow hibiscus. Gleaming copper bells. A silver plate. Golden raisins and melting gud in halwa.

All out of my reach. But I have no reach. I am stuck. Elevated, ensconced among beautiful things that tell of abundance, of feasts. Dyes upon dyes on me, on the porous stone where skin would be. Darkness, solid nothingness at my core.

But they look at me. They are pointing at me and wailing at me.

Dragging a young man before me, telling him to place his forehead at my . . . feet, they say.

A thakur slaps his son for the first time. A handmaiden scurries to tell her mistress. The mistress flies out of her chambers barefoot through a courtyard. I want the incense to curl thicker so I am spared all that I am about to witness.

She is screaming her son's name, begging him to be quiet. Alokendra will not be quiet. He says he has no need for shame because he is not a deviant. He pleads in the way of poets. Priestly poets who have sung praise into my face for generations would do well to learn from this child. For years after, servants of this household will whisper his words to the village. Only the servants will, because *this is sacrilegious . . . they say.*

"Do we not worship the king of fruits, the Mango, and bow also to the queen, the Litchi?" Alokendra sobs. "I have been raised in thrall of this delicate fruit. I have spent my years being instructed to revere its najuk skin and quivering flesh. When the fortunes of this family have been beholden to the fragility of this blushing benefactor, when we have worshipped for generations at the altar of its rosy skin and celebrated its tiny seed, why must all the sons of this family be mighty as a mango? Can I not have your love for my sweetness, my dear father?"

Ahalya Devi, Alokendra's mother who bathes at dawn and bows at my pores four times from daybreak to dusk, who wears the cleanest garbs and has not a single jewel out of place, who worships with all her breath that her husband and her sons may live long lives, that her daughters may birth sons and the women of this household may keep their laaj, their shame, and be worthy of protection or of rescue . . . she is now in lament and is striking her head against me.

But the man for whom she prays the most protects me instead. He *pulls her head away from me, pulls her by her hair and flings her body to the floor. Her beloved son shrieks and rushes to his mother, like a girl . . . they will say.* This angers his father so much the man roars that if the boy had compared himself to the fruit of their fortunes, he should also know that there was indeed an annual season of pruning and hacking away the diseased branches and twigs, and that bruised and blemished fruit were discarded. If the boy sees that filthy Untouchable again, he will be disowned and cast away from the Brahmin family. He will not be worthy of his promised university education. The father delivers a tremendous kick in the chest of his son and leaves the house to find comfort in another woman . . . they say.

And with the thakur gone, so many voices that had lain silent now rise in a cacophony around the mother and son heaped upon each other on the courtyard floor.

The thakur's men say they must get to the bottom of the case of how their young thakur boy could have been led astray. Maheshwar vows to his mother to take his assistants out in search of Heera and teach him a lesson. When Alokendra staggers up to clutch his beloved brother's feet and yelps for forgiveness for his lover, Maheshwar's face reddens.

A servant says they must find the daayan, the witch who was one of the cleaners at the wedding of the thakur's elder daughter, Uma. The daayan was named Sona. They say she saw young Alokendra and she fell in love with him. When he spurned her advances, she immediately put a spell on him, and he started to dance at the wedding like a girl. The more the thakur told him to stop, the stronger her spell grew, and the boy danced more and more gracefully, more and more delicately. He was in a reverie and could not stop, do you remember?

Maheshwar gives his first decree as the thakur's older son, whose time has come to take care of his brother's and the family's honor. He will ask the sarpanch of the village that the witch be given fifty lashes with a whip and paraded naked in the street.

Alokendra looks up from his brother's feet. He looks at me. He rises, dusts himself off, and walks up to me. Water in his eyes, blood in the veins at his temples, distortion of the features of his face. This is a human emotion. Why bring it to stone?

ROSE OIL IS spilled on the keyboard of my laptop. I jump up. I try to soak it up with napkins. I click on the keyboard but nothing moves on the screen. The letter from the man in India is stuck in my view.

Dear Sister, you may think the existence of the daayan is a myth. But both science and folklore have described such a maiden—she is usually dark-skinned but beautiful in her own way with sensual ways and big, hypnotic eyes. Men can spot such a daayan when they feel too aroused by her body and too mesmerized by her gaze. In some worse conditions, the daayan may be a churail, who are more demonic than a witch practicing black magic. A churail leaves her hair open and flowing and her feet and ankles are twisted backward. I have never seen a churail but I have witnessed firsthand a daayan, a young girl of Kumhar caste. She cast a spell on my friend in the village and caused him to abandon his wife and children. I must say, my friend's family did some terrible things to punish this daayan while her husband watched.

But in our family, the thakur pardoned Sona and brought her sentence down to twenty lashes, but she was still to be paraded naked and would be made to eat cow dung. If the men in her family resisted, they were to be tied to a tree and beaten unconscious.

INTEMPERANCE

As it turned out, Sona was none other than the sister of young Heera, who picked litchis in the thakur's orchard. When she couldn't have Alokendra, this daayan lured Alokendra to her brother, Heera, who was already a corrupt sexual being.

Heera was the son of Gareeba, who was known for singing folk songs. They belonged to the Dom caste, people who handled burials and cremations.

Isn't it interesting that Gareeba, which means "poor man," named his son Heera, which means diamond, and his daughter Sona, meaning gold? These people had such aspirations to be like us.

I am simply trying to lighten the story to prepare you for what comes next.

However, you will have to telephone me for the rest of the story, especially because you should know how the curse placed by your own great grandmother is intensifying on you and making you more and more irrational. Please don't mind my comments. You will see that I am merely a well-wisher, and you are invited to a better future in our country with its superior civilization, which promises a more fruitful and more suitable old age for you.

I also understand that you are a passionate woman, and you have certain needs. You have been and still are a beautiful woman and accustomed to male attentions. I will take care of those needs. My wife is in favour of this offer. She is a pious woman and well-versed in the Manusmriti's permissions for the complexities of such things.

I will anxiously await your telephone call.

Your well-wisher,

Brajesh

The Music

It's a Saturday morning, but the IT helpdesk is open on campus, and I rush to drop off my laptop. I am miserable at the thought of having lost all I didn't save, but I also shudder to think of Aaron in IT bringing my device back to life on that sickening page of the letter from the despicable cousin.

Back home at the houseboat, I know I must snap back to my own life, staid though it may be in contrast with the chaos of my ancestry. I am estranged from my parents and brother because I wanted to leave behind the way I'd flinch at hands and voices raised against me. Look how far I am from those hands. Hark how easily those voices can still reach me.

I will anxiously await your telephone call.

I am here now, I tell myself. Here. Now. Alone. Safe. Here. Now.

I don't need his letters to learn what happened. My visions are preceding his unrelentingly brutal narrative. Perhaps his words turn my visions darker. I could throw open some windows and step away, let out the miasma of his words, let in some air.

A friend is having a party to celebrate the arrival of summer in Seattle, and I text him to beg out of it. I cannot bear the thought of being among people who want to know more about my plans

INTEMPERANCE

for the swayamvar and the feats. My friend throws this party every year, and I usually look forward to it. He and his husband have a glorious backyard that bursts into color with dahlias they planted together years ago. I love this garden. But something about encountering the exertions of the hummingbirds I'd delighted in last summer make me feel just so wary this time around.

And so, while dahlias thrust their fuchsia depths into gasping faces, and friends gather to drench themselves in chatter and wine, I do the thing that has saved me over and over again to live another day. I pull the cream linen curtains of my bedroom shut against the summer and lie down beside my dog on the cool white sheets of my solitude.

The sunset threatens to be sweeping and spectacular. It will command all attention and will be lavished this attention by all the people of this town. Picnics would be had. Pictures of a variety of photographic prowess would be posted on social media. The closefisted public beachfronts of the city would be crammed with people in awe of their rare outdoor sweat. It is as if the whole citizenry will look up at the beautiful sky and chorus, "Look up at the beautiful sky."

I must get out of town.

In the tumult of my declaration of a swayamvar and the torrent of public opinion on it, not to mention the ghosts of my ancestors arriving unbidden to hand me a reckoning of sorts, I simply haven't had the time to think clearly. A wedding planner may gasp at the idea of a bride-to-be taking time off to think when one is already so violently late in planning a wedding, and indeed Demi has sent me links and telephone numbers for me to follow up on different aspects of the swayamvar, but the longer I have lived and the more action I have taken, the more I have longed for a ceasing of action and a surrender to thought. And it is in the very nature of thought that it be performed in silence and solitude.

I have a wealth I would not exchange for all the currency in the world in that I have a retreat, an actual place I can occasionally go to clear my head or chase a writing deadline for a book. I call Cat and leave a message to ask if her cabin on Whidbey Island is free. It belonged to her parents and was passed down to her as a wedding present. Over the years, I have had complete access to it, especially after Cat and her husband moved to New York City. Cat loved to come here in her many years as a single woman, and we came here together as friends to guffaw into the night years ago, but now Cat is in the throes of family life. She is barely able to stop by her sweet island cottage on any quick visit to Seattle, so she is glad I can inhabit it sometimes, "keep it breathing," as she says. Still, I always check with her before I head over there, just in case they lent it out to others.

Cat calls back to say the cabin is all mine.

"Or I could head to you and see how that husband of yours is faring," I say.

"Soon, soon. By the way, Karan came by," she says. "He took a day off from his writing residency and came by to see how we're all doing."

"Oh?"

"Yes. He's . . . ," Cat trails away.

I wait.

"He's sort of worried about your . . . plans . . ."

"I know. But how did he look? Is he feeding himself well?" I think of how Karan is prone to turning gaunt when he's in the middle of a writing project.

"He's well. He talked a lot about this woman, this other writer at the residency. I didn't ask him too much ... didn't want to seem like I was gathering information to relay to you. But he is glowing."

I feel a sting in my eyes, but I push past it and put a smile in my voice. Karan is falling in love.

"Well, I won't say it doesn't hurt that I am hearing about it secondhand," I say to Cat. "But I'm glad he is at least talking to you about it if not me. I can't wait to talk to him. He will call when he's ready."

"Yes," Cat says quickly. A clang of something behind her. "Okay, I have to go," she says.

By the time I arrange for my usual dog sitter and spend the early evening playing with the dog so he will forgive my departure or at least be too tired to notice and I pack and send a few emails and shop for a few groceries to bring along, the hour is indeed close to sunset. I once heard someone, a friend's aunt, a woman from Hyderabad, say that twilight filled her with dehshat, an Urdu word perhaps best translated as dread. The word so perfectly captured an emotion I had felt almost every hour of all my life, I let it invade my imagination, untouched, untranslated, on each day's twilight. But the twilights of the nonsunny days of Seattle, which passed without a sun to visibly go about setting, a sun shushed away by the skirts of gray skies, soothed me. The twilights that announced themselves in all the noise of beauty were the ones that seized me with dehshat.

WHEN THE ISLAND taxi drops me off at the rickety gate of the driveway that heads to the cabin, the sun has set and the path through the woods into the cabin is dark. The driver glances at my carry-on suitcase and my cane and asks if I'd like help carrying my things into the cabin. I refuse, gently and with a wide smile, and I say my husband is coming over on the very next ferry and he'll haul my suitcase inside. I toss it into the inside of the gate for good measure.

The driver leaves. I hate that I still must do this, keep up the pretense of having a husband or boyfriend to ward off any sort of criminal advance from strangers. Do younger women still have to give out incorrect phone numbers to persistent men, or have social media and DMs put to rest all of that, I wonder. When "following" and "stalking" have gone virtual, are we safer, somehow, or worse off?

The cabin is on some twelve acres of property that are glorious but have fallen to disuse somewhat, even though Cat and her husband have someone come around occasionally to clear the woods and tidy up. I unlock the cabin in the dark, find the drawer that has the candles I'd brought here a few visits ago, and I light them. The cottage is bathed in a warm glow and my breath starts to slow. The night is too warm for a fire, but I light a small one anyway in the small Ulefos woodstove.

I have rituals here and have learned to build rituals in the many islands and forests of the Pacific Northwest. I used to occasionally go camping on my own, although that is growing rare after the time my right knee buckled from its weakness on the gravel at a campsite in Chehalis and the nearby campers who found me after several hours had to cut their own trip short and drive me to the ER. Now, it's cabins and cottages that hold my silence.

Some of my rituals are to ward off ghosts. Incense. A verse or two from the Hanuman Chalisa. Despite my efforts to exorcise my mind of them, I still believe in ghosts. "Believe" may not be the right word. Let's just say that my imagination houses them deep-seated and rent-free. I blame this on Malti, a maidservant from my childhood, whom our parents would ask to stay back and put us kids to bed on nights they had to go out to parties. Malti would tell us the single bedtime story she knew—of a village to which many men would travel from far and wide in search of a maiden. They were drawn by tales of the maiden's beauty. She was said to have thick, long, flowing hair that smelled of jasmine and lips that quivered like roses in the first rain of the monsoon.

Even now, I can hear Malti lower her voice as she spoke of this object of desire in a story wildly inappropriate for children of ages seven and eight. Traveler after traveler would arrive late at night in the village and lose his way on this steep hill. A woman would come out from behind the trees with a lantern and they would know at once, from her hair and her lips, that this was the maiden they had journeyed all this way for. She would offer to lead them back to the path of the village and they would follow her, this woman with her hair flowing like the night and her lantern like the moon snatched from the sky into her right hand. Then they would notice that they were walking backward, not forward, because the woman's ankles were twisted and turned all the way around.

A churail! Malti would whisper this word fiercely and clutch at our faces and we would shriek with terror each time. The travelers were never heard from again. She would finish with a sigh, which meant that we children were to cover our heads with the bedsheet and fall asleep at once. My brother would fall asleep right away, but I would not sleep for hours and would be miserable in school the next day. Still, I couldn't wait for the next night that our parents would be out for a party and Malti would be asked to stay back and put us to bed.

Since then, I had sought out ghost stories. Horror was my

favorite movie genre, not because I was inured to it but because I am absolutely incapacitated for days after. I line up for sequels to *The Conjuring* and *Paranormal Activity* and all else like a moth to a flame. The new genre of horror, films by Ari Aster such as *Hereditary* and *Midsommar*, which masterfully combine grief with horror, convince me that nothing stands between us and evil.

And yet as the firelight casts shadows on the cabin's walls and the coyotes howl at the owls to go tell the spirits that I am here, alone, I kick back in an easy chair by the fire, sip on rose tea, and feel myself grow sweet and beautiful.

It took years to get to this point. I used to be frozen in terror the first few times I arrived here or at other retreats where time and breath sounded too loud in my ears. I had grown up in a noisy Indian metropolis, a screaming family, two tumultuous marriages, and the unrelenting din in my brain that was motherhood. After the divorces and sending Karan off to college, I threw myself into work, spent cheery evenings with friends, and then the silence hung heavy in my late-night hours.

I look at the pictures on the cabin walls, especially that picture of Cat and me in our thirties on a trip to Mumbai, me urging Cat to follow me deeper into the Arabian Sea on Juhu Beach. There's that photograph of Cat looking just dreamy on her wedding day and her groom looking dashing. They are in their early forties surrounded by some friends but not others. A tint of sadness hangs about them in these pictures, and I wish I could go back in time and change that for them. I shift my eyes to happier pictures with the babies that came swiftly after their wedding, first Kira and then Maeve. Cat had told me for years that she'd wanted two girls, and these were the names she'd give them. I'd longed for this dream of hers to come true. There I am in one lovely photograph of me with the toddler Kira and the baby Maeve. It's my favorite picture of us, taken in my houseboat when their family had returned to Seattle after a long break, and we had reunited. I can almost see Cat on the other side of the camera, barely keeping her shit together to hold the camera steady as she wept. Another picture is more recent—of Karan, a grown young man, pushing the two little girls on their swings in Cat and her husband's backyard in Brooklyn.

My eyes grow heavy from sleep. The bed in the guest room (I never sleep in the master bedroom) is unmade, but I don't have the energy to put on the fitted sheets. I climb into my soft cotton pajamas, throw a cover sheet down on the bed, and pull the duvet over me. I fall into a deep sleep.

In the morning, I awake to the call of that bird that I look forward to encountering every time I'm in these woods. Tuh-tooh-tah-*tee*! I have sometimes had to wait for this bird, whose name I never intend to find out. He, or perhaps his grandparent or aunt before him, had first called out to me years ago, in what sounded like "Where have you *been?*" It questioned me over and over. I even tried to phrase a response and whispered, "I don't know."

His questions kept changing over the years. Sometimes, he asked, "What-a-bout-*mee?*"

On another visit, it sounded like "Oh-don't-you-*see?*" and on another, "How-could-it-*bee?*"

Today, I can't understand what he is saying. I listen for hours.

My retreat is not dissimilar to Thoreau's retreat into the woods around Walden Pond. Some say he lived a voluntarily austere life there, and there's debate about that, but mine is decidedly laden with treats I bring with me and meals I cook to perfection. Today, I cook a rich lamb biryani. The woods grow thick with the scent of cloves and kewra water and black cardamom, and onions frying in ghee. I realize I have forgotten to bring mint leaves, but I know where in the garden to get some.

I have been here in the summer, when figs have been so ripe they have plopped into my palms on the pluck and reddened my cheeks when I parted open their flesh. I have watched for hours as a plum ripened on my windowsill. I have been here to gnaw noisily on fall's apples, a variety somewhat different from those on which Thoreau fed himself in his woods. I have let the juice of the apples trickle down my chin and dry to a sticky laminate there. I have lain on my stomach in the slippery green moss, watching a banana slug make its way out of the rain toward the canopy of a fallen red leaf. I have resisted the urge to pull the leaf closer to the slug and shorten its miserable journey. I have been here once when a rare winter snowstorm trapped everyone on this island indoors and I ran out of tea in the cottage. I thought of tea all day and vomited by nighttime and realized I had an addiction to caffeine. I have written books from here, surprised at the prose that seeps out of me when I bestow it some days of wordlessness. I have spent hours staring listlessly at oaks when too much silence in turn asphyxiates the Muse. I have wept from the knowledge that a marriage must be axed, a knowledge that is permitted arrival only when there is nothing to do but lie down and let a kettle scream itself dry on your behalf.

In such a retreat, I am not lonely. This is the only place where I am not lonely. Loneliness only settles within me when I imagine there is any other way to be but alone.

I take few showers when I am here. I get acquainted with my true scent, unmasked from beneath my usual layered emollients that emerge from glistening little beauty-store pots with scents mimicking patchouli and rose. My unshowered scent is olive and mud on my scalp, turmeric and lemon under the arms, and molasses and warm butter in the folds of my vulva. My hair is hay, my eyes look sleepy without their usual streak of liner (or lately the kohl from the silver box I deliberately left behind at the houseboat), and my lips are a dull purple without the dab of lipstick I wear in the outer world. Still, here, I balm my lips to stay tethered to the human. In this inner world, I am the woman who finds newer, more languorous ways to pleasure herself—fingers, toys, raindrops, winds, the warm sun, unfettered fantasies. In the outer world, I would soon be that invisible woman who excuses herself when she bumps into you on the ferry, but you are not expected to respond to, kindly or otherwise. Here, in my cottage, I am faerie and gnome, undisturbed genie and examined demon.

As I pluck fresh green leaves of mint for my lamb biryani, I turn my face up to the sun. I crush one of the leaves into my palms and inhale the scent. My bird swoops close and screams out something. My eyes startle open, and I look for him but now his call is going farther and farther away into the pines and I am sad I still didn't get what he said.

I WALK BACK to the cabin. Here, in the woods, my limp grows deeper. The land is uneven, yes. But it's also the unabashedness that I am gifted in solitude. Women who are so alert to the way they are seen can feel such ineffable abandon when no eyes and no mirror are turned on them.

I think often about how Thoreau, even when he would retreat to Walden Pond, would have women wanting to be in communion with him. Sophia Foord was one such woman, a middle school teacher in the town of Concord, where Walden Pond was situated. Sophia was an abolitionist and a brilliant thinker, among whose students was the little girl who would grow up to be the writer Louisa May Alcott. Foord was fifteen years older than Thoreau. She fell in love with him. She is said to have thought of them as "twin souls." She asked him if he'd marry her and was spurned by him. For years after, she stayed in love with him and wrote about this love in letters to Louisa. She died in 1885 at the age of eighty-three, a single woman. Years later, researchers would find a letter from Thoreau about this marriage proposal from Foord. The letter is not kind. It speaks only of how her proposal makes him feel sort of put upon. So little research exists of Sophia Foord's life aside from all this love and proposal business.

I am afraid that the pursuit of love and marriage and its questions has been a distraction from all the other work I could have done in the world, responses to the urgencies of elevating the human condition in one way or another, and yet here I am, tending to my heart and the hearts of friends.

Here, where thinking gives way to sensing and sensing gives way to being, ought my being not give way to peace, perhaps even enlightenment? Or are those things reserved for men like Thoreau? I hurt that those two things have eluded me. I have seen the saris of peace swirl around the corner of a room here and dart behind a tree there, just out of view and just within reach. I have always then been reclaimed by ennui or some preoccupation and been unable to give chase.

Why, now, when I have overcome soul-deep loneliness and can embrace a life of being solitary, do I still not lie back into a solitary life, a life of easeful solitude?

Why, now, do I imagine bonds and communion with a partner? Perhaps I will find one who will also understand my need for solitude from time to time. He will know that when this woman heads into a forest in a cultivated, organized solitude for a while, she returns nourished, a few pounds heavier from the feasting, but softened from sleep and turned ravishing from thought.

Will he? Do I know of any such husbands who would be content to have their woman come and go as she pleased, not merely from work and social engagements, but from disengagements? Perhaps an asexual man such as Sylvan Wilson would, but I am seeking sexual union too! What sort of man would meet me at this delicious ebb and flow of union and solitude? For what sort of man would I risk this seduction of my own seclusion?

What if I had been this way from the start, a young woman who cherished her time alone? Siddhartha would have loved such a woman.

When I met Siddhartha, I was a twenty-two-year-old girl, begging the world to send help. I found a lifeline in his lazy grin. Young man inheriting his father's bookstore in Bombay. Beautiful girl asking him if she should read Milan Kundera.

You must. And then you must let me take you to get Irani chai and brun maska at Yazdani so you can tell me your thoughts.

Maybe, maybe.

I raced through that book. I had thoughts. I had feelings.

I will take you to Prague someday.

Maybe, maybe. Oh, yes, please.

I spent the monsoon of 1992 reading every book Siddhartha placed in my hands. I was the one to kiss him first, a brazen move for a young woman raised with warnings in 1990s Bombay. I kissed him just before my train arrived at Churchgate Station so I could jump in and hurtle away right after the kiss. But he jumped in after me. Had I wanted him to do that? Is that why I jumped into the general compartment instead of the women's? Siddhartha did nothing but stand across from where I sat. He stood by the door of the compartment. At each station, I was afraid he would exit. After all, he lived in Colaba, near his bookstore, and this girl he was courting lived all the way in Bandra.

My heart raced every time the train slowed.

Don't go.

He didn't go. He watched me as I alighted at my station, watched as the girl who had dared to make the first move and kiss him climbed off the train at her station and waved goodbye, confused that he stayed on the train to go farther and farther away from his home. Oh, she realized, he didn't want to frighten her and climb off the train to follow her home.

On that day and for the nine years that came after they married, she would never know why Siddhartha took some exits and wandered past other entrances, when he took trains or planes or cars that put miles between them, and when he came close to hold their baby and ruffle her hair. What I still know is that he loved me in his own way, but he needed more solitude than I was willing to give. I held tight in fear, and he turned to sand in my grip.

I washed my hands of him but what I'd wanted was for him to be a wave that drowned me.

AFTER THREE DAYS of rest and very little contact with the outside world at Cat's island cabin, and after I have finished reading bell hooks's *Communion*, I call for the island taxi. The same man who had driven me here comes to pick me up. He smiles at me. Perhaps it is a knowing smile, perhaps a smirk, but I find myself smiling heartily back. The anxiety or embarrassment I'd felt on the entry into solitude has fallen away. On the way out, I am sim-

INTEMPERANCE

ply grateful for a quiet ride to the ferry. My mind is swirling with hooks's call to engage with the female search for love, to plant my feet in and push off with all my might into that leap of faith that is a swayamvar.

BACK AT THE houseboat, I am happy to fall into the warm wet licks of the dog. "TV Time!" I shout to him, and he jumps into position by me on the chartreuse velvet sofa. Hours of television have been waiting for me, and I dive in. These people who come into my living room are my friends, growing bigger and bigger as the expanse of my TV screen responds to decent raises in my wages. My most beloved television friends are the ones who solve the gruesome murders of women.

    I would move to Shetland to sit on a craggy cliff and write in the long hours of wait as Jimmy Perez and his stubbled jowls investigate the murder of a headless corpse washed up on shore. I would marry most of the men who investigate the murders of headless corpses that have washed up on a shore. Men roused from their sleep in the middle of the night because the severed hand of a woman with her wedding ring intact has washed up on shore and these men who must now fight their own tortured past to find the killer are my favorite kind of men to marry. They're out of the house for long periods of time, they bring home stories that will hold me in thrall, they seem to not have much of an appetite for home-cooked meals or a desire to entertain guests, and they're grateful someone is willing to work with the nature of their tortured past. A homicide detective in Brighton whose own wife may have been murdered by a serial killer? We could go to therapy together. An unsolved case that haunts an NYC detective? Maybe a fresh pair of eyes will help solve it. Alcoholism got him kicked out of the job? I don't know how to work with this one, but could you please take me to the coroner's analysis of the cause of death? I've always wanted to go.

Sometimes, when I cannot get away to the cottage on the island or into the imaginary friendships with television characters, I lean hard into the loneliness. I play Hindi film songs of loneliness on a loop.

Karo-ge yaad toh.

Har baat yaad aayegi.

If you set out to remember, every memory will return.

My blood runs cold at these merciless lyrics, and I let them wash over me as I lie in bed for as long as I can between Zoom meetings. I move to the whole playlist devoted to different renditions of "Chaap tilak sab cheeni moh-se naina milaake," a sensual love poem penned more than seven hundred years ago by Sufi mystic Amir Khusro for Nizamuddin Auliya, in which he coquettishly chides the Nizam for stealing his identity, his pride, his form, everything, with just one look into his eyes.

I dance slowly, my eyes closed, my feet in pain and yet not, and before I know it, I am a whirling dervish in my living room. The houseboat holds its breath.

WHEN I DIP a toe back into the swirling waters of my social media now, hoping that the discourse has been distracted away by some other person's willfulness, the chatter still demands to know what my feat will be. Lying about is hardly going to yield an answer to the question, so I tear myself away from the unconditional embrace of my bed and venture out in search of myself, this time in the city.

That is to say, I decide to seek ideas in my quotidian existence—

my work, my play, my whereabouts, and my companions—the clues to my desired love and communion.

I have often joked with friends that a very desirable match for me would be a man who lived in the same houseboat community me, so we could live together but also apart. So, I perk up as the handsome bald man from six houseboats away joins me on the walk up to our cars. He had once saved me from a potentially disastrous fall when the streets around our houseboats had turned to ice, as they often do in Seattle. He had offered a strong Ukrainian arm, and I had leaned on it with all my pounds, so he had to all but carry me back to safety. I understood he was younger than me, but nonetheless, we had a bit of flirtation on text message, and he had invited me to glimpse the sweeping view of the city offered by the top floor of his office building, the Columbia Tower. This was not an uncommon or weird offer in any way, as any Seattleite would tell you, but I had decided it wasn't something my soulmate would lead with, so despite his proximity to my home, I had ruled him out. Now, as we exchange pleasantries, just as I am wondering whether to include him as at least a contender and inform him about the plan for the swayamvar, I see a young woman waiting for him by his car. A pretty young woman with a perfectly made-up face that looks dewy, pillowy, and clean (all words I have learned from online influencers). He introduces her to me, and she links her arm in his.

I drive my MINI Cooper, pepper white, alas not a convertible like Demi's (whose text messages I must soon respond to) to the top of Queen Anne Hill, which is where my story in this city began. I had picked out an apartment on Craigslist when I got confirmation of being hired at the university here. When I arrived, I found it was what the Americans called a basement apartment, but thankfully not quite submerged, since its windows were level with the street that sloped downward. In my early years, I watched and learned the ways of this city, my new home, by gazing at the people who walked by my window. I watched Americans eat handheld food in public—burgers, hot dogs, ice cream, tacos. I saw them kiss openly, even those who were gay. Some of them would spot my face in the window and quickly look away, and I learned that all those other things they did weren't considered rude, but glancing into someone's home was.

I stand now at Kerry Park, a viewpoint from which tourists could look at the skyline of the city and also at the majestic Mount Rainier. The mountain is out today, as we say around here. Ah, look, I have grown to consider myself as the "we" of this town rather than of any other place I once believed was home. And yet aren't I still learning new things as I watch people around me? Why didn't that person smile back, and exactly what did they see when they looked at me? A reasonably attractive middle-aged Indian woman whose husband worked at Microsoft and kids went to Ivy League schools? A really good ob-gyn? Or could they glance at me and see a woman standing still in a swirl of romantic possibilities?

I'm just a middle-aged woman,
standing before all of mankind,
asking them to vie for me.

It doesn't matter what they don't see. I am here to see, to look for clues, and so I settle down on the bench on which I had sat in those early years, and instead of my nine-year-old Karan, who had run around and zipped something called a Beyblade on flat insides of an abstract sculpture in this park, I now gaze at other people's children. I hear squeals and whines. I listen to the patient voices of parents.

Perhaps I want a man who has parented well. Perhaps the feat would be to answer a parenting question: *How did you fail your children?*

Bleak.

What legacy of imagination did you impart to your child?

I decide I would not ask any questions I couldn't answer myself.

Perhaps the parenting feat could be more tactile, like changing a baby's diaper. (But what if diapers were different today from my time; would *I* be able to change one now?)

What story would you tell a child at bedtime?

Yes. This was definitely a contender. I fish in my purse for the journal I had started, the red one, and scribble it down.

I turn my eye to the couples enjoying a summer picnic. No, I tell myself, I wouldn't cry. What on earth? I hadn't expected to be assailed by this particular memory, but here it was—Paul, when I had just started to date him in the summer of 2005, sitting there with a picnic laid out on a blanket, complete with basket and baguette and cheese and wine and strawberries. Cat, with whom I was already close friends, would tell me later that he had told her the next day that he knew at that picnic that he wanted to marry me. He had been entranced by the way I enjoyed the food. He told her the day after the picnic that I looked stunning in my green figure-hugging dress and movie-star sunglasses, but it was the way I dipped my strawberries into white wine and the way I moaned at the freshness of the cheese that stole his heart.

Here, now, in the midmorning sun of a summer almost

twenty years and almost twenty pounds later, would a suitor still sit back on his elbows and, in a state of languorous arousal, be moved to a proposal at the sights and sounds of me falling upon a meal? Oh, but I had dispensed with the matter of a proposal. If now I was the one wielding power with my decree of a feat, I could well sit back on my elbows and test the way he licks and nibbles.

I TAKE MY arousal with me for a good dousing at the university pool, where I swim laps every Tuesday and Thursday. I don't do this for any sense of vigorous exercise. I do it because it is in the pool, deep in the water, that I can recreate the silence that has become essential to me. In the swimming pool, I am beautiful.

I go slowly back and forth in my lane. I don't know any stroke other than freestyle, and even that is imperfect. I don't know how to modulate my breath. I must look like a flopping fish sometimes to anyone watching from the deck. The lifeguards have stopped watching me with concern over the years I have been coming here. No one here knows I am a mermaid, a jalpari.

Through swimming goggles, I can barely see a thing. Objects at a distance are already hazy. All this has the effect of immersing me as if in a watercolor painting still watery in the making.

In recent months, a man swims in the lane next to mine during the same hour, 11:30 a.m.—12:30 p.m. He and I have fallen into a rhythm, swimming from opposite ends. Through my swim goggles and my fading eyesight, I have the sense that his skin is somewhat like my own in color. I can't tell if he is tall or short, young or old, but his comportment suggests youth. He is broad shouldered, and despite looking able-bodied to my failing sight, he swims at the same unhurried pace as me. Sometimes, I come face-to-face with him underwater when we swim past each other. Last Thursday, the man seemed to grin at me as we passed in the water, which startled me, not just because his teeth looked eerie in my watery view but because it was an odd thing to do when submerged in a chlorinated pool. I couldn't possibly return his smile, even if I'd had a moment to tear myself away from the reverie of water and react before we both swam off on our own way. The underwater encounter did cause a drop of water to be trapped in my ear canal, and I tried all day to shake it out. It began to sound like the flapping of a bird's wings. By the next morning, the bird was gone.

Today, I arrive earlier than usual and have the pool almost to myself. I swim for just a half hour and decide to leave to run errands for the planning of the swayamvar. The man, or someone who I think is the man who usually swims in the lane next to mine, walks in as I am leaving the pool deck, leaning heavily on my cane so I don't slip on the wet floor. To make up for not smiling underwater the last time, I nod at him and smile. My eyes are still behind my goggles and I don't register his face clearly, but I see enough to notice that he neither nods nor smiles back. I decide not to be offended. Perhaps he doesn't recognize me outside the water, perhaps he had been offended by my nonresponse last time, perhaps he is preoccupied and doesn't notice my greeting. I turn around as we pass each other, and I see his eyes on my legs. Ah. He didn't see me smile because he chose to stare at my lurching gait.

Oh, well.

I shower and drive home, and for the rest of the day, I savor the scent of chlorine that lingers in the webbed base of my fingers.

BACK IN MY home, I listen to the voices coming over from kayakers and stand-up paddleboarders. Snatches of conversation. The shrieks of revelers on boats, canoes, and dinner cruises mingle and come up to me like a chorused taunt. My mind wanders to factoids like the one a therapist had once told me about how it wasn't seasonal affective disorder that caused the most suicides in this city; it was the arrival of summer, when it sunk in for some people that they weren't at home alone because it was raining outside and too cold and damp to venture out with friends but that indeed they had no friends at all, even in the warmth.

I start with guilt then, for I am the one settling deeper into my solitary ways despite the call of friends, despite the state of relevance that is still assured to me. Silence could hardly be a bad habit. Solitude could hardly be bad for health if it made me so ecstatic. I know that when I wrap the cotton top sheet around me and let my body temperature drop enough in the stillness to next wrap the Jaipuri cotton quilt with its pink and blue florals over my torso and my head, roll myself up tighter and tighter until I turn the world almost soundless, until it becomes just a little difficult to breathe, I would be cocooned in my sweetest state of being—a loneliness chosen for the way it left me thoughtless, unseeking, unsought, wrapped away from dread, ultimately unraveled into the intimacies of hope.

In the first hour of such intimacies, the world would fall away. In the second hour, I would move between a state of waking and unwakefulness. It wasn't until the third hour that my eyes would stare open against a cottony absence of color, my body would be breathed by something outside my own breath, and the silence would spread from inside me to the outside.

I had never imagined such a state was possible. It wasn't until

INTEMPERANCE

the years of enforced solitude, that time when the whole world was gripped in a sickness, sent scuttling home by virulence, that I eased into this intimacy. It didn't arrive often. In fact, it was so willful in its attentions to me, I was beholden to its comings and goings.

And yet here I am, planning a party of my own for the sake of something as vulgar as matrimony. Isn't the pledge of matrimony to be in a state of near-perpetual togetherness? What would a husband make of my head and torso being rolled up in a Jaipuri quilt? My solitude may look silly from the outside. Or it may look like death. Its vastness may be rendered trivial to the unaccustomed eye. My space, my contortions, my breath, my stares into the nothingness of bridges and boats outside might be plundered for something as tawdry as male arousal.

I allow myself a shudder at this thought, wherever I am.

Here I untether myself from the dread of youth slipping away and feel instead the benevolent fear of losing life itself. Like runners keep jogging when halted by a traffic light so their heartbeat does not slow down, I keep bringing myself to stillness so my heart goes on.

They imagine me disenchanted, but here I am, in an enchanted forest of my mind in the heart of the city.

Is reclusiveness allowed for women? As romantic and lofty? What do we do when we no longer have to be trying to shed pounds, expected to show up for friends, be present for family, stay visible, stay relevant, stay in association? Is the sumptuousness of solitude as sexy on a woman as it is on a man? Pico Iyer writes about Leonard Cohen disappearing himself into stillness, something Iyer describes as sumptuous and luxurious. Does a woman ever really disappear?

I have parties, friends, chosen family. Choice upon choice. But here I am, seeking to be free and yet be pleasantly inextricable from the lives of others. I forsake alienation, not loneliness; I am troubled by isolation, if I am isolated at all, not by solitude.

No one is looking. No one has expectations anymore. Somewhere between the void of expectations and the abyss of irrelevance, I want to float up, one arm outstretched, to find an intimate other. I could forgo sex, perhaps, but my feet, oh, my feet! Oh, how they ache, twisted and turned around as they are. The thing about feet, let's face it, is that they are best massaged from the other end, by others' hands.

The stillness, the silence, the solitude, have fed me and then turned outward to ease an opening. All is light here where I am alone, but a different hue of light seeps in from the opening. In the refraction, I sense a future where there is both communion and quiet.

Once again, I wonder about the impending sacrifice of this silence, this loss of hours, to the companionship of a man. What sort of man would I permit to crowd into my consciousness, sully my spaces here on the bed and there in my head? Will he want words from me to describe my dread? Will he be content to leave me unknowable?

But see, only now, when I have overcome the fear of being seen by the world as the "unloved woman" do I truly desire to be a woman in love.

A recent buried memory flashes into my head. When I had crushed the mint into my palms back at the cabin on Whidbey Island and that bird had called out to me, I did, in fact, hear what it said. I just hadn't wanted to acknowledge it then. It said, Do you want *meeee?*

Of course I want you, you fool, I whisper.

THE STENCH. OH, the stench. All around me. Round me. There's so little of me, just an inch of heft and around four from the left of my existence to my right, or head to foot or diagonal. I am a circle. Ah, thank goodness, I am a perfect little . . . no, not perfect, I am imperfect. Dear God, what is that smell? It's dead in me and yet I am breathing. I'm an organic pile of something. Life giving. I have memory of once being grass and then being ground in what . . . teeth . . . not human . . . bovine. Cow. Gaiyya. Gaimaiyya. Mother cow. But she is not my mother. She doesn't give birth to me. She ruminates me through one chamber and another and another and another, then shits me out and I am a pile of shit. I am holy shit. I am picked up in the fingers of women and lovingly rolled and flattened. Rescued from flies. Turned into the shape of a peda. A cow dung cake. Laid out to dry. The sun soaks up my moisture. All around me, sixty others like me, bathing in the sun. Some went into the fire. Fuel. Generous to a poor man's choolah brewing chai.

I am picked out to be stuck, glued to a wall. A prime spot. To my left, cow dung cakes like me. To my right, cow dung cakes like me. We all hold hands, brush shoulders, plastered on these walls. Why am I here? To make this hut cool in the heat of summer.

This is all this family living in this hut gets from the cow. From other people's cows. Her dung. Never her milk.

Voices. If I focus on their voices, I could perhaps ignore the way I smell. It's already fading, isn't it, this stench.

A woman, older, wearing a tattered sari. Leaning against her lap, a younger woman, no, a girl no more than sixteen. A daughter.

"Those angry men make me laugh. Why should I be scared?" the daughter says.

"Sona, bitiya, my beautiful daughter, watch your words," says the mother.

Sona. Not a daayan seducing hapless men. Just a child.

"Do all Brahmin men have those big bellies, Mai?" the girl laughs. "Their big fat round tond protrudes so far, I could reach out and poke..."

"Shhh. Chup. Someone will hear you. Our homes are made of bamboo, not stone. And don't you dare even joke about touching them. We are Untouchables. Unless they choose to touch us women. Don't even let your shadow touch them, or they will..."

"They will what, Mai? If they do anything, I will tell them I know how much goo they make. How many huge mounds they shit twice a day. How the thakur's wife's paad smells. Paaaaaauuuuunnnn-phut-phut the lady farts."

The girl stops speaking because she can't stop giggling.

"Why... do they... why do they say we are the ones who smell bad, Mai? The other day when you took me to their palace..."

"It is not a palace. It is a big house. They are not kings or queens."

"In the big house, when you took me to help you scrub their dirt, the thakurain was walking to her puja chamber with her head covered in her beautiful orange silk sari but she gave such a loud paad I almost screamed out in fright."

This makes the mother laugh, and she slaps her daughter on the shoulder.

The daughter doubles onto her outstretched legs and giggles helplessly. Through ragged, laughing breaths, she continues, "Like she had eaten a dead mother cow the previous day. A dead mother cow and three-day-old dal."

"I will tell you why they spread tales about our smell," the mother says. "What they are smelling is the charred flesh and bones of their own dead. We cremate their dead and that scent of their sinful ancestors wafts from our pores only to their noses. They should worship us as the ones who deliver their dead to moksha. But they don't, which is why I steal something from them every day. I only steal these six drops of oil for your hair. Not their gold and their fish and mutton. Only this nourishment for your scalp. My daughter's hair is the most beautiful in the village."

The girl has stopped giggling. "I want them to smell like us," she says. "I want them to have the ash of charred bones in the cracks of their heels. The scent of burned flesh in their scalp. I want their hair matted and singed like my father's. I want their skin dark like ours from working in the sun and burning their dead."

"Chup, beti. Hush your wayward mouth. Stay far away from them. They don't want your shadow to make them impure. Good. Let them not smell you. If they smell this fragrant oil on you, who knows . . ."

"Don't be afraid, Mai . . . I will run so hard they won't catch me. I will take Heera with me."

The mother's face darkens. "How will your mai live without her Sona and Heera? Will you steal my only treasures?"

"The daughter of a thief mother must also be a thief, Mai!"

She jumps up as her mother lunges to pinch her. Hair flying. Chests heaving with laughter. She ducks and hops and puts her hand here and there against the walls of her home to leverage her leaps. Her hand lands on the corner of my being. I feel like I have been thrown into a fire.

Sona, I whisper. Sona. Be careful. Those men are coming for you.

It's as if she turns to look at me. But she is looking at a mere cow dung cake on the wall of her hut. Her mother catches up with her. She rains kisses on her child's face.

Sona, I whisper. Run.

The Cake

I wake up feeling like shit.

My head hurts, my scalp smells, and my skin feels dry and flaky. Shadows around my eyes mingle with the smudges of kohl. I look at the silver box on my nightstand. Only a pinch or two of the kohl remains.

I fight off a dizzying sense of dread all morning. To anchor back into my rising list of tasks, I finally heed the many text messages from Demi Yante and make my way to the subject of cake. Stacey at the cake shop has a practiced pleasantness that she lavishes on me at first but quickly withholds once she finds out there is no groom yet. She fixes me with an exacting gaze. She makes sure I know that she has agreed to give me an appointment only because of a call from Demi.

"If it hadn't been for her, no cake shop would have been able to accommodate you. A wedding cake must be ordered six months in advance of the bride's big day," Stacey says with a thin smile, squeezing my hand as if we'd been girlhood frenemies.

"Is there another bride?" she asks cheerily, signaling an in-this-cake-shop-we-believe-love-is-love-and-wedding-cake-is-wedding-cake energy.

No, I say somewhat apologetically, explaining the whole thing about the swayamvar, making up moments of pomp to come, adding a twinkle to my eye in the hope that Stacey would get the *audacity* of it all. But I seem to lose her at the mention of the feat.

"So, there may not be a groom?"

"There may not be a groom, but the hope is that there will be one."

"Oh, yes, of course. But will there be guests?"

"Yes, I'm inviting everyone I know." *Was* I?

"And how many guests would that be?"

"Let's say a hundred."

"Demi said to expect 250."

"Oh, I can't imagine there would be 250 people. Did Demi explain that this isn't quite a . . . wedding . . . I mean the wedding may or may not come after the feat . . . did Demi explain all that?"

"Demi said this would be something big and the news media would be there, and she would be sure to mention to them the cake designer."

"Designer? You mean the baker?"

Stacey sighs, but not once does the smile disappear from her face. She ushers me to a little round table covered with a fresh white linen tablecloth. On it are two dainty dessert plates and two forks. Stacey explains that she is not a baker but a cake designer. A cake designer rarely does an initial exploratory meeting with a client, but Demi had called in a favor, so here we are. Demi was to have joined us, but she said she had to rush to get me a city permit.

I apologize to Stacey for essentializing her vocation.

She waves away my apology. "We sometimes make exceptions and accommodate a once-in-a-lifetime, sweep-you-off-your-feet, dazzle-'em wedding such as this one is expected to be," Stacey says. At this, she lets her eyes flit around so it looks like she is glancing around the room, although I could swear she is focusing her peripheral vision on my face, my grays, the cane in my right hand, and the absence of an engagement ring on my left. She doesn't stop smiling. I come to realize that my role would be to answer rather than ask questions.

No, the groom wouldn't be joining us for the tasting, I say. Stacey clicks her fingers, and a young woman emerges to sweep away one of the plate settings. (This seems like an unnecessary flight.)

I respond to Stacey's rapid-fire checklist.

Yes, I hope there will be a groom. Let's just say yes.

No, no, it's not a bride. You're fine, you haven't offended me. It's a groom. He'll be there.

No, I haven't researched designs. I am a researcher but for, like, social science.

Sorry, no, I haven't researched cake designs.

Yes, sure, a sculpted cake with sugar flowers. Why not?

Yes, yes, fondant should be better than buttercream, yes? I love The Great British Bake Off.

Three dollars per slice? Oh. Jesus. I suppose . . . why not? It's a once-in-a-lifetime, sweep-you-off-your-feet, etc. etc.

No, not lemon.

No, I'm really not sure why, but not lemon. I understand it's a lovely end-of-summer flavor, but it doesn't suit my Indian palette, I guess. I think of lemon as belonging in savory dishes, not sweet.

Umm, no, I don't think I'd enjoy having a henna-style decoration on the cake.

No, not chocolate. I've always thought that's a children's birthday party thing. No? It isn't? Oh, well. But not chocolate, no.

Dark chocolate . . . okay, maybe.

Oh, that's so kind. I agree, I should not settle for something I'm not ecstatic about. Thanks for reminding me of that, Stacey.

Yes. Perfect. A summer-berry white-chocolate cake with hints of cardamom and rose water. Love it. Yes, yes, yes. And if I choose to wear a red sari as a wedding dress, maybe you could top the cake with raspberries?

A cake topper? No, I don't think I want a bride-and-groom cake topper.

A family heirloom? I don't have . . . I could try . . . to find something. (To my surprise, I find my throat constrict with emotion, and it's just as well that Stacey is writing notes and not looking into my eyes.)

Stacey hands me a tissue. She raises her eyes, and although the smile has stayed all this time, she announces that she will throw in an extra slice for me to taste today, so four slices rather than one. And she might add a special, surprise, magical ingredient at her whim on the day of the wedding. The tastings are offered just to get a sense of preferences with the matchings of flavors and the levels of things, she says, her voice trailing off behind her as she leaves me seated there with a *cake fork* (it has three tines and is curvier than a silly salad fork).

INTEMPERANCE

It is only then that I turn my attention to a young white couple seated at the table next to me. I've barely paid attention to them because they've been speaking in whispers this whole time.

"I don't even fucking *like* cake," the man says.

"I know, handsome," says his fiancée. "I should have remembered. Maybe we can ask them if they will do pies instead?"

"Don't embarrass me here. We're at a cake shop. Let's just look at the cakes. Why didn't you take up my mom's offer to help you with all this? I don't think they want dudes here."

"What? They love it when the groom comes along! And I . . . I wanted the cake tasting to be just the two of us. Like a date."

"The two of us and a pushy baker's shop assistant trying to talk us into add-ons."

"I'm sorry."

"Whatever, we'll figure it out."

"Thank you!"

"How much longer here? I gotta be back at work in twenty minutes."

"Well, they'll bring us the samples, we taste them, and then say what we like."

"I'll just leave it to you. You taste the cakes and pick whatever you like. Just keep it in our budget. But also, don't embarrass me with the guests on my side of the family. I don't want a repeat of my first wedding and the totally basic tastes of my ex."

"Oh my God, honey, I can't taste all the cake slices myself! Don't you want me looking lovely in my wedding dress?"

"Then just take an itty-bitty bite of each slice. Can you even stop at that though? Just kidding!"

They kiss.

"Okay, gotta go. And seriously, call my mom."

"I will. Bye, hon. I hate how hard they work you."

AND THEN, THERE we are, two brides-to-be holding two *cake forks*, one of us with a groom in flesh and blood who has disappeared into thin air and the other with an airy dream to manifest a suitor. We avoid one another's eye.

Stacey returns with the shop assistant, who lays out three slim slices before the young woman and four before me:

Dark chocolate cake with raspberry filling

Lemon cake with blackberry jam and blackberry buttercream.

Pink champagne cake with Bavarian cream filling and raspberry topping.

White chocolate cake with blackberry jam and cardamom buttercream.

As the two of us try hard not to devour the slices in one noisy, porcine mouthful each, Stacey tells us why we should choose little special touches (gold leaf designs for me; a keepsake cake-cutting set for the other woman). The young bride-to-be discreetly punches numbers on a calculator app on her phone. Once the cake deliverers arrive on site, Stacey says, there could be more design work involved—placing flowers, icing details or assembly, especially if it was a long distance or rough roads between the shop and the venue.

"There's nothing worse than a cake disaster on your wedding day," Stacey says.

"Look," I say, setting down my *cake fork*. "Here's what I'm thinking. If, on the day of my swayamvar, no suitor shows up, or no suitor can perform the prescribed feat, it's still my birthday, and I will marry the cake. Build me a cake worthy of my hand. Craft me a cake that I could murder on my wedding night."

The other bride-to-be spits up Bavarian cream across the table she laughs so hard. Stacey does not find any of this funny.

The Videographer

A documentary filmmaker has asked to meet with me to discuss the possibility of shooting some video of my swayamvar for a film she is making on disability, love, and desire. Certainly not, I had wanted to say to her, but something is now making me curious about my resistance. A quick web search tells me this queer Black filmmaker is accustomed to being told to shut up and go away but is unaccustomed to actually doing that. Her documentary on medical gaslighting won a few good awards. Her picture on her website—frank faced with a playfulness to her eyes draws me in. I call and make plans to meet her at any restaurant of her choice, and she suggests Cafe Flora, a vegetarian place I love.

When I arrive, Vee is already seated in the patio area. She is in a wheelchair. She's in a pink sundress I could kill for. The afternoon sun is dancing on the blond highlights in her curly hair. Vee compliments me on my balayage and tells me where she got hers. Her nails are shellacked in a coral red and they match the nails on her toes. Her makeup is flawless. I compliment her on that and say I one day hope to learn about the right makeup for my face. It's been on my to-do list.

"Have you seen my makeup tutorials on TikTok?" she asks.

INTEMPERANCE

No, I say. Clearly, I've been missing out, and I plan to correct that the moment I get home.

"Lunch is on me," I say, beaming at her as the server brings us menus.

"Of course not," she says. "We have funding for the film. This sort of preliminary interview is included in the budget."

She asks me about the swayamvar. I tell her I have the logistics in place, more or less, thanks to Demi. "But I'm still gathering data for the actual feat. Or feats."

Vee says she knows a little bit about the swayamvar tradition because she asked her wife about it. Her wife is Indian. Her name is Padma.

"But I don't want you to think I'm asking you to be in my film because I fetishize Indian culture or something. I have principles. Like, I won't take any money from Padma even though her parents loaded. And I mean loh-ded."

"I . . ." I start to speak but don't know what to say.

What would I like to know about her, she asks.

I want to broach the conversation about disability—mine, hers, and what will be on film. But I don't know where to begin. I haven't read up much online, I say. I tell her I read a few things about her award-winning documentary. I congratulate her and say a few other polite things. She watches.

"I'll tell you my story of disability," she says, "but please don't think you need to immediately tell me yours." Vee tells me she had a terrible case of endometriosis some years ago. She smiles at the frown on my face and says, "It's not uncommon to be unaware of the disease. It's when a tissue similar to the tissue that normally lines the inside of your uterus—the endometrium—decides to grow outside your uterus."

"Ah, yes," I say. "I think I have heard of that. Does it . . . hurt?"

"Oh, baby, you have no idea. It *hurts.*" Not everyone with endometriosis needs to use a wheelchair, she says. But she just couldn't bear the pelvic pain.

"And why should I?" she says. "When I can get around in Smooth Sasha?" She taps her motorized wheelchair.

I laugh out loud. "You named your *wheelchair?*"

"I sure did," she says. "And I make all those same physicians who gaslit me say hello to Smooth Sasha now before I pay them my dollars."

We laugh together and clink our lemonade flutes.

Vee tells me she had spent a whole year going from doctor to doctor, each of whom told her it was all in her head. One guy told her it would all get better when she had a baby.

"*When?*" I say. "Not *if?*" I can tell the rage is rising in my cheeks.

Vee nods. "When."

She tells me she gaslit herself at first. She was wracked with self-doubt. Maybe the trauma of being estranged from her family after coming out as queer was just catching up with her with these phantom pains, she told herself. Maybe she and Padma could start a family even though neither of them wanted kids and Vee had never wanted to get pregnant. Maybe yoga. Maybe acupuncture. Maybe veganism. Even when she met the physician who stopped treating her like she was a liar, Vee had refused the cocktail of painkillers she was offered—fentanyl, morphine, and epidural ketamine.

"And then I had a diagnosis. This weird, women's disease. Not researched much because men don't have it. Does it even exist?" She went through five surgeries. She was treated with nerve blocks. She now takes that cocktail of meds.

"But . . ." I'm here. "I gave up my job as a therapist. Or at least it's on hold for now while I parse through why I, a trained psychologist, hadn't believed myself. But I still love to talk and to listen. And as a child, I had loved the home video camera my father gave me. So, I combined those two loves . . . and boom."

She laughs one of the steeliest laughs I have ever heard. I am awed by Vee in the true sense of the word.

She had made the documentary film and now she is making one on disability and desire. She says she understands her status as being somewhat on the fringes of the disability world. "Like, I am interviewing people who were sent away to nursing homes as children who were born with a disability. Sent away by their families. They were overmedicated with chemical restraints. Left them groggy. Controlled. I mean, today's gaslighting of women who speak of unexplained pain comes from the same place of wanting these inconvenient people to go away."

In her earlier film, Vee had especially highlighted the gaslighting of women of color. "A whole other intersectional clusterfuck of a universe, that one," she says. Black women are far less likely to be given a diagnosis of endometriosis than white women. "Black women are told by their physicians that they have pelvic inflammatory disease, a sexually transmitted disease, rather than endometriosis. You see what they're implying?"

I look at the cheer of the restaurant around us. Gorgeous floral wallpaper in the interior, a fountain gurgling water near us surrounded with fauna, skylights, sunny toddlers with well-dressed mommies, grapefruit juice glittering on trays rushing about. I look at Vee with all the medical trauma within her story but her appearing here, now, looking unflappable, impeccable, easygoing. She looks back at me, and I know I appear the same to her.

For this new film, she wants to focus on disability, joy, desire, intimacy, she says. She wants stories of women and nonbinary people with disabilities who enjoy sex and love and beauty. Women who scream their wants from the rooftops, she says.

We both fall silent. I wonder if I am wasting her time, not just here in the restaurant but also as to whether I am a good candidate for her film. I steer her away from asking me to commit to being in her film. I ask her about her makeup routine. She dives into a long, step-by-step tutorial. The server comes, takes our order of tofu scrambles, sweet potato fries, and salads, and Vee jumps back and forth between ordering and talking about makeup. At the end of it, she says, "I'm still chasing glass skin. You know? Like the Koreans? But thanks for asking. Biggest tip—don't use too much concealer. It just looks too damn obvious when it creases under our eyes. Like, nothing screams forties more than . . ."

She goes on about concealer for a bit, but I am taken aback. Everything that I imagine people don't want to say in disability activism, Vee is saying about aging.

She seems to read my thoughts. She grins. "I'll shut up. I shouldn't talk this way about our bodies, I know."

I am so disarmed by the lack of a certain propriety I had expected—a serious *correctness* of some sort, a lack of silliness if not just playfulness—that I don't know what to say. I grin back and say we should talk about what we were here for.

I hadn't meant to sound stern, but I did. Vee's face falls and then she straightens up in her wheelchair.

"I . . . I'm sorry, I just meant . . . ," I say.

"Oh, no, no, you're right. It's hard to get a word in edgewise with me. Ask Padma. And we really, really need to talk about the film. I'm so excited."

"Well . . . ," I say. "I just realized I am not sure I can do it." I tell her that despite what it may seem with the whole swayamvar thing and all, I am really a private person. I hadn't intended for it to become so public.

"And the whole disability thing . . . ," I say, not sure what I intend to say next.

"Yes?" Vee says, searching my face with her perfectly crafted, daytime-smoky eyes.

"I mean . . . the disability part isn't, sort of, front and center."

"I see."

She holds up an aioli-dripped French fry and taps it against the one I have in my hand. Like a cheers or a high five.

"None of us, none of us disabled people, feels like we are the right kind of disabled," she says. "People want us to be either supercrips or invalids. Those who overcome and triumph, or those who waste away."

My stomach has started to churn. I see my father cheering me on to climb all the way up the five hundred steps of the Ekvira Devi Temple on a family vacation in Lonavala. I begged to be excused, but he wouldn't let me "give up." When I finally made it to the top, exhausted and aching, he roared with enthusiasm and made the family applaud. I see my mother telling me to wear long skirts to hide at least some of the sight of the way my foot flopped and buckled before finding the ground.

I return to Vee, who is in the here and now, the here. And now. She is telling me I could bail at any point on the film and would get to call the shots as I pleased. "Except the camera and directorial shot I mean," she says, tucking into her salad.

She says she wants to shoot some footage of my life around town in places and situations that hold meaning for me. She says she will also do some sit-down interviews. She would also like to follow me around as I prepare for the swayamvar. The permissions and consent forms from any place and people we meet would be her bother, not mine, she says.

"And, of course, I want to shoot the day of the event. I can't pronounce it and don't want to try," she says. "That's not an American lady thing, it's a crip lady thing," she says, winking.

I'm still not entirely sure about all this, I tell her. "Because you see, I have spent most of my life trying so hard to conceal my limp. To now limp about on camera, or even talk about my disabled life . . ." I trail off.

"I totally understand," she smiles. "And just for my curiosity, is that how you think of it? Your *disabled life?*"

"I mean, it's just a phrase that came to mind."

"Oh, and just to clarify, you wouldn't be limping about on camera." She uses air quotes again when she says, "limping about," and her smile is deeper now.

She says that if at any point I decide I've had enough of her and her crew, or something is making me uncomfortable, I can just walk away, no hard feelings. She says I can refuse to answer questions, that I can shut her down if something offends me, and that, if at the end of it all, when I see the completed footage and the treatment and the final edit, I don't like the completed project for some reason, she will artfully remove all shots and any mention of me from her film.

"I will also give you any footage you want from our shoots if you like something. Even if you walk away from the project."

I thought of Demi asking if I had video clips to upload to the website she'd made. I could weed away some sorts of men if I uploaded a video of me talking about my disability. Heck, maybe I'd draw in only serious suitors if they had a better sense of . . .

"How does that sound?" Vee says.

"It . . . ," I say.

She leans forward in her wheelchair. She is so tiny. She looks like a . . .

"I look like a child right now, don't I?" she says.

"My goodness," I say with a long exhale.

"You don't have to say yes because my tiny little body and my big smoky eyes make me look like a child you are going to turn down," she says.

I shake my head and chuckle. "Well . . . I suppose I want to show that loaded wife of yours what you've got."

Vee laughs. "Oh, she knows what I've got."

The people at the tables near ours look over as we laugh a bit too loudly.

"She loves you, doesn't she?" I ask Vee.

"She does. Padma is a financial advisor, and she says one of us must do something better than chase wealth. Tip the balance between good and evil. She loves my little social-justice-warrior heart. She calls me the Protector."

I stare at Vee as she sips on her lemonade. I am disoriented at what she just said, like the universe is jostling me about a bit.

"I am running out of reasons to refuse," I hear myself say. "Your film sounds fucking awesome. Let's do this."

I watch as Vee whoops for joy and whirls her chair around. People in the restaurant look over. They look away quickly when they notice her wheelchair.

VEE WANTS TO start right away, so we make plans for her to come home that evening with her crew. I move some of my furniture around so her wheelchair will move around easily. She brings along two young men—film students—she tells me, introducing them as Diego and Mark. They lift her wheelchair carefully onto the houseboat. The two of them remind me of Karan.

DIEGO AND MARK get busy around my floating home, excited about the shots of the light on the water that surrounds us. They pet the dog to settle him down, plug in lights, and declutter a bit. I decide to stay hands off.

I know my home is photogenic, despite the clutter. Space is scarce on a houseboat, so every piece of furniture must be chosen with care. In all these years of living alone after Karan left for college and I downsized my already little life, I have learned exactly where I like to place my mug of tea, where I like to sit for hours and at what angle of recline with this footstool or that, how I want my books on the sweep of bookcases behind me as I look into the nothingness and the abundance of the waterscape ahead. The space is a negotiation between practical storage shelves in the open kitchen, a lavender-gray accent wall in the dining area, fuchsia silk curtains in the loft bedroom (which is getting harder to climb with the passing years), and a large bathtub in the bathroom, which seems like such an indulgence for this small home, but that's just the point. A huge cowhide ottoman-style coffee table in white and a chartreuse velvet sectional sofa sit like jewels in the light of the living room, which changes all day as the sun moves on the lake outside. I have risen early on some mornings when I know the moon lingers in the sky, and I lie on the sofa to stare, listening to the water sound like it's making love to the underside of my home.

My art is both political and apolitical from all over the world. Nothing expensive. Everything meaningful to me. I am proud when Vee and her crew take all this in and let the camera linger.

When I am settled in my favorite corner of the chartreuse sofa, Vee asks: "When did you find out you were disabled?"

I have to think about this for a bit, and I am conscious of the camera zoomed in on my thinking face. I tell Vee I was disabled by polio when I was eleven months old, a baby traveling in a train with her parents.

"But I asked when you found out," Vee says, smiling.

"Oh," I say. I knew what she'd asked, and she's way too smart to let this go. "I only found out I was disabled when children called me a cripple in the school playground."

I talk for a while, and then I'm telling her how, when a young girl has an affliction in her leg and has so many doctors and therapists and even a faith healer take a look, some hands are bound to wander to parts other than just the lower and upper limb. I have wondered—what if it had been my arm that was disabled? My neck? My ears? My eyes? Would I have been safe from predators then?

You wouldn't, Vee says, even though the camera stays on me. So many of the people she has interviewed speak of sexual abuse, she says. Those with mental health issues more so.

We talk about how to be disabled and female is to have the gaze be turned up twice over. At any point, someone could be staring at me with a sexual gaze or a repulsed one. I stayed pinned by this gaze for years as a child and a young girl, sometimes immobilized by it, crushed by it so much that I didn't want to walk in the streets of my hometown in fear of someone shouting out, "Langdi!" which is the word for a lame girl or lame woman. But to me, the word implied someone limping so much more than me, someone writhing in pain, a beggar child, grotesque, howling. Dim-witted.

In a voice turning shaky, I tell Vee how, in my childhood, my parents and my brother teased me as being not very bright. I didn't excel at school. I barely scraped through, despite burning the midnight oil. My parents employed tutors. I'd sob and skulk into the Catholic church attached to my convent school to burn a candle to Jesus. I truly believed Jesus sat by my side during exams. When the result arrived, I was careful to blame myself, not Jesus.

I have never cried about being disabled, I tell Vee in response to another question. Not even as a child with polio. Not even when a car crash caused by a hit-and-run driver smashed the ankle in my strong leg and left me limping deeper than ever, and also now in pain. I have never felt anger over any of it. Not even when I am a woman openly angry at so many other things now. I have barely registered frustration when I trip and fall or when I can't climb stairs without a struggle.

What I have felt is shame. Even when I am all alone for no one to see my effort to walk in a way that makes my limp imperceptible or to see my struggle up a hilly street, I run hot and cold with shame. The shame is consummate. It rushes like a violence to my cheeks. It turns over like a dead bird on my tongue. It keeps me young, in the way of a child who wets themselves when a teacher scolds them in front of their classmates.

My mother would say that there was no running from it, that in Hinduism your birth as a lower-caste person or a disabled person are a punishment for the sins of a past life. So, I was a sinner as an infant, twisted and marked as a girl by the sins of a past life about which I knew nothing. Disability was also a thing that happened to poor people, not to middle-class people like us. It happened to lower-caste people, those people, there, who didn't clean themselves the way we did.

As a girl, I learned quickly to be pretty, turn up the radiance of the gift of my light skin, keep the gazer's eye on the beauty of my face, up and away from the hideousness of my legs, all sinful.

I shudder now, for all that was lost to me and all that pinned down on the identity of others not given the privilege of escape. What would life have been like if I hadn't been consumed by all this? What if some of us could recover a fraction of the time spent trying to hide our disabilities or caste, or overcompensating for them by being a sweet girl, a clever girl, a woman laying out achievement after achievement in her adult life?

I watch Vee's face. It has softened more than I have seen all day. Perhaps it's my story. Perhaps it's the descending sun outside my window.

She asks me to go on. The dog jumps onto my lap. The camera zooms into his face and then back at me. I know I look my most beautiful when I am nuzzling against the dog's head. Endorphins offer an inner glow.

I tell Vee about the excitement my parents felt at getting an appointment with a polio specialist in Bombay when I was fifteen. I remember my mother asking him if I would be able to carry a child in pregnancy. When the specialist swiftly responded that yes, of course, there was no doubt about that, she asked more specifically if I would be able to place my legs in childbirth position and push. He smiled. He said yes. He seemed patient with these questions of hers. I was grateful for that. I would have felt bad for my mother if he had been short-tempered with her.

"As a child with disabilities, especially as a girl, you learn to calibrate and negotiate the inconvenience you are causing others. My mother's embarrassment. My father's sadness and sense of failure. A schoolteacher's pity or their frustration at my slowness. A sibling's sense of obligation to be your proxy guardian when the parents aren't around, keeping you from being teased or taunted, beating up kids who dared.

As a girl growing into womanhood, I was grateful to boys who focused on my prettiness and not on my limp. When I met Siddhartha, I joked about how, in traditional arranged marriages, a woman would be asked to walk around the room so the family that had come to see her would ensure she wasn't lame. I kept it light, but I used the joke as a way to demonstrate my walk to him.

"He laughed. We laughed. But we both knew I was offering him an out. He stayed. He was in. I thought of all the aunties of my childhood whispering to my mother that no one would marry me without a hefty dowry. I remember my mother's silence. There was one aunt though..."

I think about the aunt who had rubbed kohl into my eyes as a child and what she'd said about my limp and beauty. A twisted message now, but true to its time. I had no other memory of this aunt. Where did the family lose touch with her over the years? Why?

I tell Vee about this aunt. "But this memory only returned to me a few days ago. Most front and center for me were the aunts and mother who thought I would have difficulty finding a husband. So, when Siddhartha asked me to marry him, I felt triumphant. He said he wanted not a single rupee in dowry, let alone a hefty one. But somewhere deep inside, I also wondered if this man was drawn to me because women with disabilities are imagined as passive, demure, childlike. And then he found me hungry, wanting too much, immoderate in my lust for life."

When I gave birth, my leg quaked and shuddered for days after. I didn't tell my mother and I didn't tell Siddhartha. I focused on my baby, and I watched the dates on the calendar like a hawk, showing up early for all the immunization appointments for the bonny boy.

When Siddhartha grew tired of domesticity and disenchanted with me, I set him free. I moved to America and learned to draw men in by asking to lean on an arm because the street was slippery or the stairs difficult. Men love that so much. They leap into the task, offer more of an arm than needed. "It's fucking adorable," I say, pouring my favorite Bread & Butter cabernet sauvignon in two glasses for Vee and me. Diego and Mark say they will pass. Hardworking young men.

We move to the deck, and I continue. "When I met Paul, I told him I had never run. I told him I would never know what it felt like to climb a mountain or even a steep hill and look down at where you came from, find it more beautiful than what you left behind. Distance for me is meticulously measured and weighs heavy. Two miles of walking is an achievement, filed away in my own mind, not to be shown off when friends are posting their running speed online. The pain in my bones and the thrum in my blood feels like punishment and reward. I told Paul everything. He fell in love with my dead-serious honesty until he turned himself dishonest."

And now, as I set a feat for a swayamvar, I wonder—if a man

offers me his physical support and picks me up from the airport or alleviates my rising discomfort and pain, what other feat will he expect of me? Do I have to be more sexually available? Offer physical pleasure in exchange for physical comfort? Or do I still get to be as moody as other women?

Vee interrupts me. She asks if I wonder if women who depend on men for financial support are also made to feel this way.

I hadn't thought of that, I say. I am surprised I hadn't thought of that. And I am in the business of thinking. I am in the thrill of thinking. When the exterior started to shrivel, I roamed into a deep and lush interiority. When I write, I flex muscles of the imagination. I lighten a load; I take flight. I create something that feels physical, a germination of cells in a way.

And what kind of man do you want, Vee asks me.

"I want a man who will feel I am the sexiest thing alive," I say, aided somewhat by the wine. "And yes, I want to be a thing to him. An object of desire. I want his knuckles to turn white from the effort it takes not to rip my clothes off in public. I want him to growl with his mouth at my neck and my right thigh within seconds of us being alone together."

I am startled at the whoops and cheers from Diego and Mark, apart from Vee. I laugh and go on.

"When the time comes, I want him to bring me the hospital bedpan. Lift me from the wheelchair into the bed. Help me when I am struggling to pull up my pants. When I finally give in, stop straining against it, I will wrap myself in the silks of disability. I hope my man will find me in an altered sense of beauty. I hope he will be in thrall. In a wheelchair, I expect to be undistracted by mobility, surrendered to my searing intelligence, holding forth with my startling acumen."

I exhale. Vee laughs along with me. Diego and Mark nod quietly.

"Women with disabilities reorder their priorities, their pace. I am reordering my desire. Parting it open," I say.

I tell Vee how a man once told me that men only look at the face, tits, and butt when they meet a woman. They don't care about what's happening below the knees. I wonder now what a suitor at a swayamvar might consider. A young suitor in India may be hesitant about what people may say about an able-bodied man marrying a disabled woman. Couldn't he get any better? Wasn't he man enough to get a full woman? In America, he may wonder about medical bills. About care. Nursing help.

I am not afraid to look like a dependent woman to be cared for. I am told that men all over the world like feeling needed and don't like women who are too independent. Such women seem aggressive and unfeminine. Men like their women to be physically weaker and smaller than them but not so weak as to be disabled. Not a woman in pain.

"In India, a husband could hire human hands to aid you. But you will feel like a supercrip. In the US, you can get around more easily. I am a big fan of the Americans with Disabilities Act. A broken elevator is an aberration to be decried if encountered in most places. But you know, self-sufficiency can be lonely making."

Vee says I haven't answered her question. She'd asked me what kind of man I wanted. But I had described how *he* would see me. How did I see him, she wanted to know. What does he look like?

I fall silent. I don't know how to answer this, I say. Could I dwell on it for some time?

Of course, she says. Vee asks me, when I buy a wedding ensemble, will I be a disabled woman or a beautiful woman? And, of course, both of those things can be true and often are, but which one will lead me in the choice? Which one will throw its weight around?

I have always, always loved fashion, I tell her. Somehow, my disabilities have freed me, at least to some extent, from the idea of a perfect body. I cherish my body. I feed my body. I lavish its cravings. "Women who work out so hard and pass up the creature delight of cake or half a loaf of sourdough bread used to soak up olive oil... I have seen them throw quick glances at my belly when I reach out for another slice of sourdough and spread butter over it. They look so lovely in their fitted jeans over flat bellies and hard butts, but oof, I love the butts of loaves, crusty and soft and warm from the oven."

Vee laughs hard at this. "Amen," she says. "We're all getting disabled. Aging is the great equalizer. The inevitable disability that comes for us all. But then, with disability, nondisabled people also hate to hear that you're not going to get better. And boy, do they hate to hear that you're okay with it. I mean, we have huge industries offering women ways out of getting wrinkles or getting fat or old. If women are spending thousands of dollars or hundreds of hours at Pilates every year, you should be miserable about your condition being permanent, right?"

"Yes! I wish we could call a meeting of all women and decide that we just don't care anymore. We sign a pact to enjoy food, to keep our money, to exercise for health and fun and not for punishment. I remember in the show *Ally McBeal*, a young white male lawyer finds the jowls of aging women a turn on. He also has the singular ability of making women orgasm by stroking the flesh on the backs of their knees."

I wonder what Diego and Mark are making of the turn in this conversation, but their faces are hidden steadfast behind cameras.

Are you disabled in your dreams? Vee asks.

"In my dreams, I somehow know how to fly but I don't know how to run. I have never run in my dreams, but for some reason, I am not limping either."

Sona. Run.

I blink. The words that just flashed into my head don't make sense for a moment. I shake my head and focus on Vee's voice.

What is the most recent incident in which you felt disabled? Vee asks me.

I don't have to think too hard. "It was when I was limping through the City of Love."

"Is that a metaphor? Like . . ."

"Oh no!" I laugh. "It's literal. It was me limping through Paris."

Vee slaps her knee and chuckles.

I was on vacation there as part of my sabbatical a few months ago, I tell Vee. Some of my friends from Seattle joined me there. I was walking up the hill in Montmartre, when my right ankle twisted almost all the way around. Like a . . ." I was about to say, "like a daayan or churail." I am startled. I shake off my thoughts. Return. Look into the eyes of Vee, the Protector.

"At first, I didn't want to tell my friends. They're all beautiful, the men and women. But limps, especially the painful ones, have a way revealing themselves. I assured the friends I would ice and medicate and elevate, and soon, I'd be limping painlessly through the City of Love.

"It was the best joke I could make through my pain. And remember what I said about recalibrating and navigating other people's discomfort? They slowed down, my friends, and offered their hands for me to hold as I stepped on and off curbs on the narrow streets in the Marais. We darted into shops with expensive clothing. We crossed the street to shops with tastefully decorated windows displaying shoes and purses. My friends asked me from time to time if I'd like to sit down at a café. 'We're here for people watching too, remember?' they said.

"They were kind also as we all climbed the cobblestone street that winds up in Montmartre to Sacré Coeur. Somewhere along the way, though, I started to fall behind too many times. I was using my cane to leverage me along, but it could only do so much. One friend suggested I take an Uber for the remainder of the walk up to the square. I said no, I was fine, I could keep up. The friend who was conducting this little tour of the neighborhood pointed out beautiful buildings and spoke of the history of the neighborhood and his own history in it, arriving in Paris after divorcing his husband of seventeen years, healing as he roamed these captivating streets.

"I was loving his tour, but my breath grew ragged as the pain from my ankle rode up to my calf. I wanted to say this out loud to my friends, but they looked so happy, their faces radiant in the City of Light.

"Eventually, I called an Uber and cheerily told my friends I would see them up the hill."

At the square, I was immediately disoriented. It was a Saturday evening, and this place was as crowded as Mumbai's Crawford Market. Tourists like us were lined up to be seated at restaurants. I waited and waited but my friends were nowhere to be seen.

They eventually called back to say they decided to wander

around and explore a bit more before arriving up the hill to the square. Are you comfortable and enjoying people watching, they asked.

"I said yes even though I could have told the truth and said no. But you know what, Vee, a pinch of moisture welled up in my eyes and I had to remind myself of the resolve my therapist had taught me for years—that I am loved, that people enjoy my company, that they feel fortunate to be my friend. That I am not seen as a burden to be disposed of. Other people have their own battles and their own reasons and insecurities that drive their decisions and have nothing to do with how I imagine they are treating me. Look strong. Feel strong."

The friends took another hour to finally arrive. I had gone through choices of cutting remarks I could make to them, but when they arrived, they look exhausted and annoyed. The Google map had them walking around for a half hour looking for me. I was no longer the victim of this evening.

"'Almost perfect,' I said, springing to my feet. 'I needed the rest, thank you.' I playfully linked my arms with my friends' arms. They were stiff, but I knew I would soften them.

"So, you see, I feel disabled often. I am reminded of it frequently. But I have come to realize that the word 'disabled' suggests, quite correctly, that something has been done to me from the outside, not from within. Just like we may disable our phone, we are disabled by the structure and expectations of the world. If only our ability were evaluated as our ability to love."

Vee is silent. She joins her hands together over her heart. Then she suggests I show her some of my favorite "pieces" from my closet.

Even though I am embarrassed at the clutter in my closet, I start to enjoy the gaze of the camera and then eventually forget it's there.

The scents of past celebrations linger in the chikankari embroidery of my pink chiffon sari. I hold the coolness of the gold zari in my kanjeevaram saris against my face. Is it the eye of the camera upon me or is it because a reel of memories starts to unspool in my own mind that I fall quiet and lay out my saris one by one on my bed? Twelve saris. Only twelve saris in three decades of middle-class womanhood. I recall a "challenge" started by a friend in Bangalore a few years ago—the Hundred Sari Challenge, she called it. It caught women's imagination and was perfectly paired with the height of popularity of Facebook. Well-to-do Indian women across the world were posting photograph after photograph, up to one hundred saris and beyond. I had only twelve. My mother didn't speak to me anymore. Or was it that I didn't speak to her?

My husbands were gone. Nobody gave me saris anymore. I wasn't invited to Indian family dinners by the ample tech community that lived in Seattle's wealthy suburbs, maybe because I was a single woman and most of these events were husband-wife-husband-wife, husband-wife fucking boring dinners. I am relieved not to have to go to these, but I would like to be invited so I could decline. I didn't wear saris that much anyway, not even when I was a young woman in India. I found it hard to move in saris. I felt like a diminutive version of myself. Trapped. Straitjacketed. I would never say this out loud.

The sari from my wedding with Siddhartha is in my closet, but I don't want to bring that out. Too personal, too mawkish, and on-the-nose for this documentary film. The latest sari I acquired was on a conference trip to Calcutta, a gorgeous sari made from Bhagalpuri silk. That's about as close as I'd wanted to go to the world of my ancestors in the villages not too far from Calcutta. The sari still smells of silk cocoons and shop incense. It is untouched and I haven't gotten around to tailoring a matching blouse.

I crawl into my bed and lie down among my saris, fully comfortable with the camera now. I reach out for the silver box on my nightstand and lace the kohl into my eyes. I tell Vee to let the cameras run, no matter what. I shut my eyes and turn my face into the Bhagalpuri silk.

BHUK! WAS I *thrown into a fire? No, I myself am fire. A flame. Light in the darkness of this home. I have been here before. Sona's home. Where is Sona?*

I see her mother. Another woman stands with her but at a distance.

I have seen the other woman before. Alokendra's mother. The Brahmin wife. Plump, fair-skinned, with the border of her silk sari covering her head. No, it now also covers her nose. She is holding her nose with her sari to block the smell of this home. Sona's home. She is standing on tiptoe, barefoot. She moves her weight from one foot to the other. Is she in pain? No, she is trying not to soil her feet. She is trying to stay pure in what she believes is a home of impurity. She is trying to stay Untouched. Unmoved.

She is speaking to Sona's mother. Phulmani, she calls her. Both women have tears in their eyes. Streaming tears. Their faces are turned same in pain, but they believe themselves to be different.

"What have you done with my son, Phulmani," the Brahmin wife says. Her voice is cold under her tears.

She continues, "What spell has your daughter cast on my son?

Where has your son taken my son? Return Alokendra to me at once and I will beg the thakur to spare your family."

She keeps repeating words with the same demand until the demands start to sound like pleas. Soon, she is bleating.

Finally, Phulmani speaks.

Even I, a single flame that can only burn in its lamp, know that no Dom-caste woman has used this voice on a thakurain before.

"Where are you rushing to with all these words, Ahalya Devi?" Phulmani says. "You have come to my home for the first time. Would you like to sit down? Drink a kulhad of water from my Untouchable hands? Tell me how I should honor you as my guest without dishonoring you with my impurity." A hollow laugh.

Ahalya Devi gasps and sputters the word, "Churail!"

"This churail bows before you, o Durga Goddess of Strength," Phulmani says. How many times have I bowed before you, Ahalya Devi? For generations, we Chamar women have offered you our respect and sought your blessings by touching our head to the ground beneath your feet. But you were always too preoccupied with your ritual baths and fasts to even bless us. We must at all times know where the sun is in the sky and measure our distance from you so that not even our shadow falls on your body, but you? You pretended not to hear me scream when your men smashed our clay pots and ripped up the baskets my husband wove for your own prayers at the Chhath Puja. Your men came looking for your son, but they wanted to kill mine. They wanted to take my daughter and make her eat cow dung and parade her naked in the village. Did you rush like this into the house of the sarpanch who gave this decree? Did you rush like this and wail at your own man?"

Ahalya Devi has fallen to the floor in shock, the same floor she was trying not to touch with her full feet.

INTEMPERANCE

"Phulmani . . . you will regret this . . . ," she says.

Phulmani does not hear her voice. She says, "The men and women of this family have done backbreaking work for you. We have been given no wages for generations by your family because a father's father's father on our side may have borrowed a silver coin for a daughter's wedding and couldn't pay it back because you never wanted him to pay it back. You wanted our slavery. I don't know any other way of being, but I know this way of labor is painful. It has pained my body, but I only knew it to be painful to my soul when I saw my Heera condemned to the same life."

Ahalya Devi is shouting now—"I don't have the time or the heart for your complaints, Phulmani. Tell me where you have kidnapped and hidden my son!"

Phulmani sneers. "I could ask you the same thing. Do you think you can send someone to find our sons? Perhaps you have the luxury of believing your son can be returned. And how about mine? What foolish dream can I have? Can I imagine Heera dancing at the village mela again? Can I imagine him leaping from bough to bough in your trees or eating sattu from my palm again? And who will marry Sona now that your men have declared her a daayan and said she will be paraded naked in the streets? Will you come to her parade? Or will you be lying around, eating mithai, and listening to the music of the white men who rule over you?"

Ahalya Devi is now breathing in the scent of age-old sweat in every fiber of cloth in this dwelling.

Phulmani does not show any mercy to the Brahmin woman. "Our sons are gone. Disappeared. The hatred of your men has taken them. Dead or alive, I don't know. Taken or escaped, I don't know. Even my daughter is gone. Your Brahmin husband could not love your son because the boy was najuk. My son's ways made me scared for him, but they didn't make me angry at him. They did not make his father hate him. I did not have rules and aspirations for him as you did for yours. My son could have lived a long and quiet life if it hadn't been for your Brahmin son's eye falling upon him. And yet a storyteller who may tell our sons' story someday will begin the story with your son. Go home, Ahalya Devi. I cannot bear to look at you.

Ahalya Devi can no longer meet Phulmani's eye. She says weakly to Phulmani, "You must have so many curses for my people. Can you ... forgive me?"

Phulmani laughs cruelly and says, "If a Dom-caste woman's curses had any might against a Brahmin, would we not have been your masters by now? Wouldn't I have lulled my son into staying with me so I could summon him right now to put his arms around my neck and tell me he is sorry for losing all sense of time and being gone for so long? Get out of my house and go home to your puny men, Ahalya Devi. I hope you will protect at least yourself and your daughters and daughters-in-law from them. Don't look so sad at how your Brahmin men have treated us. Go home and think about how they have treated you. Everything you allow them to do to you and your girls and your girly boys, they come out and do to us. Go home and pray to your Goddess Durga for the day your man dies and we can cremate him by that flame that my family keeps alive so that your deaths may be sacred."

Phulmani points at me. Bhuk. I flicker to attention. I was dying out a moment before, muffled into myself in shame. Ahalya Devi turns her head to look at me. Her reddened eyes on the hot amber of my face. I recoil, bend backwards, the air almost knocked out of me.

She stares in silence at me for a moment, shocked. Bhuk. Bhuk. I steady myself. Does she see me?

INTEMPERANCE

Do you see me, my par-daadi?

She looks almost exactly like me. Not the flame, but me, whoever I am, somewhere in time and shape. She wears the same age around her pampered face. The same flesh spills over the waist of her sari.

She tears her eyes away from me, looking confused at the long dwell of her gaze on nothing but a flicker of fire.

The Blessings

The room is dark. I sit up with a start. Vee and her crew are gone. What did they see? Had I been convulsing?

A text message on my phone. From Vee. "We let ourselves out. Hope we didn't wake you when we shut the door. You looked so deep in sleep. If this picture is too invasive or intimate, we won't use it."

Attached is a shot of me taken from what seems like the ceiling (how on earth?) lying in my blue jeans and navy linen shirt on my bed of saris. I'm not in the most flattering pose, with my mouth drooling, my hair unkempt and a sliver of belly fat served up for view. Not quite the princess bride in her chambers. I have to catch my breath.

In that moment, if I hadn't already done so before, I fall deeply in love with the woman in the picture. I send it to Demi to post on the website. I connect her to Vee so they can post clips of me talking about my legs and pain and wheelchairs to come.

Another ping. On my email. From that man in India again. I consider deleting it. But perhaps there's a better way to stop him? I decide to steel myself against his spewing and to look for some coherence between what he's been sending me and what . . . what

INTEMPERANCE

seems to overtake me when I rub that kohl into my eyes. Which one is telling the truth?

Dear Sister,

I am pained to see that I have not received any response from you still. This is the last message I will write to you. I know you will be moved to telephone me after reading the rest of the story of the curse.

Three days after the thakur slapped his son and stormed out of his home, Heera was found lying on the shores of the Ganga, bleeding from his head, whipped at the backs of his knees, and with his ankles broken and twisted like a churail. He was still alive. They say Alokendra wept at his lover's broken feet so loudly and in such a ladylike manner his own family had to drag him away and throw him into his chambers to be kept under lock and key.

However, two days later, both Alokendra and Heera went missing. All searches proved futile. To this day, no one knows what happened. Both families searched high and low but never found any dead bodies.

Alokendra's mother, Ahalya Devi, was so distraught she is known to have broken all the rules of a Brahmin zamindar's wife and run all the way to the hut in which Heera's family lived. There she found the mother of Heera and Sona, a woman named Phulmani. Who knows what happened between those two women, but Phulmani . . .

I ALMOST DROP the phone, my hand is shaking so much. The names, the narrative . . . how could I have seen something in my fugue before this man told me this piece? Or had I read this email before and forgotten about it?

. . . but Phulmani is said to have insulted Ahalya Devi and threatened to murder her. She put a spell on Ahalya Devi so she would carry a curse all the way home and deliver it upon our clan. Poor Ahalya Devi did the daayan's bidding. She ran all the way to her house and beat her chest in the courtyard. Her sisters-in-law tried to hush her, wipe her tears, drag her into her chambers, but she was contaminated by the lower caste now. She wailed and shrieked and said: I curse this family on behalf of another mother and from my own heart. May no woman married into this household ever bear a sturdy son. May your daughters henceforth be twisted. May they be willful and wayward. May they be daayan and churail. May they bring your Brahmin family shame upon shame. May they be cursed with intemperance.

The men and women of the household muffled their laughter and hid their smiles. No one wanted to laugh at a brokenhearted mother, but the foolish woman seemed to have forgotten that a Brahmin woman cannot be a daayan, she would always be pure, and her curse would go nowhere.

But her curse was powered by Phulmani's curses. It came smelling with the fumes of a daayan's hut. It all came true. So, this is the curse I have warned you about, my dear cousin-sister. Think back to your own life. Do you not see the ebb and flow of waywardness? Aren't your words and actions selfish? Haven't your decisions to roam away from your country and be estranged from your family of origin and choose poorly from among men been characterized by a terrible intemperance?

What will you do if the victorious suitor ends up being a Muslim or a black man? And as you have seen from your last marriage, a white or Christian man will never see you as an equal. There is still time. Call off your swayamvar. Show some moderation like the

INTEMPERANCE

more respectable Brahmin women of your ancestry and break the curse.

Break the cycle of shame in the family. Return our clan to its days of glory. As you will see from the progression of the family tree I am briefly listing below, all the way to your own birth, our clan's shine has been in decline.

Some say Ahalya Devi need not have cursed the family because her son and his instigator were not killed. The gossip over the generations is that the young daayan Sona convinced the two young men to run away together so that she herself could escape with their help. When the thakur's men came to collect Sona for her rightful punishment, they found that she and the boys were gone. The father, Gareeba, showed the men that the two saris they had saved for the girl's marriage and the mother's single gold bangle were missing. Those who believe this theory of escape base it on the fact that they found a fisherman's boat missing on the village shore of the Ganga the night the daayan and the boys disappeared.

For years after, some relative or the other who arrived from a farther shore would bring strange rumors. The most outlandish of these was that Alokendra, Heera, and Sona landed in Banaras, where Alokendra became an apprentice to a famed male kathak dancer named Kalkaprasad, who taught thumri and the dance of seduction to tawaif women. These women were the most sought-after courtesans (today they are mere prostitutes). Heera worked as a guard in the tawaif dwelling, hauling away men who dared to threaten violence to the women there and also the men who tried to haggle over the prostitutes' rates.

In that dwelling, Alokendra and Heera were allowed to be lovers among the other sexual deviants. Sona took up work as a handmaiden to the prostitutes and was spared their profession herself because the three of them lied to everyone and said she was Alokendra's wife. It was easy for the three of them to keep up this ruse. Then Sona declared to the boys that she desired very much to be a mother. Some say she paid one of the prostitute's clients to impregnate her, and the man came under her daayan spell. The more popular view was that she shamelessly asked her brother's lover, Alokendra, to impregnate her, claiming that their ruse would look more believable if they had a baby. It is said that the red moles on her illegitimate child's back signaled his lineage to Brahmin blood.

They say Sona and Heera and Alokendra wanted to educate the child the way Alokendra would have been educated if he had stayed with his family. Sona is known to have been especially stubborn in wanting an education for her child, so she took the offer of a job with a frequent client of the tawaif house, a mithai merchant whose family's fortune was built on their legendary rasgullas. She followed this man to Calcutta. No one bothered to ask why Alokendra, her so-called husband, would let her go. Lower-caste people are allowed more indiscretions than us. But do they have our gift of superior intelligence for an education? Sona's ambitions met with misfortune and her son was only clever enough to study to matriculation (even this is probably because of his father's genes). The boy chose to join the sweet merchant's shop and grew to be a dependable and beloved member of the merchant's family. A daughter of the merchant's family fell hard in love and pleaded his case as her suitor—he was, after all, the son of a Brahmin, said the Bania-caste girl.

This half-blooded son's half-blooded son went on to fulfill his Grandmother Sona's desires for education. He went to Bombay to study in the best of colleges there. He, Dr. Amar Thakur, became the principal of a school for boys, teaching them English, history,

INTEMPERANCE

and social sciences. Young men who graduated from this high school would say that the most useful lesson he taught them was how to tender a sincere, meticulous, and unconditional apology. What a strange thing to be known for.

They say he had a daughter, and she is also a teacher in Patna. I believe her name is Ananya or Ashanti or something like that. So, you see, all these people have gone on to use the generosity of the quota system for lower castes and make a good life for themselves.

ANANYA. I HAVE seen that name recently. I put down my phone and go to my dining table to fish out the envelope in which the silver box with the kohl arrived. From one Dr. Ananya Kumar, with an address in Patna, Bihar. Sona's granddaughter? And . . . maybe my grandniece, if the lineage was traced to Alokendra? Somewhere, in a home and family I never knew, a young woman was sending a distant aunt a strange package? Why? Was she related to the aunt in Patna who laced my eyes with kohl? Why were these women not more a part of our family circles?

I have to read more.

Maheshwar Thakur, who had exposed his brother Alokendra's love and broken Heera's ankles without lifting a finger on his own hands (because his were meant for prayer), was pleased that his fourth child was a daughter. His three older boys—Rameshwar, Siteshwar, and Parameshwar—would have a sister to look up to them, to teach them how to be protectors, like Lord Vishnu, the Protector. She would tie raakhi on their wrists. He named the girl Parvati.

This girl Parvati, contrary to her name, was no goddess of fertility. When she was just ten years old, she kicked one of her brothers so hard in his private parts he almost lost his masculinity! That kick was thereafter blamed for the misfortune of the boy, Rameshwar, who was married off the next year and sired only girl after girl. One of his six daughters, the one named Aadarshini (which means the "one with values") fell in love with the rising Bollywood cinema industry and ran away to Bombay to try her luck as a film star. She became a starlet and changed her name to Shiny. What Shiny? No shine for her. She didn't mind being a starlet and never the big star. It is said she looked back at the life of her cousins on her mother's side of the family and shuddered at the drudgery. When she was killed in a freak car accident on Marine Drive in Bombay in 1968, she was in the middle of seducing a young man who was smitten by her long and slender neck.

She had lost touch with her father's side of the family, but she is known to have sometimes talked in a drunken state about the fact that her Uncle Siteshwar sired no children and died the day after his wedding by consuming poison. She wondered what became of his widow, who was pronounced a daayan (she was not a Brahmin woman) but was rescued from a terrible fate by some mad old crone in the village who smuggled her away in the middle of the night and transported the widow to her parents' home.

I hope you are still following me, my sister. These associations of yours are important for you to understand and appreciate so you can rescue yourself from the curse. Let me continue—the Bollywood starlet Shiny's Uncle Parmeshwar, meanwhile, had become addicted to opium and drove the family's litchi cultivation to the ground, losing acre after acre while siring girl after girl, but none within his legitimate family. The quality of litchi in the orchards plummeted—an outbreak of toxins in the yield one year poisoned fourteen schoolchildren, who died of encephalitis. But it should

INTEMPERANCE

be noted that this was mainly because these were malnourished children susceptible to infections.

Only later would it be revealed that the reason Siteshwar had consumed poison was that he had been in love with Bhanu Devi, his sister-in-law, whom his brother Parmeshwar had married to spite him. The reason Parmeshwar had consumed opium until he lost his mind to it was that it was rumored and, he had some evidence of truth, that Siteshwar had had relations with Bhanu Devi the year before the wedding and Bhanu Devi had given birth to an illegitimate son, who was now being raised by Bhanu Devi's mother, who claimed that the boy was hers. The mother would claim this until her dying day, on which occasion she finally revealed the truth to the boy and asked him to go claim what was rightfully his in the thakur estate. But there was nothing remaining to be claimed, and by then, the clan's reputation was so muddied that few cared that this illegitimate son—Samarth—married a good and pure Brahmin girl to try and resurrect the family's reputation.

By now, of course, you recognize yourself as the daughter of Samarth and your mother Jamuna Devi. I, meanwhile, am descended from the lineage of Uma Devi, the sister of Alokendra and Maheshwar. Uma Devi escaped the curse, which her mother only made after Uma Devi had married and left the home. Given that the curse was from her mother, it did not befall her. And yet we have all suffered by relation and association. Where once we owned land, we are all now in middle-class jobs.

I do not have to repeat here the rumors about how your father was discharged by the Indian Army for leaving his post during wartime against the Pakistani Army, refusing to kill their soldiers in combat. I am sad that the shame of it made your mother so angry that she could not tolerate the whims of her own daughter over the years and drove you out of her house. I also don't need to tell you about the rumours about your brother. I do not believe that his pakadwa vivah, his forced marriage at gunpoint, is a failure. I don't believe that he has stayed in the marriage helplessly when he could have hired the best lawyers in Mumbai for an annulment. I fight with anyone who says he only stays in the marriage because he is a gay man, and the woman he married is submissive and grateful and allows him to beat her and cheat on her all over the place. But it is true that the two of them refused to have children, so that is the end for the clan.

Here is the main lesson to take from this diseased family tree. They say if Sona the daayan had just taken her rightful punishment instead of mesmerizing poor Alokendra to steal his own mother's jewels and help her and her brother escape, there would have been no curse on us. Such was the natural course of crime and punishment back then. If she had taken her deserved punishment, her brother would have been let off with a warning and could have lain low. He could have married a girl from his own caste and had a simple life. Alokendra's mother would not have lost her mind. There would not have been a curse on the family. Can you imagine the glory of our clan if all had been as it should? Can you imagine your own fortunes?

Still, dear sister, our extended future family's prospects are good in Bihar and in the whole Hindu rashtra. If you break the cycle of selfishness in the women of your family, you will be welcomed home even now. Our prime minister has changed the nation, and he needs intellectuals like you as his advisors. You must have heard how Muslim females are taking over public spaces and holding rallies to make false claims of oppression of themselves and their criminal husbands and sons. They are occupying land in Delhi willy-nilly and filling the streets with stench and filth and the blood of our Mother Cow. They say they do not want our just and progressive modern leader to amend the citizenship criteria. Why are they so scared? Do they have something to hide?

We need researchers and scholars such as you to set the academic records straight in the US and in India. You are a respectable and accomplished lady. You are not like the pseudo-intellectuals and the secular libtards who have surfaced in India, rampantly parading their lives as lesbians and having children out of wedlock. Should you make the sage decision to return to the motherland, you will be given complete protections and live out your life in the comforting embrace of your extended family. Do not forget you are descended from none other than Mother Goddess Sita herself. Even after two failed marriages, if you were put to the test of fire, you would come out pure. Living without a husband in America leads to corroding the cultural threads of Indian civilization.

Come home with your son. Our motherland needs such men as him—young, articulate, virile, masculine, and devoted to the truth. Your son should be protecting you as well as Bharat Mata, his motherland. We will teach him to have a missionary zeal. He may not have physical strength (the curse is still strong), but he has the education to show the world how we upper castes ended up being slaves for one thousand years under the Muslims and then the British. We can correct the ills and put the nation first. We need you in the think tank we have instituted, the India First Foundation (IFF), gathering luminaries and intellectuals like yourself from around the world.

As I have said, I am here for all your needs. Don't waste your passion on men who take advantage of you and then leave you. Please promise me you will not feel upset but will see this as my concern for you, my dear sister.
Jai Shri Ram.
Yours sincerely,
Brajesh

The Dress

I am gripped by a desire to bedeck myself. Steep myself in all the waywardness of the girls and women who gave a slip to their punishments, turned their curse into blessings, and may have lived or died doing whatever they willed. I want to bedeck myself like a bride and a daayan. I want to fly through the skies of this unsuspecting town, a cackling churail.

No more than two weeks to go before the swayamvar, and Demi's texts have been more and more insistent. I scroll up to a post from a couple of days ago about a pop-up bridal store that has come to town. Do you think you will stumble upon your perfect bridalwear here? Demi had written. Three questions marks, three exclamation points, and a tiara emoji.

The next thing that pops up on my phone is a message from an unknown number on WhatsApp. I idle over whether to delete it before it lands some spyware or some such thing on my phone, but I see my name in the title of the message and the words "old lady," "sex," and "shame." I see that the message has been forwarded to me by the unknown sender with the words "This is being shared all over on Indian WhatsApp. So sorry some miscreants have done this to you."

In the life of a single woman in her fifties are some mornings when she lies in bed in a state of repose, drifting in and out of slumber, responding to this pending message or that, sipping tea, reading the papers, pleasuring herself, eating medjool dates, or all of the above. These are well-earned acts of remuneration for the toil and trauma of the decades that came before. However, vestiges of the sort of low-grade anxiety that hummed like white noise in those decades often curl up around her in her bed on these fifties mornings.

So, now, as I blink at this message that has just arrived, I realize that if I don't click on what promises to be a hideous video, my anxiety could turn into a full-blown, beastly dread.

In the video is a tacky stick figure animation of an elderly woman hobbling with a cane. My headshot from the university website—taken by our university photographer on what I had thus far recalled as a pleasant, mirthful spring morning posing in front of bursts of cherry blossoms on campus—has been superimposed on the stick figure of the woman. The soundtrack is one I have seen on TikTok videos that come out of my homeland—a fake rendition of uncontrollable, breathy laughter. I watch as the stick-figure woman in the video puts a stick-figure garland around the neck of a stick-figure young man, depicted with a stick-figure perky face and a full head of stick-figure dark hair. The young man bends her over and starts to fuck her from behind. Superimposed on my photograph is some sort of animation that makes my face look like I am moaning in pleasure. Then the animation does a clumsy cut to the man fucking the stick figure, and it's now a white-bearded, coughing man who looks like he is on death's door. Cut to my face shown as screaming in horror.

"Happy swayamvar to Indian American lady professor!" the

video flashes at the end. Laugh-crying emoji and the fake laughter crowd the screen.

I turn the phone over on its face and smother it into my pillow. A cloud builds up in my eyes. My body is cold and my face is hot.

I am about to hurl the medjool dates from my stomach onto my floral cotton sheets when my brain kicks in with two thoughts.

The first is my therapist's training of me in cognitive behavioral therapy—"*Are you okay in the here and now? Are you safe and well in your lived reality?*"

Okay. Safe. Well? Well . . .

The second is an avalanche of questions—is the young man depicted as getting old by fucking me? Or was he replaced by an older man? Is the implication that I cause men to age as they fuck me? Or that I am promiscuous and they are two separate men in the same fuck? Or that the woman imagined a young man only to discover it was an elderly man? Or are the two men depicted as a son and a father?

My brain craves a clear narrative.

Of course, I'm also wondering who made the video and how many times it has been shared and how many people in my outer and inner circles have viewed it and which of these people is likely to forward it to Karan, and isn't there a mathematical formula that will tell me, like an algorithm . . . fuck that . . . isn't there a whole bibliography in my own research about this sort of thing—and worse—happening to women in the online sphere? So, now it came for me full steam. And why should I be spared when girls were paraded naked in the streets by my ancestors?

And then I feel tears welling up in my eyes and now they're streaming down my cheeks. But what is this thing I am feeling that is not clocking as sadness? I am not recoiling with shame.

I am just so floatingly relieved to be in these circumstances in my life where shame of the kind imposed from the outside just does not ... stick? It is no longer the silence that surrounded me for days when I told an assembly of relatives that the old patriarch of the clan had tried to undress me, a nine-year-old, in the bathroom. Shame is no longer a riptide that pitched fifteen-year-old me out of the Mumbai BEST bus four stops ahead of my home because I couldn't bear the stares of the passengers after my breasts had been groped by two laughing men. Shame is no longer the cinderblock weighing down my legs when I wanted to run from a party at Karan's friend's parents' mansion, where the host cornered me in the bedroom when I went to fetch my coat and forced a kiss, and his wife walked in and icily asked me to keep my hands off her husband and this is what single moms do and she thought I was different.

No, shame is now water off a swan's back. And my tears are out of sheer, staggering gratitude for every single thing I did and undid that brought me to this point.

Yes, I want to bedeck myself. I remember I had promised Vee that she and her crew could come along to shoot footage of the search for the bridal dress. I call her and ask if she can be there this afternoon.

The pop-up is set on Capitol Hill, opposite Elliott Bay Book Company. The company's name—Madhuban—is spelled out in the window in champagne-colored sequins and pink rose petals. My heart skips a beat. When I push the door open and hold it open for Vee and her wheelchair, the lightest waft of rose incense settles on me. Muted flute plays on the sound system. Gossamer ensembles in pinks, oranges, yellows, reds, creams hang from freestanding racks. Georgette and chiffons, silks and brocades everywhere. Not too many. These are exclusive pieces. I am a little girl now, grinning from ear to ear.

"Do you have an appointment?" a young white woman in a white silk kaftan asks us, breezing over in our direction.

I say, I'm sorry, I didn't know we needed...

"We're doing appointments only. We'd be happy to set one up for you for our next event."

"Event?"

"Pop-up event," she says. "We have another one coming up in six weeks," she says, eyeing Vee and her crew, her arms wide open, not to offer a hug, but to sort of contain us in an invisible bubble to be rolled back out to burst on the street. The bubble couldn't burst in these lovely interiors.

"I don't need any help. I'll just look around..."

"We don't work like that. The bride and/or bridesmaids are to come here with an appointment. Your daughter... or... sorry... daughter or niece etcetera can make an..."

"It's not for a daughter or niece," I laugh. "It's not for an etcetera. It's for me. I'm the bride-to-be." I laugh again. Apologetically. Feigned.

If nothing else had done it so far, this look on her face makes me want to call the whole damn swayamvar thing off. It's as if it isn't just my age that she finds objectionable. It's my jeans, my makeupless face, my ambling in here as if I were an aunty who had rushed out to buy garam masala mid-cooking. If I were an old bride, where was the meticulous planning, the sense of humili...

"I'll take this one," says someone walking up behind her. "Hi, bride-to-be. I'm Maddie. Short for Madhavi."

Maddie is wearing a Maharashtrian-style nose ring that rests on her thick mustache. She is dressed in an ivory silk shirt knotted high on her waist. Three inches of midriff later, she is rocking the flounciest lehenga I have ever seen in a pistachio green with pink flamingos embroidered on it.

We do introductions and she leads us to the interior of the store, where we are ushered into a private space decked out like a princess's chambers. Fresh marigold flowers everywhere. Ivory-toned brocade curtains. Ivory-toned brocade loveseat. Someone brings in rose milk in copper tumblers. The camera crew falls upon all these things. Vee and I look at each other and I know we both are too stirred to sip anything.

Maddie is asking me questions to which I don't have responses. Did I want to pick something off the shelves, or would my bridal piece be custom ordered? Did I know which of the designers featured today I was interested in? Surely, I would be returning for a fitting? Or was this a rush job? Would I have bridesmaids? And a sangeet ceremony? Was I planning a whole trousseau?

I explain the whole thing about the swayamvar.

It's a pop-up wedding, I say.

Maddie sits down on the loveseat. She sighs. She puts her hand to her heart. She rubs her hands. Glee.

"We are honored you chose us," she says. "Let's do this."

I say I don't want her to get in trouble for breaking the company rules ... should I just look for something online?

"Sweetie, I *am* the company rules. I'm the proprietor of Madhuban. Let's go right for the red Banarasi silks, shall we?"

Maddie brings flower upon flower of bridalwear to me as if from an enchanted forest. She asks me questions about colors and textures.

It is delightful to work with a bride who has dressed herself for long enough that she knows her colors and drapes, Maddie says.

INTEMPERANCE

I dare to tell Maddie I don't want to wear a sari, that I have never been comfortable in one, that I feel too diminutive ... no ... diminished in one, somehow.

Maddie brings me a red lehenga made from Banarasi silk. Golden gota motifs. Sheer chiffon dupatta.

She is torn between Kheer white and Sindoor red for me, she says. "What did you wear at your previous weddings? Anything you want to repeat? Or would you like to do it all differently? Also, we do have a donation program if you want to pass your wedding dress on later to a bride with fewer means."

I say yes to that instantly.

Her questions ebb and flow with everything she learns from me in a few minutes. She takes notes as I scrunch up my nose at thick brocades and splashy florals, ghoonghat veils and virgin whites, anything that speaks to a lifetime of dressing and undressing as a negotiation between me and the patriarchy. I'd worn a rich turmeric-yellow sari for my first wedding, per my Maithil Brahmin family tradition. I'd worn a lacy eggshell-white wedding gown for the wedding with Paul.

"Let's make this one all about you. Smell the silk. Feel the chiffon on your neck. Does it feel like something you will take out of your closet and drape on yourself from time to time? Stand before the mirror to look at yourself through its transparency?"

A woman's face suddenly flashes to mind, a mirror and a face and a mirror and a face. I grab the arm of the silk loveseat to be steady again.

"Does the fabric feel like it's the best version of your own skin?" Maddie is saying. "Something you'd like to touch on a night when you are by yourself and want to ... you know?"

I get the sense Maddie isn't just saying all this for the camera.

She had indeed felt these weaves in the silks, embraced them perhaps more than those of us who were given them in gluts in our girlhoods and womanhood without permission or guilt or punishment. I ask Maddie if she dreams of her own wedding day.

She does and she doesn't, Maddie says, smiling at me through her squinting eyes. Early in childhood in Houston, it was her older sister who was being sold dreams of a wedding. Her immigrant parents came from Ahmedabad in Gujarat, and her sister was told they would have a grand wedding for her someday back in their hometown, with five gold necklaces stacked on her chest, sixteen different types of sweets for the guests, and miles of dancing.

Maddie was called by a different name then, and when she asked her parents about her own wedding day, she was told that boys didn't dream of such things. Boys in their family of jewelers focused on taking over their fathers' business and getting rich so they would have their pick of pretty girls whose families would line them up. Maddie spent her childhood watching her sister get dressed up for Navratri, in ghagra after ghagra sent from Gujarat. Swirling skirts of peach and pinks and yellows. Maddie would help her sister pick out the bangles to match with her outfits.

In their teens, her sister would let Maddie try on some of the ensembles and would giggle when Maddie tried on the choli, where the fabric that was stitched to cup young breasts would lie floppy at Maddie's chest. When Maddie burst into tears one day about this, her sister hugged her and promised never to laugh again. She helped Maddie stuff socks into the choli, turned on Dholi Taro on the speaker, and danced madly around the bedroom with her.

"It was the best day of my life," Maddie says, trying a fuchsia dupatta against my skin and meeting my eyes in the mirror to see if her satisfaction at this mix and match was mirrored by my own aesthetic fancy. I nod with glee. We smile together in the mirror.

"It was also the worst day of my life," Maddie says. Her mother had walked in on the dancing sisters. Her mother was confused and angry. Her father was asked to come home at once. He was not confused, only angry. Maddie's sister was told to stay away from her brother. Maddie was sent to Ahmadabad for "treatment."

"I will spare you the details of that," Maddie says, no longer meeting my eyes in the mirror with her own. "Because things are so beautiful now," she says. "Look at all this," she says, sweeping her hands around the pop-up store.

Her father had paid for all this. But what he had really paid for was for Maddie to leave their lives. When Maddie had returned from Ahmedabad with their family's reputation torn to shreds and a suitcase filled with silks, organza, and tulle, she was dispatched from Houston to New York to live with an aunt who was similarly debauched, a lesbian who had been divorced by her husband (Maddie learned from the aunt that it was she who had divorced her husband, but that version just did not fit the comprehension of their clan).

When her sister got married and had her dream wedding, Maddie wasn't invited.

"Can you imagine, in this day and age, how much intention it would take to cut a daughter out so totally that no family news reaches her even on social media? Not even from her sister, who once doted on her?" Maddie says in a soft and steady voice.

I can, I say to Maddie.

Maddie and her aunt found out a month later from a visiting distant relative who had needed her aunt's place for an overnight stay in New York. The wedding was held in Ahmedabad with five gold necklaces stacked on her sister's chest, sixteen different types of sweets for the guests, and miles of dancing. Maddie knew exactly how her sister had probably been warned not to even write to her. Anything could be seen as an affront to the groom's family.

Maddie's father had thrown money at the Maddie problem. "When men have so much money, they lose sight of other ways to love," Maddie says. A rich man does not pause to ponder, Maddie had found. A man raised with money has not developed faculties other than finance.

"I don't blame just the money, of course," Maddie says. "It's money and culture. And most cultures already leave men poor in matters of tenderness, no? How could my father love me or see me? How could the women around him have any other currency with him than what had brought them to him or kept them with him in the first place? Wealth is a family system. Wealth is perhaps the most wretchedly unquestioning form of love. Not unconditional. Unquestioning."

Maddie had taken her father's money, nonetheless. "I guess it was my dowry," she giggles.

She went to fashion school at the Parsons School of Design, got an apprenticeship at a top design house in Mumbai (where she had fallen in love twice and had the most satisfying sexual experiences with "one mushtanda after another, thank you, Mumbai!") and here she now was, "finding the perfect maang tikka for you."

She lays a half-moon maang tikka on the parting of my hair. A jadau peacock and a swan in uncut diamonds with entwined necks rested on my forehead.

"So . . . I don't dream of a wedding for me," Maddie says. "I don't dream of marriage. I dream that more brides would just have party after party, like, where they just appropriate wedding rituals to serve their own fancy. Do what you want with the institution of marriage. Settle into it, stamp on it, swallow or spit it out. Just promise me you will look like a fucking apsara through it all."

When I emerge from the dressing room in a red Banarasi lehenga with a blouse that shows a roll of flesh at my midriff but also draws the eye upward to the cleavage in which I routinely love to trap an ice cube on summer days, Maddie, Vee, and her crewmen fall silent. I feel the camera zoom in on my face and then pan down. I sashay. I swirl. Maddie drapes the fuchsia dupatta around me in a way I tell her I could never replicate on the day of the swayamvar.

"Well . . . ," Maddie says, her eyes dancing. "May I attend your swayamvar and dress you for it?"

I gasp at this. Even Vee lets out a whoop. Of course, I say. It would be my honor.

Maddie turns up Pandit Ravi Shankar and Philip Glass on the sound system. Mixed in with Ustad Zakir Hussain. Flute, violin, cello, tabla. I stand there for a moment. Misty eyes, quivering skin, thundering body, racing heart.

Maddie asks more questions. Was I right now wearing the bra I would wear on my wedding day? How about the shoes?

My face must have fallen. The camera is still on me, or I would have burst into tears. All this has been so beautiful I had forgotten that no footwear I ever wore with an Indian ensemble carried me with the elegance I felt within.

I say this to Maddie, keeping my voice even.

"You know . . . ," Maddie says. "The trend these days is for brides to wear sneakers under their lehenga. Bridal sneakers. I'm thinking cream-silk body and gold-sequined shoelaces. What's your shoe size?"

ON THE WAY out, I bump into the dancer, whom I had forgotten to email with a thanks but no thanks three weeks ago, the day the din of the swayamvar began. Nevertheless, Shakti looks delighted to see me. "What a phenomenal thing you are doing, my sister," she says. "This swayamvar will heal so many of us. And I hope you have a blast."

I start to apologize for never having written to her. She waves away my apology, and then, with dancing eyes, she says: "You can make it up to me."

I want to kick myself, but I ask her what she means. I imagine she wants me to read a draft of a nephew's poor-little-rich-boy college essay.

"Please let me host a sangeet for you," she says.

"No way," I say. "I am doing this swayamvar as a tiny thing. It's not really a wedding or anything. I'm not some bride. A sangeet will feel like a mockery." I also feel a pinch of guilt for ignoring her many invitations to get-togethers over the years.

"What if I plan it as something that's not a mockery? We will do mehndi and dance? No spectacle or anything. Just pure joy to match your joy? Can you trust me?"

I think of what Demi had said to me about trusting. "It's so nice of you . . . but . . . can you promise me it won't draw all sorts of gossipy energy? I just don't have the stamina for that."

Shakti's face lights up. "Nothing but positive energy. It's my promise to you, my jaan. And give me your wedding planner's contact. Then you don't have to worry about any little detail. Just show up and sit back and be pampered."

"Oh, and can you . . . could you make sure that the woman I met last time . . . at the dance class . . . Janaki . . . could you make sure she doesn't attend? I had a weird encounter with her."

"Janaki? I don't know who that is. I thought she was someone who came with you. I had never seen her before."

I stand there gaping at her as she turns around to invite Vee and her crew to the sangeet event. She asks me if that is fine with me; she doesn't want to violate the offer she just made, of avoiding a spectacle. I look at Vee's face, mad with anticipation. I nod. I go home to submit myself to the other state of being, summoned in soot and camphor, that has begun to feel real as my own reality seems to turn liminal.

WHEN I SEE *her, my first instinct is to shut my eyes. She is naked. I should avert my gaze from her face and her shoulders, the top of her breasts, but I am trapped as a gazer. I sense nothing but the image in gaze itself. I can see nothing but her, looking right at me, into me. And yet it isn't me she sees.*

Sona is a woman in her twenties now. She is watching herself as she rocks back and forth, heaves up and down, round and round. Her face is flushed. Her hair sticks to the sweat on her neck and her breasts. She looks into me and watches her own ecstasy. I stop resisting her delight in her own view.

She sees herself unscarred. Strikingly beautiful. Her hair thick from her mother's tending with stolen oils. Her mouth playful in a new way. Open in a way fear does not allow. She is unafraid and in full claim of this moment. She does not look down at her lover. She is peering into me to see her love for no one but herself.

I thrash about with my view to see who is beneath her, try to catch a glimpse of a naked man, but I am contained in an oval maw, in the inches of a frame. I can't hear anything. Her scent must be everywhere, mingled with his, but I can't smell. I can only see so much as what is permitted from where I hang. Pieces of her skin are hidden from me, not because her skin is blemished. No, her skin is in its prime and is flush with the waters of youth and lust. Water has its way with us all, and mine have seeped out to tarnish my face, taunting my gaze where I stare out de-silvered.

    I try to rattle and crash to the floor so I can turn to shards and see at least some broken truth, see the man beneath her and the stories of the room, but I am affixed firmly to the wall. Sona smiles slowly. All this could be yours someday, she seems to say, taunting me for the rules that keep me bonded to my careful state.

The Vidaai

The phone is ringing. It's Cat.

"He's dead now," she says.

I had wondered for months what words she would choose to break the news to us of her husband's death. I'd imagined her saying—

He passed away last night.

He is no more.

He's breathed his last breath. No, she wouldn't say this.

He's no longer with us.

We have lost him.

Our beloved Paul has left us.

WHEN I FLY into New York for the memorial, Karan is at the airport to receive me. I'm not surprised Karan would want to be at the memorial. I am pleasantly surprised he offered to come pick me up.

"Trust Paul to make it convenient for me to be at his funeral," he says after we have hugged, and he has taken my carry-on bag from me. It has taken him no time at all to drive to New York

City from Saratoga Springs, where he has been doing his writing residency.

Karan has talked over the years about Paul's seemingly effortless manner of putting others first, and this comment now is wry, heartbreaking. He wants me to commiserate with him. My child wants us to mourn together the death of his former stepfather.

Cat's husband used to be my husband. Paul. Cat is the one who will be his widow. A sob rises in my chest at the thought of my best friend as a widow of the man she loved so dearly, a man I didn't quite love as much when I had my turn. Karan hears my sob, and he reaches out his right arm from the driving wheel to pat me on the head. It's tender despite the awkwardness of the reach in traffic.

I know some of the people assembled at Cat and Paul's home, and I don't know several others. I look through the crowd to find Cat sitting in Paul's favorite chair. Her face lights up when she sees us, as much as a grieving widow's face can light up. It's been more than six months since my last visit to their home. Cat looks strikingly older. Her red hair is graying, and she seems bigger than ever, barely fitting into the large sofa chair that Paul's medium frame occupied over the years in their tastefully furnished Brooklyn apartment.

Cat heaves herself out of her chair and stumbles toward me just a little differently from how I stumble toward her. When we embrace, I feel her body shaking. I feel its weight against me, and I pull it in deeper. This body of hers, large, ungainly, desiring, and yielding, had been such an indelible part of that terrible conversation we had had that night when our friendship shattered. When it left me bereft for more than two years.

You did not see me as a threat because I am fat. I was just your fat

INTEMPERANCE

friend who would never find a man. You never thought any man could ever love me, least of all your man.

All the shouts and shrieks of that rageful night the two us best friends fell apart now thud quietly against our chests as we press our grief against each other.

Paul's wives, someone whispers in the room, followed by an *oops* for being unwittingly loud.

Cat's body starts to quake against mine. She is laughing. I start to laugh with her.

"Paul's wives," we say together to the man, who looks mortified. Somewhere in that room, I catch Karan's eye. He smiles at me.

I release Cat so I can hug the daughters she had with Paul—Kira and Maeve, six and four. They run up to Karan, and he crouches down to receive their hugs. His eyes shut to savor the moment. His eyes are swollen, I notice now. He must have wept the last two nights since Paul's death and all morning today.

Cat had asked if I'd like to do a eulogy. I said I didn't think it would be appropriate. The truth is I am disoriented. I want to be in observance and in a state of observation. Solitary among people. Grieving on the fringes.

I already knew Karan would want to do one. Paul and Cat had asked my permission to ask Karan months ago. I wasn't surprised. I knew Karan and Paul had stayed close over the years. I had encouraged it. In all the comings and goings of husbands and fathers and outer family, I had wanted Karan to maintain ties that I didn't tend to for myself. I wanted that Karan be held in all the love that could come his way. All the love that was his to give and receive, beyond my own despairs and destructions.

Karan and Paul spoke on the phone more often than my son and I did. This man had taught my boy to fish and hike. Karan confided in him about his crushes and dates. Before Paul's diagnosis, they traveled together to Egypt and were hosted by Paul's friend Khaled's family. At Karan's college graduation, Paul and Cat sat two rows ahead of me, cheering and dabbing at tears while Siddhartha (who flew in from Mumbai) and I sat together in silence, making videos. Paul bought his former stepson a pair of expensive Italian leather shoes when he got his first job, no matter that it was as an administrative assistant in a publishing office.

THE MEMORIAL IS planned at an Italian restaurant Paul loved in midtown Manhattan. I had been to this restaurant with him and Cat and the girls every time I visited them in New York or traveled here for a conference. Paul always ordered the same thing, and that's what's being served to the guests at the memorial tonight—French onion soup, roasted cauliflower, lobster risotto, and for dessert, affogato. The wine is flowing freely among the fifty or so invitees. Cat has planned this well. Paul had had the time to give her instructions. What might it have been like for Paul, picking out wines for your friends and a former wife and stepson to drink while you are home alone, turned to ash in an urn on your widow's nightstand?

I watch Cat's face in the glow of candlelight at the table. She is not in black as I'd expected. I didn't know that a memorial service that was more a celebration of life didn't require me to be dressed in black, and I had missed Cat's text that told me of the dress code. As a result, I am self-conscious that I look more like the widow in my black dress with lace at all edges. I look like a mafia widow. Cat is radiant in Paul's favorite color on her, an emerald green.

I am startled at this thought, this self-involved moment in the midst of so much sorrow. I reach out to squeeze Karan's hand.

INTEMPERANCE

He links his warm fingers with my cold ones. He did this as a child and hasn't done it in years. The last hints of the distance and disapproval he has shown me these past few weeks melt as our fingers find a mutual temperature.

He and Cat and everyone else are listening to a eulogy being given by Paul's best friend, Khaled Masoud, an Egyptian American professor of history at our university back in Seattle. Khaled and his wife had been close friends of ours, but we had grown apart in the years since I divorced Paul. Other friendships had gone the same way, and in the early years, I wondered if they all resented me for driving Paul out of the city. A part of me was still bothered that they would not feel sorry for the woman who was cheated on, for that was the only part of the story they knew. Why had that not been enough for them to come around to my side?

Paul and Cat moved from Seattle to New York a year after I divorced him. I heard about their move in an email sent by the dean to all faculty, wishing Paul well in his new position as a professor of Philosophy at CUNY. I knew our colleagues were relieved that at least one of us was moving. I imagined they'd have preferred that *I* be the one to move. Everyone loved Paul. I would have liked to think that it was a race thing, that of course the white male faculty member, the nice guy who was a good fit, the professorial twinkle-eyed affable academic who was trailed by students as he walked between classes, was the one they'd prefer to keep in their community. Or maybe it was misogyny—blame the woman for her husband's cheating. But I couldn't hold these convenient ideas with any genuine heat in my chest because I knew he truly loved this institution and showed it in the way he spoke to every student as if they would be the next great philosopher, the way he could be forgotten but never feel ignored or passed over for a chairship.

Some may have described him as mediocre yet lovable, but he wore his mediocrity with that rare quality of humility.

Which is probably why I never came to love him. Among the many idioms my father dropped as wisdoms in my growing years was this one—bin bhay hovay na preet—there is no love without awe. A worrying idiom from a violent man, but shaken off from his twisted use, it stayed with me for its original prudence. Paul did not fill me with awe. He did not fill me with love.

We had been married for six years. It was his first marriage and my second. He brought love to the marriage, and I brought a desire for stability that muddled what was in reality a yearning for solitude.

The day I came upon Paul and Cat folded into each other had stunned me more than anything else in my life. I revisit that moment often, not to revive the pain in times when I am seeking gratuitous self-affirmation but with a sense of curiosity. I have never quite put my finger on what I felt in that moment. What I know is that I had never suspected that they were cheating on me. I say "they," because it was both of them, my husband and my best friend, who had cheated on my trust.

In hindsight, I probably serve as some sort of record in the "the wife is always the last to know" cliché. There had been slips and hints for months. Paul offering to drop off the extra serving of dinner we'd often make for Cat and bring back the cupcakes she'd bake for us. Cat sleeping over at our place when I was at a conference (I had actually felt grateful that she'd keep Paul company, especially since he'd been so lonely and had suffered more as an empty nester after Karan left for college). Paul and Cat going for morning walks together while I lazed in bed, grateful to not have to walk the puppy, silent about how it was getting a little difficult

INTEMPERANCE

to recover from the ache in my legs at the end of each long day. Books Paul was reading found lying around at Cat's home—on her sofa, in her bathroom, on her nightstand. No, none of these had raised any suspicions for me at all.

When I say they were folded into each other, I do not mean they were in bed. They were dancing. Paul had taken Cat's serving of dinner over to her place. I had felt guilty for making him do it over and over. I had decided to go over to surprise them and laugh about how I, too, was quite willing to walk in the Seattle rain the way they loved to do. I was being spontaneous and was going to drag us all out to go get ice cream.

I found parking a block away from Cat's craftsman home. As I walked over, I saw them aglow in the light of Cat's living room. I still wonder why my first response had been to smile. Perhaps because I came upon two people I loved, these two people who were my chosen family in this nation that was in the grip of an epidemic of loneliness, these two white people I called Home.

I halted. I stood there, sure that they would look up and see me in the window. I saw their faces and knew then that they did not sense the passing of time the way I ceaselessly did. Time was passing far more slowly for them than it was for me. Even though I was familiar with every expression on these two faces I had watched closely for years, I had never before seen what they wore together in that moment. The tenderness took my breath away.

THESE TWO BELOVED faces wore a love that was theirs alone. Paul was stroking Cat's face as they moved. His other hand was wrapped firmly around her large form. She was in her ratty pajamas and her fleece nightgown, the one we both had laughed over for years because it barely came around to the outer edges of her chest, but she still loved it. Paul was barefoot. Cat's eyes were shut. I imagined her eyelashes were fluttering. They danced like that for a while as I stood there turning to mist. They shuffled from side to side, and then Paul stepped away and twirled Cat.

She twirled. Light on her feet, sweet as a ballerina, my friend twirled.

I knocked on the door. I heard shuffling inside. I didn't answer when they asked, in turn, who was there.

When Cat opened the door, Paul was seated on the sofa. He stood up. They both knew I knew because my face was already bathed in tears. They knew every expression on my face, and the one they saw in that moment was relief.

OH, OF COURSE I had been self-righteous. I had summoned up anger. I wanted to be convinced I was in rage, wanted to play the part of the wife whose husband had cheated on her with her best friend. I had thrown some of Cat's dishes to the floor. Cat did not protest or try to stop me. Not all the ones I threw were shattered, because there was not enough force in my arms. I had spat in Paul's face.

The two of them had wept too. They looked afraid and sad and small. They apologized, over and over. They did not look at me or touch one another once. They didn't deny anything.

I moved into a room at Hotel Sorrento for a week, and Paul insisted on paying for it. I let him. I asked to be left alone. I canceled my classes.

Paul moved into Cat's home. Karan asked if he should come home from college to be with me, but I said absolutely not; he was to focus on his studies. But something in his voice told me that he was the one who needed me then, to tend his broken heart at the loss of his stepfather. I'd flown him home and hugged him and cooked his favorite, jambalaya. When he asked if he could visit Paul and Cat, I had felt a pinch, but I'd let him go. I'd waited by the window for his return. When he returned, I watched him walk up to the door and turn his blissfully happy expression to one that he imagined would be more acceptable to me, something neutral and accommodating. I contemplated slapping his face with all the bitterness that I was entitled to have, but I instead drew him into a hug at the door and told him that I wanted him to always reach for all the love he could have, that I was still learning to love, but he could enjoy his head start because, unlike me, he didn't need to unlearn something first.

I didn't go to the farewell reception the university held for Paul. It was still all too fresh, the divorce with him and the estrangement with my closest friend. Cat had reached out many times, with texts and calls and even once a knock on my door that I didn't answer. Even today, I know it was for the best that I didn't muddy my reckoning with words of apology or atonement from these two people I loved. In the two years that followed the betrayal, my solitude had emerged as a palliative. In the clarity it offered, I had flashes of such pain and beauty, I fell in love with me and them and the whole damn world.

I saw how much Paul had ached for me. I saw how much Cat had loved me and wanted to be loved by me. I had given neither of them what they sought from me. Paul was a distraction from my deepening intellectual life. Cat was the fat friend who bore witness to my growth, while I saw her desires as unattainable and thus never to be discussed with any sense of thrill. In my solitary months and years, I moved from considering the whole episode as the treachery of white people on a virtuous brown woman to realizing that I was the one that held power over them. These Americans whom I loved in my own way had been afflicted by an intergenerational loneliness that they didn't talk about. I, in turn, even as I made myself solitary and chose isolation, imagined better and better worlds for myself. They had watched as I outgrew them, and they had turned to each other for a comfort that included in it a mutual love for me.

When I heard Cat was pregnant, something she'd desired for decades, I had flown to their home in New York, knocked on their door, and told them I loved them and wanted them to marry. I knew they hadn't done it yet for fear of hurting me somehow. I couldn't bring myself to attend their wedding, but I sent a happy Karan.

IN HIS EULOGY now, Karan speaks of the first time he'd met Paul. "Just another professor from my mother's university getting drunk among a clutch of academics in our living room," he says. People chuckle.

Clutch. His new book must be coming along well. I release a long breath. Karan is speaking about the time he was nine years old and watching his mother fall in love with this white man. He says he was confused and afraid, but Paul had a way of talking to him like he mattered more than anyone else in the world. Paul would ask him what he was reading and why he had picked that book. Paul would bring him books to read—manga comics, Harry Potter, Wittgenstein—and would read them alongside Karan. The two of them had their very own book club. Paul taught him how to tie his shoelaces. He taught him how to swim. He took him camping even though Paul himself hated camping. Paul asked him if it was okay for Paul to love Karan's mother and ask her to

INTEMPERANCE

marry him. When Karan said he wasn't sure and asked Paul to wait, Paul waited two years before asking again. By then, Karan had forgotten that Paul and his mother weren't yet married. He hadn't noticed that there hadn't been a wedding.

"Because we were already family," Karan says. The room sighs.

"Paul was already my father. He never stopped being my father. He told me once that he felt like the best version of a man when he was being my father."

Karan's voice breaks on those last two words. When he returns to his seat next to me, I lean over and kiss him on his temple. I inhale at this spot of his thinking mind. I place a sigh against the wind still held in his windswept hair. I push a soundless wish at his temporal vein, for peace and love and mad happiness to heal any wounds of my time that impeded on his.

Back at their home, when the last of the guests have left and her parents are resting in their guest room, Cat hands me a letter. From Paul.

I ask her if she's read it.

No. He asked me not to, she says.

Dearest one,

I'm gone. You're still there. You will have years and years, won't you? We always said you were built like an ox. Hearty, despite all the ebb you have come to feel in your body now. Yes, Cat tells me everything. But you already knew that.

I blink.

You have waved away my apologies for years, but this one comes to you from a dead man. Even you, heartless as you are (can you be hearty and heartless at once?), will not rip up a dead man's letter nor spurn his apology. I may not have hurt you, given that I did not reach that deep into your love, but I disappointed you. Maybe all I did was inconvenience you. Whatever it was I did to you, I did worse to Karan by shattering what the three of us had, and these terrible regrets I take to my grave (or, well, to the incinerator).

Cat has told me of your plans for a swayamvar. I tried really hard to stay alive long enough to come watch that beautiful spectacle. Cat and I even booked plane tickets. She and the girls will be there, and I expect to hear all about it. If I weren't married or dead already, I would line up and lift all swords from stones, shoot the eyes of fish on a wheel, duel each suitor to have another chance to be with you. By the way, I read this line out to Cat (I will not cheat on someone again, even emotionally, even in epistolary form, even in my ashen state).

I know you sense that many men will arrive at the swayamvar, or you wouldn't have announced one. I am told you are uncertain of the feat you will set for them in order that you make the right choice. I have spent these past few days musing over this. Among some other things I had to wrap up before my departure, this one offered a pleasant preoccupation. I have this to offer, unsolicited and mansplainy as it may be—in all my years as a boy and man, the thing I have found most difficult to do is render a heartfelt, unconditional apology. I have noticed such a lack in all the men I have known. It is as if all societies, all cultures, all religions agreed upon one thing and one thing alone—men were never to feel the crushing, soul-stirring remorse that could flatten empires or egos.

If I may summon up the nerve to offer some advice to you,

INTEMPERANCE

from this safe distance, I will ask that should you find a man by whatever feat you design, you turn upon him the same luscious love you turn upon yourself. Such love is formidable. Few of us come to regard ourselves with such beauty in our lifetime. It is beyond my imagination what such a love would do if also turned upon a partner. What would the world then look like? I hope you find out.

Yours,
Paul

The Bridal Shower

Karan has offered to drive me to the airport even at this unearthly hour of 5 a.m. He is a late riser and plans to spend an extra day with Cat and the girls, so I am especially touched by his gesture. In a hug that feels like it should never end, I tell Cat how much I love her and how I really don't want to return to Seattle and definitely not to run around doing a swayamvar. She tells me what she has told me many times in the last few months—that she has grieved Paul's death in the past year of his diagnosis of interminable and swift pancreatic cancer. She is ready for whatever new pathways the grief takes her on, but she would not miss my swayamvar for the world.

"Paul also insisted I be there," she says. "So, that is that. Got it?"

"It's four days away," I remind her. "I don't expect a seven-day-old . . ."

My voice trails off. Cat smiles.

"Widow. You can say it," she says.

When I don't say anything and just hold her closer, she strokes my hair and says, "We'll be family forever. You, me, Karan, the girls. They will bring new people into the fold. We will be family greater still. That's a phrase our eloquent Paul liked to use for all of us. Now, go find us a new man to enjoy!"

Her laughter mixes in with my own to make one of our favorite sounds. Then, clutching me even closer, she says, "I promise I won't steal this one from you."

A bleary-eyed Karan comes downstairs with his car keys to find his two mother figures doubled over, covering their mouths with their hands to muffle their screaming laughter so they wouldn't wake the girls. One of them is clutching her crotch so she doesn't pee.

Karan and I ride in an easy silence for a while. When I see the sun rise over the Brooklyn Bridge, I burst into tears. Karan asks if he should pull over, but I say I don't want to be late for my flight.

"You have a right to feel it, too, you know," Karan says, squeezing my hand.

"Feel what?"

"Grief. He was your husband too."

A gasp catches in my throat. I look at the gold of a clueless sunrise falling on Karan's puffy face. My beautiful child. This kind man.

"I can't imagine you ever had true closure," he says. "I know you forgave them, and you all moved on, but ... correct me if I don't know these things yet, but it seems to me that you never really got the chance to truly detach. I always wondered about how you could forgive them. But ..."

"Yes? But?" I say, bereft for my child but also somewhat lost for myself.

"But I was grateful you did. And I realized only recently that maybe you did it in huge part for my sake. I mean, I know you loved them both, too, and they loved you so much, but you might have called it good and decided to detach to heal, except you knew how much I loved Paul and he loved me. And how I didn't want to let go of Aunty Cat. You kept them whole for me. You kept them uncompromised for me. That . . ." His voice chokes.

"That is a woman who knows love, Mama," he says.

He lets me cry in breathless sobs for the rest of the ride, like a child without a mother to run to but a son for witness.

When we arrive at the airport, he gets out of the car and helps with my bags and then, smiling, says he has some news. He's in love, he says.

She's a writer too. They met at the residency. That's why he hadn't called or written for a while. He's sorry.

I reach out and tuck a lock of his hair behind his ear. For years, he has drawn his head back out of my reach at this gesture, but he allows me to do this now. One hue of love softens you to another hue of love.

I tell him I'd like to miss my flight and take the next one. He shakes his head and says there's a thing called a telephone, and he will call me from the car on the way back, after I've gone through security.

So, I can't see his face when he talks about Femi. And I feel the loss of that lay itself atop the many losses our modern lives assemble because we let time and efficiency override our human impulses. I don't see the way he would have shyly averted his eyes from me when he said he's never felt so breathless and silly around anyone before. I can't squeeze his cheeks when he tells me she is a way better writer than him. "Like, *way* better. But I will enjoy trying to catch up," he says.

"Or you could just make peace with her being better." I smile into the phone.

I don't see him shake his head at his mother as he laughs at that.

INTEMPERANCE

"Mama?" he says.

"I know. I'm sorry I keep pushing it..."

"No, that's not what I was going to say. I want to say I hope you find that right man. Make them work for your affections. Find the most outlandish feat. I know there's someone out there who will leap as high as you want. Make him leap."

WHEN I CALL the dancer to cancel plans for the sangeet, she tells me she had heard last night from a woman named Cat, who said I might try to cancel, and she has been instructed to override my protests. Cat has already paid for a henna artist, Shakti tells me. "Cat said to tell you it was a gift from Paul."

Damn you, Paul.

SHAKTI HAD PROMISED me it would be a small ceremony, but when I arrive at her mansion in the chauffeured car she sends for me, her block and two blocks around it are littered with guests' cars. I am seized with panic, but the chauffeur is already backing away from me as I stand, solitary and wracked with dread, in the driveway. Shakti rushes out of her door to me. She is with a few other women I know, past friends who fell away, and present acquaintanceships navigated every now and then at this desi event or that. These are doctors, homemakers, vice presidents, philanthropists, professors, painters, software engineers, interior decorators, singers, and an author of a book on how to raise children who thrive. So much past and present toil assembled in this house, very few failures ever spoken of. They're chanting something and have rose petals to throw at me and little jasmine garlands to tie around my wrists before I enter.

I am egregiously underdressed for my own celebration. When I mutter this to Shakti, she says it would be egregious if I had dressed any better than the plain white kurta and jeans I'm wearing. It's your mehndi, she says. And haldi, she says, ushering me into her garden, where she seats me on three giant pink cushions piled high under a canopy of flowers. The flowers are delicate orchids. "The bride needs to be dressed as plain as possible, in clothes she can throw away after the turmeric stains them," Shakti says.

I'm not throwing away these favorite jeans, but she doesn't need to hear that.

A woman I used to meet up with sometimes for an occasional cup of chai and truly mind-numbing conversation about whose kids have made it to which college, says, "But you don't have to tell this bride that! Doesn't she remember it? She should know it better than all of us! Third time round, no? I mean, hats off...."

Ah. This is why I no longer meet up with her.

The woman goes on. "Maybe I should just give her my husband. He can be so annoying sometimes."

A few titters.

Shakti says, "Well, your husband would have to compete for her hand. Can he perform any feats at all? Or will he fail the round that rules out annoying men and go back home to you?"

I have never heard her sound this icy. She is holding the woman's hands now, as if she has just said the most loving thing to her. And then Shakti smiles, and says, "Come, come. Enjoy this lovely event. We are fortunate to join our friend in all this, no? But I totally understand if you want to leave?"

If the woman had wanted to leave, for some reason she is unable to say it, and I wonder if her family or her husband are beholden to Shakti's family or husband in some way. Dear God, these terrible alliances.

The unfunny woman looks like she is holding on to a cliff. No, the cliff is holding on to her. For funsies.

I watch the other women's faces. There's a hush over the garden that was only seconds ago filled with shrieks of greetings and dialed-up delight. They all look like they're deleting the comments they had prepared for any "roasting" they had planned for me. I have been to a few of these women's events, mostly birthdays in recent years. The roasts are brutal. Occasionally funny, but mostly nakedly brutal.

Shakti smiles sweetly at everyone as if she had just asked the woman if she'd like to choose between mango lassi or Rooh Afza. She lets go of the woman's hands and ushers them all to sit around and make themselves comfortable. Food will be served to them, she says. We will sing soon, she sings.

I hadn't actually felt so stung by the unfunny woman's comments. I'd just wondered why she felt compelled to make them. I had witnessed her do such things before to other women, and perhaps I recalled her making similarly clueless, fumbling comments when I was a single mother bringing little Karan to a Diwali party here, a Holi celebration there. Something said loud enough for husbands and kids present to hear—about how I managed a sex life while having the full-time responsibility of a son?

What is this woman's role in this clutch of community? The town gossip? The instigator of roasts? The clown, the unfunny clown? The aunty-est of aunties? The keeper of traditional values? Has she assumed this role on her own, or has she been appointed? Where does she feel free?

I don't have another minute to dwell on the woman because

a henna artist is holding my hands now and asking me to point to the pattern I'd like. I make a quick but pleasant choice of a pattern with birds and flowers. I ask the young woman her name, but she doesn't seem to hear me, probably from the din around her or the focus on her work.

The cool touch of mehndi fills me with an emotion I mistake to be longing at first, but then recognize as dread. I've been here before. Once and twice. The woman's comment wasn't funny, but she also wasn't wrong. All this pageantry, all these symbols of certainty laid into my palms ("If the color on your palms sets in really dark, it means your husband will love you forever!"), the forgotten and remembered scents of herbs that promised a life of passion and unbroken promises.... I could let them move me to tears or I could lighten up. Lighten the fuck up until I am nothing but air and dread.

The next thing in this garden takes my breath away. Dancers, kathak dancers, dressed in plain red cotton churidar-kurta-dupatta ensembles run up to a clearing before us in the garden and, for the next fifteen minutes, perform the most jaw-dropping choreographed dances representing the meeting of Radha and Krishna.

My eye is drawn to the ghungroo on a dancer's ankle. A single bell catches the rays of the setting sun and glints into my eye. It bobs a bit more than the other bells on the red velvet because it has loosened, almost about to fall and roll away altogether. Then the dance has ended and the bell and the dancers walk around, stepping heel to toe, heel to toe, both hands locked on one sit of their waists, readying for their next dance. Oh, I am definitely coming back for more dance lessons.

I feel so overwhelmed with this gift of art that stirs every good thing in my soul I don't notice right then that the henna artist is

INTEMPERANCE

facing me, not the dancers, and that she not once turns around to look, to have her soul stirred, lest her focus be nudged, and a single curve of a bird's beak be out of place on my palms.

After the dance, the guests—almost fifty of them now—are served chaat and mithai in dainty little plates. Waitstaff circulate in a tidy rhythm, offering this or that, even though most of the guests refuse hearty portions or seconds. Shakti sits by me and feeds me spoonfuls. When I protest, she insists and says this is how brides are fed when their hands are filled with herbal paste. I want to say yes, I know, I have eaten like this twice before, this is my third time around, but I decide against the callback.

Shakti is called away for some hostess-related issue. I look around me, and all the women are chatting with someone or other. So much chatter. Some of them are taking selfies with each other and occasionally come by and take one with me. I want to recede, go cry somewhere like a grieving widow. The whiplash of circumstances, from losing a former husband yet being no one's widow, to readying to be a bride yet having no groom . . . What. A. Circus.

I ask the henna artist if she'd like a plate of food. She could take a break, perhaps. She shakes her head without looking up from my palms. She pulls my right hand closer to her face. I say I'd like to go to the restroom, so she could take a break anyway. She says she is the one who would accompany me to the restroom, to help me with my underwear, so I don't mess up the mehndi on my hands.

"Unless you'd prefer someone else," she says, still not making eye contact.

"I have no one close to me here," I say. "No family member.

These women are all acquaintances. This is my third time, and it's a swayamvar, so I don't even know if there's even a groom or a wedding at all."

That works. She looks up at me.

"Why no family members?" she asks.

"All estranged," I say. "At least, my blood relations."

"Do you want to go to the restroom?" she asks.

IN THE RESTROOM, she is businesslike as she holds both my arms and raises them high up, away from any business that's going to go down. "Palms facing the sky," she says. "You won't believe how many brides ruin their mehndi on a trip to the restroom." Then she pulls down my jeans and underwear, her eyes averted. She steps outside the door as I pee. She's relieved when I say I can manage for now without toilet paper. I couldn't possibly ask her to double up as a sort of nurse.

"May I ask you a question?" she says in a low voice as she zips up my jeans.

I nod.

"How have you managed without . . . with being estranged from your family?"

"It's really hard at first and then gets easier. If the family has been abusive, you still miss them, but you heal and heal and heal, and the healing makes you love them in deeper ways, real ways, not the ways in which they taught you to love them. Then you miss them some more, but you've also met yourself as a healed, whole person and you love her and never let go of her hand."

I catch a glimpse of myself in the bathroom mirror, my arms raised up, my palms to the sky, as I say all this in a rush. I look like a cartoonish pop messiah or a desperate TikTok self-help influencer.

She is staring at me, unblinking.

"Are you all right? Are you safe?" I ask her.

She nods. Her real name is Salma, she tells me abruptly. Not Ambika.

Had she told me her name before? Maybe I just didn't hear her response when I'd asked.

She gets more work in some places as a henna artist with a Hindu name, she says. "Even though henna is originally a Muslim custom," she smirks. I get the sense she isn't trying to explain, just trying to fill me in and give context for something she's about to tell me next.

Salma asks if I can step outside and duck into the back of the house for a few minutes so she can smoke a cigarette. As she takes a long drag, this young woman probably no more than twenty-five, she tells me she plans to run away from her home tomorrow. She plans to elope with her boyfriend of six years. He's Black, she says, and her family and community are not having it.

"My family is not even that conservative Muslim," she says. "And Jamal is also Muslim. But it's just a racist thing in our South Asian communities, isn't it?"

I nod. I'm alarmed for her, and I want to make a whole lot of solicitous inquiries, but I stop myself. She doesn't need an aunty. She's chosen me as a sounding board, chosen this strange aunty bride who is being gossiped about at her own mehndi ceremony.

Salma tells me she was studying architecture but was more interested in doodling pretty designs. She decided to quit her studies to start her henna business. "Like Mark Zuckerberg," she grins. "But my parents didn't see it that way." She says she has done mehndi for the daughters of many of the women at this event. Sometimes, the celebrations are just brimming with joy, she says, and Salma feels very much part of it all. Other times, she is treated like servants are treated in India, like her work is lowly. She is invisible. Some families try to haggle with her when it comes time to pay. Some brides arrive up to six hours late and everyone expects Salma to just wait, because "it's a special occasion." One bride hated the design she'd picked and dramatically slapped her hands together to ruin the hours of work Salma put in, then refused to pay. Salma has started drawing up contracts.

I ask her if our host, Shakti, is paying her adequately, if Paul and Cat had been quoted an adequate amount. If not, I am happy to pay, and pay extra for this ridiculous service she's just now had to provide, aiding me in the bathroom. Salma shakes her head vigorously. Shakti is paying her double of her usual charge, she tells me.

"Why double?"

"I should probably not be telling you this, but she paid me so I would take extra care of your feet and make the henna extra beautiful over your scar-tissue. She told me you were beautiful, and that the community has benefited from the risks you have taken in your life. She said her daughters and her friends' daughters will not have to think too much before making certain life decisions because women like you have already done those things that are considered taboo. You have already absorbed so much of the gossip that it won't feel like a novelty when her daughters break the rules or break some cycles. I was excited to meet you. But I didn't want to talk too much right away. I hope it's okay that I have shared all this...."

INTEMPERANCE

My eyes have welled up and I raise a hand instinctively to wipe away a tear.

"Uh-uh!" Salma says, stopping my forearms in midair with the reflexes of Jason Bourne. She wipes my tears with her hands. She's accustomed to dealing with all sorts of fluids in this business of adorning brides-to-be.

"She's powerful," Salma says, continuing to talk about Shakti. "I love how she shut that catty woman down. No one messes with her. Shakti is badass."

"Pure love and pure rage," I say. Pure Shakti.

Sometimes, her heart breaks at these events, Salma says as we walk slowly back through the gorgeous living room with its spectacular split-level views of the water. "Many times, the mothers, even the educated, professional, modern ones, push the daughters to go over the top, put the henna designs all the way to the elbows and knees, even though the brides don't want it. Brides start to cry. Brides turn meek and obedient," Salma says. "They're always hungry. They want to fit into their dress. They want to fit into some role. They've signed up for some sort of contract of their own, it seems. And their hands sometimes feel so cold, and I feel a current running up my hand. Not exaggerating."

These rituals are so meaningful, she says as we arrive back at the garden. "The solah shringar and all," she says. "The sixteen adornments of the bride. Henna is just one of them." Salma had always wanted a simple wedding for herself. Even so, she had always wanted a mehndi and sangeet. She's been holding brides' hands year after year, wedding season after wedding season. She'd love to let her own hands sit idle for hours, give them over to another woman's attention, let her mind wander as tiny darting fish appear on her palms. She'd love for her mother to feed her as her henna dries.

"But tomorrow I will have to rush from my place straight to the marriage court. My parents keep track of me, like, there's literally a tracker on my phone," she shrugs. "They aren't abusive, but, well, define abuse, right? So, yeah, my suitcase is packed and hidden in a friend's car, and I leave tomorrow to marry Jamal, and no mehndi ceremony for me. Anyway. Let's go back to your ceremony," she says, crushing her cigarette under her toe and popping a cardamom pod from her kurta pocket into her mouth.

No one seems to have noticed that we were gone. Vee and her crew are interviewing women at the party, and they're lining up. I shudder to think of what they're saying. It doesn't matter, I remind myself. But when I enter this world, this community, once mine and now distant, it starts to feel like it ought to matter. It unsteadies me.

Salma says nothing for the rest of the time that she adorns my hands and then my feet and ankles. Women come by, sit beside us, ignore her, and talk to me about my plans for the swayamvar. They plan to attend, they say. Are they allowed to take pictures and post? Am I nervous? Am I really expecting men to show up . . . of course they would show up . . . but proper, eligible men? Am I going to the temple to pray in the morning? What is the feat? Will there be just one or . . . ?

Salma does not look up at me once through these conversations. When she is finished, she sits back with a sigh. "I like to wait a few minutes to make sure it's all setting properly," she says, giving me instructions for drying and then removing the henna.

"Salma," I say in a quiet voice, leaning over to her. "Tell me what you love about Jamal."

Her eyes widen. She grins. She looks over her shoulder and then, with her own voice lowered, she leans closer and says, "He is a very serious guy, but he laughs so much around me. I love myself around him. I love who I have become over the years we've been together. Successful, but also sure of what I want. And there's this thing that happens when we're together—we really, I don't know, we really *look* at each other. Like, eye to eye. Like, totally present. You know that emoji, the smiley one with the three hearts around it? I don't even know what it's supposed to mean, but I feel like that emoji." She starts to laugh and then straightens up and holds my arms up again, almost like two women high fiving. She's still smiling.

"Salma," I say to her, being careful to keep her name down to a whisper. "I wish you had the adornment of the mehndi for your big day. Look, I have the mehndi and don't even know if the love of my life will be there tomorrow. But you know what? As far as adornments are concerned, I would do anything to have my face look like yours right now. Brimming with joy. That's what that emoji means."

"Does it?" Salma says, squinting her eyes at me sideways, teasingly.

A COMMOTION STARTS up outside Shakti's home. People rush over to the entrance. Salma and I stay seated where we are. Salma looks nervous.

Vee's crew comes over to tell us a couple of media people are outside with their cameras. One of the women had posted selfies on social media and used all the godforsaken hashtags that had grown around the swayamvar these past weeks. "Tomorrow!" her post reminded people. "Look how we've all gathered in our fineries to wish our poor sister, this fifty-five-year-old lady, better luck third time round!"

Shakti comes over to apologize. She looks stricken. It was that gossipy woman, she says. "She slipped out a while ago after causing this..."

"It really doesn't matter," I say. "This is not your fault. In fact..."

I go outside and address the couple of media crews there. "I am not the only bride planning to get married tomorrow. I am not the only person looking for love. If I don't find my match among the men performing feats, there is still so much love for us all to celebrate. And if you're really, truly interested in this whole swayamvar, send me the best of your eligible men."

I hold up my henna-adorned hands, stand up on tiptoe as best as I can, and, with a limpy twirl, give them the best brimming-with-joy emoji face I can.

The Vows

I am a love letter again, so brief and so willing to be in service of love. . . .

Praanpriye, my Heera, do you want me?

You spurned the gifts of gold I brought you. You are afraid that your father will accuse you of stealing from the thakur. But how you exaggerate when you say my father's men will cut your family members to pieces!

I turn shy when I dance and you watch me. Do my feet falter now? What was the song you sang for me the other day? Why have I never heard it before? I want to lay my lips on that throat over and over again.

I hide you from everyone and you reveal me to myself. My nights are now silver and my days are gold. And there you are at my dawn and dusk, you diamond upon diamond.

You dream of us living together somewhere in a land and a time when all our longing is seen as beautiful. That may not happen for us, but our progeny will love like madwomen. They will want and want more.

Our love will show them how to love.

If my people come for us with axes, let us make a boat from these litchi leaves that look like tiny boats. Do you want to take *me somewhere, Batohiya? Let us ask our common mother Ganga to hide us in her sari and take us to her home of origin, take us to our nanihal. There, I will do the thing you love most—I will make you laugh. Have I told you it my favorite sight in the whole wide world, this sight of you doubled over in helpless, noisy laughter at something I say that you find funny? I will make you laugh in the river and your nose will spurt water, just you wait and see.*

Heera, Heera, Heera, I chant by day. Heera, Heera, Heera, I moan at night.

The Cleanse

I know it isn't right to wake up a student with a phone call in the wee hours of the morning, but my head is noisy from people and people and people, some of them gathered to take pictures outside my houseboat now, and I crave the silence of being underwater.

I am surprised when Kristen replies.

Hello?

Her voice sounds like the first hello ever said into a telephone in the days after Thomas Edison invented the instrument.

Ah, yes. That makes sense. These kids don't get phone calls, only texts.

She sounds relieved to hear, then, that it is just me and not a national emergency alert or a cousin calling with news of a death in the family. The surprise at my end is that she agrees to my request. She doesn't need to. I have no real power over her. She is no longer a student in one of my classes, just a former student who switched from a sociology major to public relations. She is an athlete, a swimmer. She is a lifeguard at the university swimming pool.

When she lets me into the pool at 4:30 a.m., she leads me in through a back entrance where there would be no CCTV.

She doesn't ask any questions about why I need to swim at that hour. She's probably seen some of the social media chatter. She probably has a menopausal mother, or at least a perimenopausal one. Or maybe such a request has been made of her before. Or maybe she just doesn't care about the details. She hasn't even noticed my henna.

I ask her not to flick on the terrible mega fluorescent lights of the pool hall. She hesitates in the dark, and then, in a sleepy voice that has me mentally ask forgiveness of her mother, she begs me to be careful to leave the same way we had arrived and to please not slip and have any accident in or around the pool. Bye.

I sit at the edge of the pool and quickly stuff my hands and feet into the Ziploc bags Salma gave me to protect the drying paste from water in the shower. I don't anticipate these things would work as well in the swell of water in the pool, but I nevertheless double the scrunchies she supplied to seal the plastic around my wrists and stretch them with a grunt around the bags at my ankles. I struggle out of my clothes in the dark and pull on my bathing suit, everything clumsy and slippery.

The water instantly does everything I need it to. I sink my head into it like into the cradle made by the breadth of a sari on a mother's wide lap. The ripples of water in the pool seem to rise to greet my body and pull its exhaustion into their embrace. Where have you been these past few days, child? What have you done to yourself?

I swim for what seems like an hour. I have forgotten my swimming cap. The water tickles my scalp and teases the thoughts right below it. I have also forgotten my swimming goggles, so the chlorine pinches at my eyes. This gives me the sensation of having wept for hours, although I haven't. What an odd comfort. The

INTEMPERANCE

Ziploc bags on my hands and feet make my freestyle difficult and ridiculous. I want to rip them off, but what is an intricately beautiful motif made with an ancient herbal paste on my palms would just be floating bits of gunk and orange streaks of water in the pool when the athlete swimmers arrive for practice in a couple of hours. How would Kristen explain that to her supervisor? So, I get used to the awkwardness of the bags and even begin to find the sound of their thwack-drip-thwack on the water pleasant.

In the dark and the silence, the soft chiding of the water and the rising beat of my heart begin a song of their own. All I must do is remember to bob my head out at every fifth stroke to catch my breath.

Outside, the sun may be rising. I could stay here, in the pool, for the whole day. No one would know as they came and went how long I'd been here. I am under no obligation to go through with the wretched swayamvar. No contracts have been signed, no promises made, no particular groom to be abandoned at the altar. Did they even use the word "abandoned" for grooms the way they did for brides? No families to be shamed.

Cat and Karan will be arriving straight from the airport, and on not finding me there, Cat will know what has happened and what to do. She'll make cancellations for me. Demi will understand.

I flip, push off, stretch, shimmy.

Cat would give Karan a task to keep him busy. ("Go tell the suitors their services are no longer needed." Karan would get to be Telemachus after all.)

Cat would take charge and spin a narrative. Her calm voice and no-nonsense demeanor would stem the gossip, at least for the immediate hour or two. She may even appease everyone by asking them to partake of the cake and bubbly, shake a leg, perhaps, and go merrily on their way. This freshly widowed friend of mine would do all this.

Flip, push off, stretch, shimmy.

I could always apologize later to my friends and to Vee and her crew. Dear God. That would be awful. But I couldn't be expected to go through with a whole . . . this *thing* . . . for the sake of a documentary, surely? Maybe the story arc for Vee could be darker, in this instance, with no sense of . . . what was the therapy-speak term for this . . . toxic positivity? Do documentary films need happy endings?

Flip, push off, stretch, shimmy.

The baker and music and flowers and venue were all paid for. I didn't owe anyone anything, literally or figuratively speaking. I could always craft it into some sort of joke. A prank. An intellectual exercise.

Flip, push off, stretch, shimmy.

Of course, I had never meant to go through with it, I'd say. That would be preposterous. I am a public intellectual, a sociologist. I simply wanted to study the discourse around all this. Yes, this was all a ruse, and I apologize for the lack of prior consent and for any harm done to human subjects.

Flip, push off, stretch, shimmy.

The pain is so sharp, I gasp under water and swallow what seems like a quarter of the whole pool. I break to the surface and kick and splutter. At first, I think I have hit my leg against something, which is why the pain is in my calf. I dive down and open my eyes underwater and see I am in the middle of the pool with no obstruction in sight. My next thought is wilder. A shark. But this is a swimming pool.

The pain is screaming now. I gasp again and swallow more water. I start to thrash about in an effort to shake the pain off somehow. I try to remember anything I've been taught about how to deal with a cramp in the middle of swimming.

I have been doing all the wrong things with this swim. Long bout of swimming without a break. Had I almost fallen asleep underwater? I hadn't drunk any water for hours! I had imbibed alcohol at the sangeet! Dehydration leads to cramps.

I grope for the wall of the pool and feel nothing. I open my eyes again and see that I am somehow still in the middle of the pool even though I have been trying to thrash my way to the side. A pang of pain makes me scream first on the surface of the water and then turn silent into bubbles as I dive in to snatch at my leg and pull it toward me as if it was an object both separate and attached to me, both beloved and antagonistic in the way it sends bolts of pain to my brain.

Holding my breath and trying not to swallow more water, I claw at the Ziploc bag but the scrunchy proves difficult to strip off. Water is seeping into the bag now, and yet I can't rip it open. My feet feel cold, or numb. My fingers start to lose motor function.

I could drown. That would be one way to get out of a swayamvar. If Sati could immolate herself to protect her husband's honor, well, I could drown myself to protect my own before any hint of a husband comes along.

Even as my brain starts to shut down from the impending drowning, I imagine people saying I had died by suicide. Karan's face swims into view.

I try to swim again, but my cramping leg drags me down again and again.

Someone taps my shoulder underwater. I whip around to see

the woman from the bar, D with the red lipstick. She is swimming in my bridal lehenga, all afloat in red and gold and fuchsia. Draupadi, she says under water.

Next to her is her friend, whose gray-blond hair is floating up in swirls all the way to the surface of the water. Penelope, she says, as bubbles from her mouth dissolve on my eye.

Someone seems to hold my elbow for a moment. I could have sworn it is Janaki, the Sita who tried to murder me. But it's Demi, no, Damayanti, seeking her good man in place of treacherous gods. The pool fills with more and more beings. Vee is there, Vishnu swimming with his wife, Padma. Maddie—Madhavi—in love with herself. Shakti, with powerful strokes. Salma is there, an Ambika abducting herself away for her own runaway wedding.

I blink my eyes as my head is heavy with a watery darkness and then, everywhere, in the water and air, I see only diamonds. Among them, the most serene figure of all, the woman from the bus, Saraswati.

It is the most beautiful thing I have ever seen, this parade of my summoned bridesmaids with their warnings and their blessings.

This is not how it will end.

I push with all the might still available to my legs and my face breaks to the surface of the pool. I am in the center of the deep end. There was no one else in the pool. My leg still throbs with pain. If I could just cut it out of my body, I'd . . .

A swan swoops down on me and slaps my face with a whole universe-size span of its wing. The slap doesn't hurt. It feels like air and silk. The swan settles into the water right before me and stares the fuck straight into my eyes. It turns away from me, sticks its left leg high up into the air, tucks its drop-dead-gorgeous neck

INTEMPERANCE

inward, and begins to slowly swim away from me, toward the shallow end of the pool, using just its right leg.

I stick my left leg high out of the water. I paddle with just my right leg, my poor, beautiful, weak right leg. I grit my teeth against all pain. I crawl through the water with every ounce of strength left in my upper body. The swan makes it look easy. It isn't. But here we are, this great white bird and I, synchronous swimmers against all sense of time.

The Garland

I arrive home a soaking rat. Not quite the bride-to-be. In the wee hours of the morning, the photographers are gone, and I have a reprieve before they return. I have but a few hours before I must go out and meet my mate or meet my mistakes.

Our love will show them how to love.

Before I begin my solah shringar, my sixteen rituals of bridal finery, I have a dog to walk. And I have a few emails to send.

I had believed that leaving my family and building a new life away from them had been enough. But the unrelenting outreach of a man emboldened in his Brahmin dominion in the politics of recent years in the motherland was not to be shrugged off. So, I take each message from the cousin and, after a quick search online, send them to his daughters and his son on all the platforms on which I can trace them. I graciously accept his invitation to join the family WhatsApp group and post screenshots of his letters there, the best parts in bold. I send his messages to anti-caste friends and activists on social media who have long asked for women of clans like mine to blow the whistle on our men.

I have much more to do and an aunt and cousins to trace in family histories from which they have been erased or in family circles they have chosen to depart, but for today, I am a bride.

I'd asked to do all the morning rituals alone. I want no one, not Karan, not Cat, not the generous Maddie, not Vee and her crew, no one, to watch me readying for the morning. Even the dog was handed over to Karan, who'd bring him to the swayamvar later. The dog had a role to play in the feats, this soul-knowing companion of mine for a quiet decade.

AS I DO on every birthday in recent years, I make myself a single serving of halwa. I inhale as the scent of semolina roasting in ghee fills the air around me. I toss in golden raisins and halved cashews. I grind cardamom seeds, gently prying open each green pod. Oh, this aroma... I have asked that fresh cardamom powder be mixed in with my ashes upon my death. I add crumbled gur to sweeten the halwa with its earthy molasses heft. I sit on the deck of my houseboat with the piping hot halwa and close my eyes for every slow mouthful.

With ghee and cardamom still on my breath, I unwrap the bridal ensemble from the white tissue paper placed in the grand blue-gold box in which Maddie had delivered it. I lay it all out on my bed. My first thought is that the dress is like a whole woman in itself. She could show up at the swayamvar, and no one would notice that I wasn't inhabiting the sweeps of the lehenga, the wraps of the dupatta, the curves of the choli. But then, when I slowly put it on, I become adorned for a special day, something that has pale shadows in the past but is unmistakably, shamelessly radiant now. I am blood and gold, river and fruit, fire and flower. I, in the mirror, am the kind of person I'd want to marry. I, in my skin, am every withering cell kindled with curse and blessing alike.

WHEN DEMI TOLD me to do one thing for the wedding on my very own, it had come to me instantly. A little thing, but one that asked a new skill of me. I would make the groom's garland with my own hands. This symbol of all swayamvar ceremonies from all of time, this garland that declares the chosen one, would be my first gift to my man.

I am fortunate to have a florist right across the street from where I live. I am fond of saying to people that I live in a houseboat around the corner from a florist and a French bakery. It makes my life sound grand, urban grand. And it is, isn't it, for here I am, dressed in every beautiful thing in the world, stepping over my lake and crossing the street to The Flower Lady to assemble a garland for a suitor.

I clutch my cane and, following a hidden path behind the houseboats that the media cameras don't know of, I almost bound across the street to the florist; the sequined tennis shoes gift me buoyancy. Vee and her crew are there, ready to roll. The florist, a woman who has owned this business for decades and is still open to surprise and delight, has set up a little work area for me in the corner of her shop. She ushers me to a seat by a window and sets down on the table before me a thick needle, a pool of thick thread, and a wicker basket filled with marigolds in orange and yellow. They're in season, she says, and she has basketfuls for me to take to the ceremony as I'd requested. She recommends I throw in a pale pink rose every now and then in the string I am ready to assemble. I, too, am open to surprise and delight, and who am I to argue with a flower lady?

Assembling a garland is not as simple as one would imagine. But I have watched videos and am ready. I thread the thick string into a double loop, measuring it at an approximate four feet long, and tie a knot at the bottom. I pierce the needle into the bottom of the first marigold, and it falls apart. I recall that I am to pierce it heart first.

I pierce the first marigold and then the next and the next. Three orange. Then two yellow. Then a pink rose. My head is soothed by the rhythm. The marigolds have arrived just this morning from a farm in Rogue River, Oregon. How do they have the same scent—of buried gold and sun-soaked citrus and of life itself—as the marigolds whose little white hearts I secretly ate in my childhood? I tear off the slim petals of a single plump orange marigold and reach its white heart and quickly put it into my mouth. It could have pesticides in it, pumped in by the mighty genetic modifications of a first-world country, but if I keel over and die right now, they would say I died eating flowers before I could meet a promise, and that thought makes me smile and slows my breath to a pace just this side of a pleasurable death.

The marigolds are moist. The moisture mingles with the henna pattern on my palms and the scent all around is so intoxicating, I start to lose all sense of time, and all that matters is the piercing of a sliver of steel, past pain into beauty, three into two into one, until I have a circle with the circumference of my two arms outstretched in an embrace. I bring one end of the string to the other. I tie them together and so I have a garland, a varmala, a necklace for a groom, a string of flowers seeking a neck.

I dip the tip of my ring finger to the corner of my eye, where I had rubbed the last wisp of kohl that remained in the silver box before leaving my home, and I place a speck of this in the knot of the garland.

THE WATER IS *dark, cool. I push against it and rise, and push and rise. Darkness and depth. Then air and moonlight. I push against the floating debris of life from the shore—temple flowers, ash and bone of humans, feces of cow and cowherd. I emerge into the air that carries the breath of two lovers. I sweep over the surface of the water and hear the language of dread and hope. Then I am in the water again and I work harder now, propelled by a hand that holds me at one end, strong, urgent, scared, still pulsating from the holding, just moments ago, of the hands of his lover. When I arc through the gulping silence of gray water, a gold coin shimmers past me, eddying down, down, into an abyss, where the wish it carries may break a curse at tomorrow's dawn or an eternity later. When I am risen to air, the sounds of two young men and a giggling girl. The fear of children. Brazen courage of youth. In a generously dark night, a white hans, a swan flying above the boat. Beside me, in and out alongside my rhythm, a mighty fish, the blind beast of the Ganga. This is no ordinary voyage. A new thrill courses through the cracks in my being.*

They say I am wood, fashioned into a lifeless oar, and my purpose is to serve my master, the boat. But I am gifted the dance of darkness and light, now immersed, now free. Tethered inextricably to journeys of love and life on this ageless river. In service of death on some days, but not on this one.

Oh, and the Swayamvar

I arrive at Golden Gardens Park's beach to the smiling embrace of my dear people, new and old. Karan is standing there dressed in a yellow silk kurta, holding on to the leash of an excited dog. Beside him is a young woman holding his hand. Femi, I say, drawing her into a hug. Karan asks if I have noticed the music playing around us.

"Shehnai," I say with a gasp. "Oh, you sent Demi my music...."

"No," he says, pointing at a man playing the instrument live. Karan tells me it's a gift from Siddhartha. "He wanted to do this, and I helped," Karan says. They've flown the musician in from Lucknow and are hosting him here for a week.

I walk over to the musician with Karan and Femi. I tell him that if the day didn't bring a single other sweet surprise, this one alone would hold my heart for years. The man is elderly, and he places a hand on my head in blessing. Karan is misty-eyed now, this child of Siddhartha's and mine and Paul's and mine, more and more a man growing into his best as a man in love.

Cat, in a gold dress. The streaks of gray in her hair are gone. The red hair is magical in the late-afternoon sun. Kira and

Maeve are wearing pretty, white dresses and holding little baskets of rose petals in their hands.

This family of mine is beaming.

A few women from the sangeet last night are here, two of them accompanied by their husbands. Shakti, with all her family. Somewhere, Salma is meeting her beloved Jamal and the clock is ticking.

Vee and her crew are everywhere, shooting their film. Demi has a handful of young people running about. Demi herself is standing under a canopy next to an outrageously large cake, and as I walk by her, she says: "The cake designer threw in a layer of a special summer fruit. I hope you like lychees."

Maddie is there, resplendent in a pink lehenga. She looks like an apsara and is surrounded by friends she has brought along. All around are also more friends of mine from the university and from among parents of Karan's childhood friends. There are friends alongside whom I live on a lake and friends with whom I marched in the streets in protest.

Demi approaches me to discuss the run of show. Look, she says, pointing to a sweep of people gathered on this glorious morning on the shores of Puget Sound, total strangers who have laid out picnics on blankets or are idling in their kayaks and sailboats on the water. Of course, there are people on the beach and in the water that have no clue what is going on with this gathering and are just doing their own thing on this fine late-summer day.

A few cops dot the scene. Demi asks me for forgiveness. Because, look, there are some people holding up signs. Most of them have hearts and rainbows and rainbow hearts. I particularly love one that says, "And my swayamvar is next week!" But there are some at which Demi tells me not to look too closely, so I don't.

I take a deep breath and ask Demi, "And ... the ..."

"The suitors are lined up there," she says, pointing at a row of men standing side by side.

Eleven men have shown up to compete. I am a little disappointed in the number and the look of some of them, but I will keep an open mind. Demi steps up with a mic and announces that this is a swayamvar and there will be five rounds of feats. As stated on the website, she says, the feats have been planned to offer accommodations for disabilities and can be modified for other viable needs. The last man standing will win the bride's hand in marriage. He may ask the bride any questions he has for fifteen minutes, and if all goes well, a ceremony will be performed immediately. Legal certification to come later. If anyone has objections to the rules, they are free to opt out now or at any point before the nuptials.

A man steps out of the general crowds to walk toward me. Demi and the police rush up to him. Demi returns to ask me if I am willing to speak to the man. He looks vaguely familiar. Unthreatening. Ordinary, and yet ...

He says his name is Hans. He says he wandered over here and had no idea of the nature of this event. He says he has swum next to me in recent months at the swimming pool. He has been waiting to see me at the pool for the past couple of weeks so he could apologize, he says.

Oh. The guy from the pool.

"I was so bothered by a little incident that you probably don't even remember. You smiled at me, and I was so lost in thought that I didn't smile back at you in time. When I did, you had looked away. Now, I know this happens between people all the time, but I feel like it creates a sort of tug in the universe. It's a fleeting one, but just a little bit sad. Do you know what I mean?"

I nod. What a strange man.

"It may be presumptuous of me," he says, "but just in case it caused any sort of annoyance or wistfulness for you, I wanted to apologize."

I nod again.

"And to be completely honest . . . ," the man says, scratching the back of his neck, his head tilted down to his chest, his eyes looking up at mine, "when you turned around, you may have seen me . . . well, I was checking you out. I was looking at your behind. I thought I could be discreet, but what you saw was lewd. I'm sorry."

I laugh out loud despite myself. I send up apologies to all waves of feminism, but I laugh out loud not only at his admission but at what had been my own misconception in that moment at the pool. I search for words to say, and settle for, "I understand."

Hans says he had kept an eye out for me and had been disappointed to not see me at the pool in my regular swimming hours. Then, this morning, he had walked into a flower shop to buy a plant for his home, and he had spotted me sitting there, stringing flowers into a garland. He says he had been about to step up to me then to talk. His apology, he says, may not mean anything to me, but it was something he had been taught to do no matter what by a schoolteacher in his boyhood in Bombay. And then he had halted in his tracks when he saw my face. He was mesmerized by the bliss of concentration he saw there.

I have a flicker of a remembered sensation from this morning with the garland, a sense of a shadow falling over me and then a twinge of loss when it receded.

The man says he found himself following me here. He'd been waiting for a moment in which to step up and tender his apology, which seems useless now.

"But I needed to explain before I make a request that you may want to refuse if you think I am strange or lecherous or stalking you or something. I want to ask if I may join the suitors."

I let out a surprised laugh. "Aren't you . . . a bit young?"

"Does that bother you?"

Hell, no it doesn't. "No, it doesn't."

I add, "But you haven't had the time to consider this whole thing."

He says that is true, but that it is also true that he has had a lifetime.

The Wood-Chopping Round

Demi's helpers bring out an axe to a stump they have sealed into a pit in the beach. They bring out logs of wood.

Cat walks up to stand by my side. "Forearms," she says under her breath.

"Forearms," I say.

Ten of the now twelve men step up from the line to compete. Man after man chops wood or tries to. Some of them are swift and exact and strong. Ripples of muscles. Wood cleaved from wood. Crowds cheer. Protesters shout. A couple of the men make a go of it, but ironically. Laughs all around.

One of the contestants who hasn't stepped up is juggling. Demi walks up to him to say this isn't the feat being asked to be performed. He looks confused. He steps up to the microphone and says he was told to come here this morning to perform feats. He plans to perform all the feats he knows. He's good at them. I signal to Demi to let him be.

Hans is the other man who has chosen not to join. He says

he will forgo the wood-chopping round because he has never chopped wood before and is too afraid to wield an axe.

The man who emerges as the best woodchopper is a sixty-something named Mike. The crowds cheer for him and he flexes playfully, signifying a Greek god or something. I look over at Karan, who rolls his eyes, but I find this man charming.

No one is ruled out in the wood-chopping round. This raises cheers from the spectators, but a couple of the suitors make disapproving groans and throw up their hands, including Mike. Seated in a blue velvet chair, I make notes in my red journal.

The Kayaking Round

Demi's helpers bring out single-user kayaks with the help of a kayak company that operates on this beach. This is Seattle. Most of these men know what to do. The instructions are for the suitors to kayak three rounds in a tight circle designated in the water before us. Some suitors get right to it. Flip the kayak into the water, climb in, oars up, start to kayak.

Hans is the only one to ask another suitor for help adjusting the foot pedal. When the other suitor ignores his request, Hans asks if I would be willing to help. I am taken aback. Demi's helpers step up to help him, but I halt them. In all my wedding regalia, I walk the few steps over to his kayak bobbing on the water. I set down my cane, gather my lehenga up a few inches to save it from the water, crouch down as best I can, and help him (God, he smells good). I send him along his way.

As I walk back to my throne, I notice a familiar face in the crowds near me. Sylvan Wilson. He does a little salute and his eyes twinkle.

The suitors kayak. Round and round. Some think this is about speed. Others show their elegance. Invariably, with the circle being so tight, their kayaks bump into each other, get in each other's way. A loud "fuck you" here and a "back off" there. Some of these men are no longer competing for my hand.

My hand is making notes.

I rule out two men. Mike is still in the running. Hans is still in the running, although he doesn't look so happy. The man who was juggling is now loping about the beach and performing perfect cartwheels.

One of the two men who was ruled out continues to shout, "Fuck you!" now at Demi, at the booing crowds, and at me. He has a point. He was the most efficient kayaker of them all. He is led away gently by a cop.

The Garland-Sewing Round

One man doesn't want to participate in the garland-sewing round, so he takes his candidacy out of the running. I am a little disappointed, since this was the most handsome of them all. Like, hot. I could have feasted on his form for years.

The remaining eight men are seated at a long picnic table. Inspired by *The Great British Baking Off*, I have fashioned this as a "technical round," complete with a page of written instructions. They are asked to make a garland for me that matches the beauty of the garland I have made for the winner. I find it endearing how the men apply themselves to the task. They are given twenty minutes to complete it.

This is when Karan is instructed to let the dog off his leash. The dog runs up to me to be pet. Then he runs over to the picnic table, where the suitors are working on garlands and where a few dog treats have been hidden. The dog sniffs around among the flowers in their baskets and between the men's feet. Some of the men ignore the dog, others push him away, and some pet him on the head and move things around so he can get his treats. Karan then retrieves the dog. I watch the dog. I watch the men. I make notes.

For reasons not related to the distraction with the dog, two men give up on the garland-making halfway. I am pleased to see that Mike isn't one of them. Hans loses some time because he steps aside to assist a few frustrated men in threading a needle, including Mike. He finishes stringing the flowers in the garland but is unable to complete the knot in time. One man says this should mean Hans gets eliminated. "Or at least ding him in some points," the man says.

I nod. "Yes, I say. I am tallying points in my journal."

The Wit-and-Wisdom Round

Demi hands me the mic and I pose a question to the six remaining suitors: "What story would you tell a child at bedtime?" They are given five minutes to respond. They are to write their answers on the notecard they are given.

"Cinderella," *because of the happily-ever-after.*—Mike

A *bedtime story my mother told me about a brave boy who fights a lion.*—Anand

"Monkey Business," *because it's a story from my South African culture.*—Ethan

"Beauty and the Beast," because women need to know that some men may look like beasts but have hearts of gold.—Simon

This is a hard one. Who is the child? What does the child love? What has the child experienced that day?—Hans

I used to make up bedtime stories for my kids when they were growing up. I'd make up feminist versions of fairy tales where the princesses were the hero.—K. J.

I am stumped. I did not have a rubric for this feat, just my gut. I decide to let all six suitors proceed to the next round.

The Eye-to-Eye Round

I have been apprehensive about this round. I did not take Cat's suggestion of having the suitors take turns holding me, but I came up with a variation. "Inspired by artist Marina Abramović, the bride would like you to hold her gaze for two minutes without looking away," Demi says to the six suitors.

For the next several minutes, I stare into the eyes of one suitor after another. One of them doesn't last thirty seconds. He starts to laugh. He says this is hokey. I agree and let him go. Another one starts to weep and says he's had enough. I offer him a break and tell him his weeping doesn't rule him out. But he really is done.

Mike's eyes dance as they hold mine. I feel intoxicated and can't stop smiling. He winks at me at the end of the two minutes. Sexy.

K. J. holds my gaze with an expression of deep compassion. At the end of it, he tells me he wants to take care of me in my disability and aging process so I can go out there and slay dragons.

Hans holds my gaze with a frown playing on his forehead. The frown eases halfway through. Tears rush up from somewhere deep inside me and settle just a little bit in my eyes. Without breaking his gaze, Hans reaches for my hand and holds it in his.

Some of the other suitors start to boo. Parts of the crowd join in.

"No touching!"

"That's cheating!"

"You didn't say we could do that!" Anand shouts.

When the two minutes are up, Hans holds my gaze for a few seconds longer and then turns to the people and says yes, he agrees, he is willing to be disqualified.

"Are you saying you'd like to be eliminated?" I ask him.

"No," he says. "But I understand if you eliminate me if I violated the rules."

There was no rule saying you couldn't hold my hand, I say to him and the other suitors. Cheers and boos in the crowds.

Anand says he is no longer interested in participating. Rules are rules, he says, even unspoken ones. He doesn't want to end up with a woman who plays games.

I turn to the remaining four men. I tell them that none of them has won, and they should go home.

K.J. is angry and says I have wasted his time. "What a bitch," he says. "She has no idea what's good for her."

"Too much drama," agrees Ethan.

Mike shrugs and walks away.

The man who was juggling and cartwheeling is now walking a tightrope and has attracted a little audience all his own.

INTEMPERANCE

Hans says he regrets I went to all this trouble and none of them had measured up. Would I be doing this again? he asks.

I say no. I smile into his black eyes and throw the garland up in the air, as far up as I can. He laughs and leaps high into its little galaxy.

I join in his doubled-over, snorting laughter as my garland catches on Hans's ear, then wraps around his beautiful, long neck.

Acknowledgments

My profound gratitude to Yashica Dutt for reading multiple drafts of this book. Your wisdom, generosity, and teaching were invaluable to my crafting of this story. Deep gratitude also to Sunita Manas (Sonia didi) and Ananya Sen for journeying with me into real and imagined villages and to the river. I am thankful for the warmth of the home of my ancestors in Bhramarpur in Bhagalpur, Bihar, where the women of my family gathered to heal us and nudge this narrative into place.

Many thanks to my dear friend Joseph DeFilippis for taking me on walks through Paris and asking the best questions on an early draft. Thanks also to Claire Dederer and Jodi-Ann Burey, whose words on my drafts were witty, timely, and so crucial.

My gratitude to Seattle University—the Roundglass India Center's Raman Family Grant and the Endowed Mission Fund helped me with travel, and my colleagues and students there continue to be an inspiration. This book was generously supported by fellowships and residencies at Hedgebrook, Ragdale, the Atticus Hotel, the French chateau of Abigail Carter, the mountain home of Heidi McFarley, and the Goan home of Deepa Narayan and

ACKNOWLEDGMENTS

John Blaxall, all of which gave me the space and the delectable comforts so helpful to writing.

Reading the work of Shailaja Paik (*The Vulgarity of Caste*), Suraj Yengde (*Caste Matters*), and Yashica Dutt (*Coming Out as Dalit*) helped me immeasurably. Conversations with my father, aided by my stepmother, informed parts of this book and had me witness a reckoning in real time, for which I am grateful. Conversations with colleagues and friends such as Francoise Besnard, Sharon Suh (who pressed bell hooks's *Communion* into my hands), Amber Flame, Nalini Iyer, Anna Vodicka, Smeeta Hirani, Ruchika Tulshyan, Novera King, and so many others, all lit sparks upon sparks.

Huge thanks to my editor Rakesh Satyal—I could listen to you talk about books for hours and then go sit down and work hard to write something to impress you. My gratitude to the superb team at HarperVia for all your care, vision, and art (thank you for this beautiful book cover, Sarah Kellogg). So many thanks to my agent, Soumeya Bendimerad Roberts, for loving and championing this book just two chapters in.

Walks with my dog Tagore and his friendship over the years have brought tenderness to my writing. Most of all, thank you to my son, always my first reader/editor and always my favorite human.

A Note on the Cover

TK (hold 2 pages)

A NOTE ON THE COVER

About the Author

SONORA JHA is the author of the novel *The Laughter*, the memoir *How to Raise a Feminist Son*, and the novel *Foreign*. After a career as a journalist covering crime, politics, and culture in India and Singapore, she moved to the United States to earn a PhD in media and public affairs. Sonora's op-eds, essays, and public appearances have been featured in the *New York Times*, on the BBC, in anthologies, and elsewhere. She teaches at Seattle University and lives in Seattle.

Here ends Sonora Jha's
Intemperance.

The first edition of this book was printed
and bound at Lakeside Book Company
in Harrisonburg, Virginia, in September 2025.

A NOTE ON THE TYPE

The text of this novel was set in Adobe Jenson.

HARPERVIA

An imprint dedicated to publishing international voices, offering
readers a chance to encounter other lives and other points of view via
the language of the imagination.